TICKER

LISA MANTCHEV

This is a work of fiction. Names, characters, organizations, places, events, and incidents are either products of the author's imagination or are used fictitiously.

Published by Skyscape, New York

www.apub.com

Amazon, the Amazon logo, and Skyscape are trademarks of Amazon.com, Inc., or its affiliates.

ISBN-13 (hardcover): 9781477825297
ISBN-10 (hardcover): 1477825290
ISBN-13 (paperback): 9781477825280
ISBN-10 (paperback): 1477825282

Cover design by Will Staehle

Library of Congress Control Number: 2014906850

Printed in the United States of America

For Lori and Ciarán,
who understand that we make
our own dreams come true

ONE

In Which a Young Lady of Good Standing and Impeccable Moral Character Enters the Scene

A girl with a clockwork heart shouldn't be running late, but I was. Narrowly avoiding a fruit cart, I hurtled into the thick of rush-hour traffic astride my new Vitesse. The motorized, high-wheeled cycle had been special-ordered from Grimthorpe's Custom Velocipedes, and I was still getting the hang of the throttle. Traveling at a speed one could only define as "breakneck," I defied physics and the traffic laws to swerve between a hansom cab and several irate pedestrians.

"Out of the way!" I accompanied my shout with the insistent clatter of the cycle's bell. "Coming through!"

Immediately behind me came the protesting neigh of a mechanical horse and the metallic shriek of brakes.

"Just see what you've done!" a driver yelled over the hiss of released steam.

I didn't dare turn around, so I craned my neck and raised my voice to bellow, "I can't see where I'm going if I only look where I've been, my good man!"

I had to look to the future; the past held nothing but pain and fear. And death.

The Ripley's Personal Aethergraph strapped to my ribboned leg garter fired to life, a welcome distraction. With a series of clicks, the RiPA tapped out a message.

ON THE WAY TO THE FACTORY YET - QUERY MARK - JUST TOOK A TRAY OF STICKY BUNS OUT OF THE OVEN - STOP

"Wicked temptress!" I muttered, mouth suddenly watering. The communication was from Violet Nesselrode: best friend, confidante, and the youngest of a baker's dozen of children with whom she shared ownership of the SugarWerks Fully Automated Bakery.

But I wouldn't succumb. Copernicus Emery Farthing—Nic, for short, and my older-by-a-minute twin—was going to have my tardy head on a platter the moment I reached the factory. I couldn't pick him up also bedecked in confectioner's sugar. Not this morning.

Today wasn't a working day for the Farthings, but Nic had gone to his office to retrieve some paperwork. Within the hour, we needed to meet our parents at the Bazalgate Municipal Courthouse for the sentencing of Doctor Calvin Warwick. The papers called him many things, a "brilliant young surgeon" and a "genius gone mad" most often. He'd been my lead physician since I was twelve, and for the last four years my family counted him among our dearest friends. But over the past few months, the man who'd implanted my clockwork heart had become a monster none of us recognized.

Late or not, perhaps I did need some sweet pastry to clear out the horrible taste of bile at the back of my throat. The moment no other carriages or conveyances seemed intent on running me down, I clicked the RiPA over to "Outgoing" and tapped out a reply.

HAVE A DOZEN BOXED UP AND READY FOR ME - STOP - PUT THEM ON MY ACCOUNT - STOP - WHEN NIC STARTS TO LECTURE I CAN STUFF ONE IN HIS GAPING PIEHOLE - STOP

"You're easily corrupted, Penelope Farthing," I lectured myself. Altering course, I shot straight down to the River Aire, where a left turn put me on The Strand. The air here was heavy with river damp, yeast, and steam. The other factories on the block were thin gentlemen in severe black coats and top hats, smoke curling from chimneys like cigars stood on end. SugarWerks was the sole lady among them. Her striped awnings were like skirts snapping in a breeze perfumed with spices and bread; her welcoming illumination glinted off delicate ornamentation of copper and brass.

I'd arrived and so came the inglorious task of slowing down. The Vitesse herked and jerked and finally sputtered to a reluctant halt three inches from the pockmarked brick wall. With a sigh of relief, I hopped off, propped the cycle against the building, and removed the key.

"Contrary beast!" Far from feeling peeved, I ran an appreciative finger over the gleaming copper handlebars. A year ago, I wouldn't have even contemplated riding such a thing; now, I fairly flew upon it wherever I went. It might well kill me one of these days, but so might other less pleasant things. The moment I'd laid eyes upon it in Grimthorpe's showroom, I arrived at the conclusion that I'd prefer to ride from this world to the next on its gorgeous wooden seat, with brass exhaust pipes in place of angel wings, high wheel instead of a halo.

After a short sprint up the stairs, I pushed through the door. An intoxicating sugar perfume nearly knocked me out the way I'd come in. Ding! Ding! Ding! I tapped the brass bell in rapid succession until Violet bustled in from the back room, wearing the blue-and-white pinafore that was the SugarWerks's uniform and a frown that was not. The same age as Nic and I, Violet wore her amethyst hair spiked and a brass gearring stud on the left side of her nose. On one set of knuckles, BAKE was tattooed in elaborate black calligraphy; CAKE was on the other. Today she had an aquamarine bow pinned to the top of her head, a silver cupcake and crossbones marking the spot between the two loops of ribbon. Her lip rouge was the same fruit-stain red as the raspberry tarts; I'd seen that same color on Nic's cheek quite a lot this summer, once they'd started walking out together.

"I've no idea why you're wasting your time on my idiot brother," I said by way of greeting.

"Don't think you can distract me, Penelope Farthing." She pulled a full sheet of gingerbread off a brass rack and moved it to the glass case without even a grunt to mark her effort. Tougher specimens than I learned the hard way not to go up against her in an arm-wrestling match. "I saw how fast you shot in on that infernal contraption. You're going to break your neck one of these days."

"Sooner rather than later," I agreed. "But you wouldn't want me hanging about the omnibus stop at all hours, would you? I like keeping my own schedule."

"Your purported schedule is a fearsome and terrifying thing." Violet shifted gears as easily as I might on the Vitesse. "Did you wind your Ticker this morning?" She fixed me with a stern look that was not the least bit undermined by her diminutive stature. Though Violet always wore black laced boots that added three inches to her height, I still towered over her.

"As if I'd ever forget. One hundred clicks before breakfast." If we'd been fencing at Mettlefield's Gymnasium, that would have been an advance-lunge and a point scored.

Except Violet parried deftly: "How is the blasted thing holding up with all the stress from the trial?"

In response to her question, my clockwork ventriculator thudded twice in quick succession. Never meant to be implanted in the first place, it already needed an upgrade. The pretty little thing should have been decorating a shelf somewhere rather than struggling to keep the blood moving through my veins.

I steered myself away from such thoughts by ogling the caraway-seed cakes. "It's working well enough. And even if it wasn't, it's not as though Warwick will ever be allowed to practice medicine again."

"Not if they hang him, he won't—" Violet leaned over the counter and squeezed my shoulder gently. "Apologies. I shouldn't have said that."

"It's the truth though, isn't it?" I said, trying to remember how to swallow. "There's a very good chance they'll sentence him to death."

"They haven't found him guilty yet . . ." Her voice trailed off, because everyone in Bazalgate knew he'd committed the crimes of which he was accused.

Straight out of medical school and flush with the success of a new open-heart surgical procedure, Warwick had been brought in as a consultant on my case. Everything he'd done, everything that happened afterward, had been because of me.

I twitched my shoulders, wishing I could rid myself of the invisible weight sitting upon them. "I'd better step on it and get to the factory to pick up Nic. Are my sticky buns ready?"

"Of course!" Turning to the order board, Violet lined up a series of brass alphabetical dials. She spelled out "F-A-R-T-H-I-N-G" before moving to the end of the counter and standing on tiptoe to reach for the delivery lever.

I didn't dare put my hands on the glass because Violet abhorred fingerprints. Instead, I lolled upon my elbows and mustered a half-smile. "Do you need a step stool?"

"Certainly not." She finally grasped the burnished wood handle and pulled it down. Unseen gears locked tooth-to-tooth, and hidden wheels whirled and spun until, with a hiss of steam and a trumpeted fanfare, a door opened in the wall. A SugarWerks Signature Ribbon-Striped Carry-Away Box slid down the gleaming gravity-roller conveyor belt and came to rest in front of us. Developed by Violet's father, Gustaf, to prevent small children from spoiling their suppers, the SugarWerks Carry-Away Boxes could be set to open at a given hour, unless the contents included ice custard, in which case they should be opened immediately. Violet looped a strap around the box and buckled it down tight. "You need to get moving."

"I also need to keep up my blood sugar." Though I didn't say so, needing to eat every few hours was no chore, not with my appetite and love of all things sweet. I tapped a gloved fingertip against one of the bell domes. "You wouldn't send me off with a box of sticky buns and an empty stomach, would you? My mechanisms are winding down."

"If you ate all of them in one go, you'd have dyspepsia." Reaching into her pocket, Violet pulled out a SugarWerks token and handed it to me. "Pick your pleasure and take your choice."

I flipped the token over my knuckles; as heavy as a real piece of money, it was good for use only in the Automatic Dessert Dispenser. My parents helped develop the vending machine for the Nesselrodes, and it remained the only one of its kind in the Industrian Empire. At any hour of the day, one could insert a token, open a door, and get a hot cherry turnover with the perfect scoop of frozen ice custard on top.

Mmm. Ice custard.

Pity I needed to pick something I could eat with one hand! Sending one last lingering, loving look at the cream puffs, I inserted my token, tugged at the knob, and withdrew an oft-picked favorite.

"The Figure Eight again?" Violet pulled out a piece of blue-and-white striped paper and set it on the counter.

"Don't squeeze it in the middle," I warned, passing her my selection. "I don't want the chocolate filling to mix with the raspberry jam."

"Take these and leave before I toss you outside without so much as a day-old pastry for your troubles!" After handing over the paper-wrapped treat and the Carry-Away Box, Violet used the considerable ruffles on her apron to shoo me out the front door.

Grinning at her over my shoulder, I affixed the Carry-Away Box to the platform behind the Vitesse's slick wooden seat. Then, unable to resist a second longer, I took an enormous bite of the Figure Eight. An incoming message from Nic startled me, and I nearly choked on chocolate filling.

WE ARE GOING TO BE LATE - STOP - WHERE THE COGS ARE YOU - QUERY MARK

A short time ago, he would have been full of teases and dares, offering to race me across town, betting a month's worth of shoeblacking or a box of chocolate bars. With a sigh, I transferred my snack to my left hand so I could tap out a response with my right.

WILL BE THERE IN THREE MINUTES OR LESS - STOP - KEEP YOUR HAIR ON - STOP

Firing up the engine, I pulled down my goggles and kicked the Vitesse into gear. Reentering traffic, I almost ran over an elderly gentleman who perambulated somewhat haphazardly on one leg of flesh and the other a brass prosthesis that must have been made at our factory.

"Attention, please, you demitasse of feminine frippery!" he barked. "This isn't the Eight Bells Steeplechase!"

"A thousand pardons!" I returned, struggling to rein in my mechanical steed.

I made quick work of the Figure Eight as I drove, but the streets clogged up as I approached the traffic circle known as the Heart of the Star. The roundabout connected the eight Etoile Roads, which radiated outward like the spokes on the Vitesse, and it was more congested than I'd ever before seen it.

"Take care there, sir!" I slapped my hand against the side of a cart before it could run me up a curb; negotiating the hub wasn't for the weak of knees or the faint of heart! "Ahoy, Freddy!"

Frederick Carmichael wore the charcoal uniform and namesake iron bracelets that marked his employment in the Ferrum Viriae. The largest and longest standing of Industria's privatized militaries recently won the coveted contracts for Police, Fire, and Emergency Rescue Squadrons. Frederick was the soldier who'd aided me after my last accident. That particular occurrence left me with a twisted ankle, an official citation, and an off-the-record, blistering lecture about yielding to larger vehicles. Never let it be said that the Ferrum Viriae are not thorough.

Frederick bestowed one of his infrequent smiles upon me along with a white-gloved wave to proceed with caution. "You promised you'd slow down!" The silver glint of his whistle flashed as he lifted it to his mouth.

"Progress waits for no woman!" was my retort.

"All the same," he said, jerking his chin at the sidewalk behind me. "Mind the crowd."

Looking about, I finally realized the cause for the congestion: a sizable assembly of protestors. The Edoceon Movement sprang up almost immediately after my surgery, protesting the "unnatural" idea of Augmentation. Very few paid them any attention until formal accusations were brought against Calvin Warwick, but since the start of the trial, their numbers had quadrupled. The newspapers printed their well-researched and scathing letters to the editor with alarming regularity.

Today, the jostling figures held signs that read "Instruct, Inform, Apprise," "Man Before Machine," and "You Cannot Augment the Human Soul!" Restless, they shifted against the rough wooden barricades set in place to keep them off the road. They might have remained corralled, if they hadn't seen me. Pity that I'm not the sort of girl who fades into the wallpaper.

"The Farthing girl! She's over there!"

Heads pivoted in my direction. Then it was as though someone had uncorked a bottle of effervescent hatred and directed the resulting spray at me.

"That's her!"

"The first abomination!"

"Freak!"

"How do you sleep at night?"

The verbal abuse they hurled had less effect on me than the actual bottle someone threw. Glass shattered under the front wheel of the Vitesse, forcing me to swerve. Perhaps in response to all the excitement, my Ticker paused in its good work. My head began to spin, carousel dizzy. I couldn't focus my eyes. Everything slowed down, like I'd abruptly driven through sticky toffee pudding.

"Miss Farthing?" I heard Frederick Carmichael call out behind me, followed by a more frantic, "Penny!"

But I had no words with which to answer him, and everything seemed to happen at once: the crowd broke through the barricade, stampeding toward me with murder in their eyes; Frederick dove into the melee, whistle blaring; I fell off the Vitesse and landed with a thump on the cobblestones.

"I've called for backup," Frederick shouted as though from the end of a tunnel. "Arrests are going to be made if you don't remain peaceable!"

Despite my vision going fuzzy about the edges, I could see the demonstrators hesitate, weighing the cost of righteous anger against spending a night or two in prison. Taking their signs and their barely disguised hatred, they retreated to the curb.

"Laugh up your sleeve at us all you like, Miss Farthing," a narrow woman snarled in passing. "Your precious Warwick is going to hang. The tables are about to be turned."

Frederick shooed her away as he knelt next to me. "By all the Bells, are you all right?"

"I'm fine," I lied the moment I could speak. Flashes of gold light swam around me when I tried to sit up. A full minute passed before I could manage, "But this is really becoming a habit, you scraping me off the road."

"Shall I message for your brother? Or perhaps the hospital?"

I let him set me on my feet, and the satisfying swish of silken skirts around my ankles soothed me in a way that words never could. Secure in the knowledge of six flounces and velvet ribbon trim, I let go of his gloved hand. "It was just a little dizzy spell. I have them all the time."

With a frown, Frederick righted the Vitesse. "At least let me summon you a hansom cab."

"I'll be fine," I insisted to him and the world, except I wasn't at all certain either was listening. Clambering aboard the cycle, I struggled to look poised and confident.

"If you won't be convinced otherwise . . ." He reluctantly cleared me a space in the road.

I roared past him and down the street. He yelled a final remonstration, but the wind and the engine conspired against him.

"I'll be fine," I repeated, this time trying to convince myself. The morning seemed devoid of color now, and even the prospect of sticky buns had lost its sweet appeal. There was no doubt in my mind that Warwick would be found guilty. If he went to jail, the entire country would breathe a sigh of relief; if he hanged, I'd carry that guilt with me for the rest of my days. Somewhere deep inside him still dwelled the caring surgeon and gentle man I'd known, but the blood of more than twenty people stained his hands, people he'd kidnapped off the streets of Bazalgate and experimented upon, testing different clockwork ventriculators . . .

All to save me.

Just ahead, the wrought iron gates of the Gears & Rivets Factory stood open, with half a dozen delivery wagons queued up to enter the courtyard. One of the streetcars paused just before me and disgorged a dozen workers, each wearing our distinctive emerald-and-black uniform. Beyond them, the smokestacks emitted lazy plumes now that the boilers were stoked for the morning.

Gaslight shone out of a single window. Ambrose Farnsworth, the supervisor, must already be noting the day's goals in his ledger with a series of numbers and hieroglyphs worthy of an Aígyptian burial chamber.

The Gears & Rivets Factory was a family enterprise. Mama and Papa were both mechanical engineers. Nic had a talent for small machinery, so he headed Research and Development. That left the bookkeeping to me. Since my operation a year ago, we'd shifted all the machinery over to produce the tiny fittings, gears, mainsprings, and brass plates our Augmentation team needed to build prosthetics and implants. We skated on thin financial ice because of public disapproval, more so now than ever with the trial coming to its messy and sensational climax, but we were steadfast in our resolve that the technology could be used for the good of all. Development also proceeded slowly because none of the surgeons in our employ had Warwick's spark of genius.

Perhaps that's a good thing.

Interrupting my train of thought, the RiPA fired off yet another message from my twin.

THREE MINUTES HAVE PASSED - STOP - ONE MINUTE MORE AND I AM GOING TO CATCH THE STREETCAR - STOP

I didn't bother to answer. If he exited the building, I could head him off.

Or run him over.

I could well imagine the lecture he was composing. Nic would be furious when I told him about the protestors. And there was still the verdict on Warwick's trial yet to be announced.

This day will surely get worse before it gets better—

In the second between one tick of my Ticker and the next, the front wall of the factory exploded outward. Brick and glass and bits of iron flew through the air and rained down on the courtyard. The shock wave threw me from the Vitesse, and I hit the cobblestones with a bone-jarring thud. Once the enormous and terrible noise of the blast passed and the ringing in my ears faded a little, I could make out the screams from the workers fleeing the building. Everything was chaos. Madness.

And Nic was waiting for me in his office.

TWO

In Which a Stream of Trouble Flows into a River of Mayhem

Scrambling to my feet, I ran for the door. Ambrose Farnsworth intercepted me as he stumbled out of the building.

"Miss Farthing!" he said between coughs, eyes streaming.

"Is Nic still inside?"

The supervisor shook his head and coughed before answering, "I've messaged for the Emergency Rescue Squadrons. I think the factory floor might be on fire."

"Is my brother still inside?!"

Farnsworth sagged under the weight of my question. "Yes." When I moved to pass him, he tried to hold me back. "You can't go in. There might be structural damage!"

I shook him off as though he were no more than one of my mechanical Butterflies and ran into the factory. Smoke filled the hall. Dust billowed out every broken window. Coughing, I pulled my handkerchief from my pocket and held it over my nose.

Two bodies lay prone in the rubble. I scrambled over, uncertain if I felt relief or despair when I saw that neither one was my brother. Floor supervisors, both limp and pale, but each had a strong pulse and neither appeared to be bleeding. Just beyond them, the door to Nic's office dangled from one hinge, its glass scattered across the floor. I kicked the remaining wood until it gave way, then peered inside. Everything familiar was obliterated, but the room appeared otherwise empty.

Ambrose must have been mistaken. Nic couldn't have been inside when the blast happened.

Except a faint moan from under the collapsed bookcase proved the supervisor had been right. I climbed over splintered wood that ripped my stockings and cut my legs.

"No. No, no, no." Popped Hydrostatical Bubbles scraped my palms as I flung aside shards of laboratory glass. I tried to move the bookcase off Nic, but the weight of it was simply too much. When he groaned again, desperation poured through my veins, hot and bright. With my Ticker thudding like a reciprocating engine, I heaved again and sent the wreckage flying. My vision blurred, then cleared, like a slide in a stereoscope coming into focus.

Nic's face was scratched and bloody, his spectacles broken and hanging off one ear. "What happened?" he said, blinking hard.

"I was hoping you could tell me." Circling behind him, I gathered his head onto my lap, trying to avoid touching the silver fléchettes that riddled his skin. Blood trickled into my skirts. "Hold still. Don't be an idiot."

"Get out, Penny." With the jerky motions of a half-wound automaton, he pulled off his glasses and cast them aside. Practically blind without them, he peered around us with a squinting sort of frown. "Before the roof falls in."

Even felled by an explosion, he was still trying to take care of me. He'd been doing it since we were little, holding my hand as we teetered about the house, crossed the streets, ran through the park.

I looked into his eyes, hazel mirrors of my own, and gently reminded him, "I don't take orders from you."

"That's always been the problem," he said with another groan. Trailing his fingers over the fléchettes protruding from his chest, he pulled them out, one by one. "You've no respect for anyone or anything."

And just like that, any closeness I'd felt between us evaporated like water hitting a hot boiler. Broken and bleeding, he still couldn't forgive me.

"I give respect only where it's due." I heard a door slam open somewhere in the corridor and raised my voice, the words ragged and smoke-stained. "We're down the hall! We have three men injured, and we need stretchers!"

The rescue crew appeared seconds later. "Sir, don't get up!" one shouted as they pushed past me. "You could have internal bleeding."

"You hear that, Nic?" All the panic that had incited me to action receded, leaving me cold and trembling. "Hold still."

"You need to get to safety," the second crewman advised me.

"I'm staying until you get my brother out," I said. "And I'm riding in the ambulance to the hospital."

"I don't need a hospital, Penny," Nic said with a cough. "Just a new pair of glasses. I can't see a bloody thing."

"Don't be ridiculous," I told him. Just to spite me, Nic rose under his own power and stood, albeit shakily. "Don't be a hero, then," I amended.

"Take me home, Penny," he said, voice faint but sure.

Putting my arm about him, I did my best not to jostle anything as we picked our way outside. Half carrying my twin out into the autumn sunlight, I couldn't help but wonder if the explosion was what the Edoceon protestor meant by "the tables are about to be turned."

There's no such thing as a coincidence. Not in science, anyway.

I tapped out a message to my parents, who were most likely en route to the courthouse by now.

WE ARE ALL RIGHT - STOP - INCIDENT AT FACTORY - STOP - MEET US BACK AT GLASSHOUSE - STOP

Mama was always slow to answer her RiPA, but when no answer came back after two full minutes, I repeated the message.

"They might already be inside the courtroom," Nic said, peering at the Vitesse with another one of his farsighted frowns. "You have to turn off all communications devices in there."

"Then let's hope she doesn't hear about the explosion from someone else." One swift yank at the leather straps removed the Carry-Away Box from the back of the cycle; I tossed it aside to make room for my brother. "Hang on tight."

With Nic tucked in behind me, I roared out of the courtyard and past the Ferrum Viriae Emergency Rescue vehicles hurrying to the scene. In the rush to get home, I spared no appreciation for the city's towering buildings, the turning leaves. The gears in my mind whirled at an extraordinary pace. In response, my Ticker thudded and then paused as though sorting through the possible list of suspects. Though I tried to keep my breathing even and my mind steady, my fingers gripped the handlebars until my bones begged for mercy.

Was it the Edoceon?

Because it wasn't just letters to the editor and protests in the street. Some of the extremists sent threatening notes to the house via the PaperTape machine and the regular post. One member turned up on the doorstep a few weeks back and tried to shoulder her way into the house to speak with me. Every day, the Edoceon were getting bolder and more vehement about their cause.

But does that mean they attacked the factory?

Craning my neck, I could just make out Nic's ashen features. Gray smudged the sky once again, and the haze was like the glass in my glacier goggles. "Are you all right?"

"I might not be able to see, but I can tell you're driving too fast!" His arms constricted about me when I took the next corner at an impossible speed and angle. "I don't fancy almost dying a second time today, if you don't mind!" The wind frayed the edges of his words, threatening to unravel them.

A lump the size of a croquet ball rose in my throat at the memory of Nic lying prone in the rubble. If he felt the same horrible sense of responsibility mingled with fear day in and day out, then I could almost forgive his shortness of temper, his lectures and snarls. "No one is dying today. Not if I can help it."

"Not dying is good. Not rattling the bones from my body would place a close second. You really have no business driving this thing with your condition." He shuddered, a small vibration I doubted had been caused by the Vitesse.

"I should take you to Currey! You need someone to look at you!"

"Just get me home!" The last word left him with a gasp, and my Ticker thudded again. The moment I felt his grip tighten, I opened up the Vitesse and gave her everything she had. Bypassing the Heart of the Star, I ran the cycle full tilt down a nearby alley, through ruts and puddles that splashed their questionable contents over my skirts. My RiPA sputtered with competing incoming messages. Though I was still expecting an answer from Mama, the first to make it through was from Violet.

HEARD WHAT HAPPENED AT THE FACTORY - STOP - WHERE SHALL I MEET YOU - QUERY MARK

And the second was from Sebastian Stirling.

RECEIVED YOUR SOS - STOP - YOU NEED NOT HAVE SENT UP SUCH A LARGE SMOKE SIGNAL - STOP

Sebastian and Nic had become best of friends the first day of primary school, a union that hadn't pleased any of their teachers or anyone else forced to endure their countless shenanigans.

Few people know the secret to answering multiple RiPA messages at once, let alone have the talent to do so when traveling at the Vitesse's uppermost speed, but I managed it.

GOING TO GLASSHOUSE - STOP - YOU CAN MEET US THERE - STOP

Turning onto our street caused a flower of relief to bloom in my chest. Overnight, it seemed, the trees that lined Trinovantes Avenue had burst into flaming color, vivid against the white brick facades and black wrought iron gates. Ahead, Glasshouse beckoned, sunlight glinting off the famous Rose Windows that spanned the upper story. The Artisans' Omnibus Tour never failed to point out that series to the occupants of the streetcars, noting the repeating floral patterns in sets of six, three, six.

"The number of letters in the phrase *Tempus est clavis*," they trumpeted through bullhorns. "'Time is key,' the Farthing family motto."

Perhaps realizing I was distracted, the Vitesse's motor chose that moment to hiccup and die. The contrary conveyance glided to a halt in the gutter, right between the neighboring Twin Spires and Pinkerton Manor.

"Hold on," I told Nic. For an answer, my twin toppled off the back of the cycle. Trying to catch him before he hit the ground, I bungled the dismount. A vicious rip emanated from the vicinity of my backside, but just now I had concerns beyond my wardrobe.

"No need to fuss," he tried to reassure me from the ground.

"Sorry, but I'm not buying what you're selling." Looping an arm around him, I heaved my brother to his feet and helped him to our stoop. Only when I went to insert my key did I notice that the front door stood ajar.

At another house, this might be construed as happenstance, the downstairs maid forgetting to close it after sweeping the stairs, perhaps. But not at Glasshouse. Such things would not be tolerated on Miss Evangeline Dreadnaught's vigilant watch. Above all else, our chatelaine subscribed to the motto "thou shalt not leave any detail unattended," and that certainly included front doors left open.

Reaching into my messenger bag, I pulled out my Pixii. Nic invented the personal safety device for me as soon as I was old enough to take the streetcar alone. Thumb to the resistance switch, I charged it with repeated depressions until I could make out its telltale whine. "Get behind me."

Nic squinted at me in puzzlement. "Whatever is the matter?"

I put my finger to his lips and nudged at the heavy front door. It swung inward without so much as a whisper—*bless Dreadnaught for her conscientious oiling!*—revealing another scene of wreckage. Rugs had been tugged from their proper places and left in woolen wrinkles along the hall. Occasional tables were overturned. Broken crystal and bruised flowers decorated the floor.

A few steps more and we stood in our parents' study. The damage inflicted here was precise. Methodical. Someone upended the room, turned out the drawers of the desks, rifled through the filing cabinets, removed the art from the walls, slashed open pillows and chaise cushions and even the leather armchairs. Feathers and cotton were scattered among the various oddities our parents collected over years of travel: petrified wood from the blood forests of Portola, the wired skeleton of a wolpertinger, souvenir spoons from at least thirty cities. Worst of all, the intruders smashed the hunk of volcanic glass carried back from the underwater dome city of Halcyon. Recruited to the developer's engineering team, my parents fell in love while funneling salt water near enough the volcanic activity to heat it for the medicinal spas. They shared a Submersible to the surface and were inseparable ever since.

"What's happened?" Nic gave the back of my jacket a shake.

"Someone broke in." I towed him farther into the room. Surprisingly, the perpetrators spared the stained glass Aquaria that spanned the length of the far wall, with its pale green depths and coral-colored goldfish. However, one of the panels had been shifted to the side, revealing the inner workings of the gas lamps that gave the glass waterweeds the illusion of movement. Beyond that were several large and well-greased gears, two pulley systems, and a small rectangular wall safe. The latter was open, its papers scattered over the floor and the desks. "They've turned the room upside down and broken into the wall safe."

Nic pulled me back half a step with a hissed, “They could still be in the house.”

“I don’t think so,” I said with a slow glance about to take in every detail. “They smashed the face of the carriage clock when they were here. Happened about an hour ago.”

“About the same time as the explosion at the factory,” he said, unwilling to let go of me. “I somehow doubt that was a coincidence.”

Gently prying my clothing from his grasp, I knelt in the debris and retrieved a glass daguerreotype. It was from the day Cygna was born and the only picture of the four Farthing children together: Nic and I at age eight, holding the baby between us, and eleven-year-old Dimitria standing behind. The glass was cracked down the middle, so I was quite literally picking up the pieces of our family. “I need to message Mama and Papa again. All of this is going to come as a nasty shock.”

Nic tried to pick a path between the marble chess figurines and promptly fell over the remnants of the mirror that should have been hanging over the fireplace. Behind the desk, he squinted and reached for something.

“You might want to call in the police now.” He held up our father’s pocket watch by its long gold chain. “I think Mama and Papa were here when it happened.”

Most men and women in Bazalgate society carry a watch that requires regular winding, one composed of balance wheels and screws and gears, but our father’s elaborately engraved case held instead a miniature sundial set over a compass. Given the fact that my parents would rather crash through a jungle atop an elephant than bask in wooden deck chairs, the gift served its purpose more than once. It was a unique timepiece, commissioned by my mother for a wedding gift, and my father was never without it.

My Ticker responded before I could, accelerating until I could hear my pulse in my ears. "Do you think the burglars hurt them?"

Peering ineffectually around the room, Nic shook his head. "I think they *took* them."

The pit in my stomach widened until I was afraid I might fall into it, never to climb back out. I walked over to Nic and took the pocket watch, wanting to believe that it somehow wasn't my father's. When I opened the case, though, there was the metal dial folded down over the compass. "But why—"

The sound of a boot snapping a bit of broken glass came from the hallway. I whirled about and raised the charged Pixii.

"Penny, don't," Nic warned, trying to catch hold of me.

Skirting an overturned table, I evaded his reaching hands. "Shut up and get down."

It was only a few steps back to the study doors, and I eased through the gap between them. Clouds wrapped sulky arms about the sun; in the resultant gloom, everything in the hallway was the enemy, from the broken furniture to the grandfather clock. The low whine of the Pixii in my ears settled alongside the rapid staccato of my Ticker. With the next step, I cursed the silk whisper of my skirts, but it didn't muffle the sound of a footfall behind me, another tinkle of disturbed glass before an arm about my waist lifted me from the ground. The strong hand over my mouth prevented me from calling out for help.

Like a shawl of frost, a sort of terrible calm settled over me. Twisting my hand about until I thought it might snap, I jammed the Pixii into my attacker's bare wrist.

No use lying to yourself, Farthing; this is going to hurt.

The Pixii discharged with a burst of phosphorescent blue light, and electricity shot through both of us. Every muscle in our bodies contracted, and then my assailant went limp. I stumbled forward but kept my feet. Instead of shuddering to a stop, my Ticker hammered merrily in my chest.

Nic vaulted into the hallway, brandishing a fire shovel. Still without his glasses, he'd need more than luck to land a blow, though he hadn't let that stop him. "What's happened now?"

"An ambush." It took me only a second to recharge the Pixii, and then I sat atop the intruder's chest and jammed the metal fore-prongs under his chin. "Rise and shine."

When the stranger opened his eyes, another frisson of white heat traveled from the base of my skull to every extremity, somehow just as real as the discharge from the Pixii. I peered into eyes so dark gray they were one blink away from black, and imagined ridiculous things: spreading a blanket for a picnic, sharing a pair of gold binoculars at the opera, snowy sled rides with furs up to our chins . . .

A sudden silence in my chest told me that the clockwork heart had ceased pumping the blood through my veins. I realized that I shouldn't be touching this man, though he remained very still. Almost too still.

"I'm afraid you have me at something of a disadvantage, Miss Farthing," he finally said.

"As you do me," was all I said in response. I could feel the blood draining from my face. My hands went cold. My feet prickled as though snow-kissed. Looking down at him, I whispered, "So this is what dying feels like."

The stranger caught me in his arms as I fell back, but Nic's frantic shout seemed to come from a great distance. Remembering the jolt the Pixii gave me just a few minutes ago, I tried to tell Nic to use it again. My nearly incoherent mumbles must have conveyed the message. All at once I heard the whine of the charge, felt a rip and tear of fabric at my throat and cold metal against my skin, then energy raced through me. My eyes flew open, and I gasped for air with a horrible sucking noise. I lay prone on the floor between the coatrack and the wall. The stranger knelt over me now, one hand gripping the Pixii.

Before I could say or do anything to reassure him, he charged it and zinged me a third time—what I deserved, perhaps, for attacking him earlier. I convulsed around the pain, then my world constricted to the wild gray gaze of the stranger as he took me by the shoulders.

"Miss Farthing!" He sounded like a Cylindrella record player, winding down. "Can you hear me?" He put his head to my chest and checked my respiratory functions. "Say something."

"It . . . isn't . . . nice . . . to electrocute people, sir," I sputtered.

"She needs a stimulant," Nic said, stumbling forward and tripping over the edge of the carpet. "And something sweet to bring up her blood sugar."

"Plum cake would be nice." Colors were brighter than they ought to be. I thought I could taste yellow.

"I'll plum cake you!" Nic said. "I think that scared another ten years off my life!"

The first ten were scared off the day that Warwick implanted my clockwork heart.

"How long has she been having these kinds of episodes?" the newcomer asked, scooping me up in his arms and carrying me to the chaise in the study. After depositing me on one of the slashed-open cushions, he sat down next to me, arm at the ready to catch me if I toppled off. His sturdy presence was as reassuring as the light scents of his cologne and fresh linen, but his face was drawn.

"A month. Maybe two." Nic stumbled in after us and felt his way to the desk. "Her ventriculator is already outmoded," he added as he rummaged in the drawers. "It was only a prototype to begin with, and the doctors aren't certain how much longer it will function. Warwick was developing a new Ticker for her when he was arrested."

The sharp reek of ammonia carbonate cleared the rest of the fog from my head. Indeed, I could just make out the label under my very nose.

THE BESTSELLING OF ALL THE PATENT FAINTING MEDICATIONS!

DOCTOR ABSALOM'S OLFACTORY IRRITANT

IS GUARANTEED TO ROUSE EVEN

THE MOST RELUCTANT OF PATIENTS

FROM THE DEEPEST OF DIZZY SPELLS

OR YOUR MONEY BACK!

My head recoiled, as though I'd been slapped, and several things came into rapid focus: the concern on my brother's face, the stranger's uniform of charcoal wool, the fact that I had just been attacked, and then saved, by a soldier.

"I'm afraid you still have me at a disadvantage, sir," I said.

"Marcus Kingsley," he said, offering me a small nod. "Proprietor and Legatus legionus of the Ferrum Viriae."

Thoroughly taken aback by the introduction, I blinked. We'd never met socially or professionally, but anyone with an eye to the broadsheets knew the Kingsley name. Marcus only recently inherited the military empire; still, it was common knowledge that disarming any member of Ferrum Viriae required stealth, cunning, and heavy artillery if one wished to avoid precipitous termination.

For the moment, though, I was alive and fairly tingling with it. As was he, it would seem, from the flakes of brilliant scarlet that painted his cheekbones. I struggled to sit up, not wanting him to have the advantage of looking down at me in any way.

"Thank you for coming to my aid," I said, "but could you explain exactly what you are doing skulking about our home when you ought to be supervising your soldiers at the courthouse?"

Though only nineteen or twenty, Marcus wore the air of a much older person the same way he wore his uniform: with excessive amounts of starch. He replied slowly, as though ironing out every word to perfect crispness. "Seconds after we received word about the factory explosion, one of your neighbors called in a burglary. The moment I heard it was Glasshouse, I put my second-in-command in charge and came to investigate. Tensions are running high in the city because of the trial, and against my advice, your family refused a protective detail. Where are your parents?"

A masculine shout of "Penny?" came from the front door followed by a louder, feminine "Nic, where are you?" from the hall. Violet and Sebastian charged into the study, skidding to a halt several feet away. There was a lot for them to take in, what with the house in disarray, a bloodied and battered Nic squinting at them, the collar of my bodice ripped away from my neck, and Marcus Kingsley sitting next to me on the chaise.

"Gracious, Nic," Violet said, striding toward him as she yanked off her gloves. Taking his face in her hands, she turned him toward the light. "You look as though you've had quite the time of it this morning."

"And it isn't even luncheon yet." Nic tried to smile but only achieved a grimace.

Standing, he allowed himself the small luxury of putting his arms about her and resting his head atop hers. With my breath still rattling in my lungs, I realized that if I was a cookie crumbling before his very eyes, Violet was a ship's biscuit: sturdy and in no need of coddling. Ever prepared, she pulled a spare pair of Nic's glasses from her reticule.

"Stirling," Marcus said, rising from the chaise to offer his hand in greeting.

"Kingsley." Struggling to recover his usual air of nonchalance, Sebastian accepted the handshake. As always, he was dressed like a model on the cover of *The Dapper Gentleman's Quarterly*, but his shoulder-length hair and aristocratically thin mustache were currently tinted the ice-blue of saffyre gin. His eyes were the same dazzling color, but right now they were obscured by smoked-glass spectacles. He'd inherited his good looks, cheerful demeanor, and eye for the ladies from his father. His weakness for infernal, new-fangled contraptions and rakish gentlemen came from his mother. Like both his parents before him, Sebastian was involved in every profitable venture in Industria as well as countless abroad. "Did we arrive in time for the festivities, or is this the after-party?"

"Penny's Ticker is troubling her." Nic hooked the wires of his spectacles behind his ears, his face puckering again with worry. "She needs to go up to bed and rest. I'll send to Currey Hospital for one of the surgeons."

"No, you won't." From the sturdy chain hanging about my neck, I retrieved a gold key, warm from nestling against my skin. Marcus popped several buttons off my collar when administering the jolt from the Pixii, so I merely had to nudge the fabric aside to access the brass faceplate set just under my left clavicle. Another demoiselle might have blushed, but the faceplate was located well above the ruffles atop my corset, and I'd been examined by so many doctors that I'd no patience for false modesty. I slid the key into place with a small click. "I must have forgotten to wind my Ticker this morning."

Violet gave me a narrow look. No doubt she wondered if I'd lied to her at SugarWerks or if I was lying now, but I would have died thrice over before admitting that Marcus had been the one to almost kill me, that his body pressed to mine and the heat between us had been enough to stop my heart. His gray eyes were on me as I tightened the mainspring. The muscles in my chest constricted under the combined pressure.

I am more than a pretty little windup doll.

But he knew that, somehow. There was respect in his eyes, alongside something decidedly personal. I paid back his attention with interest, wanting to see how long it would take him to avert his gaze. We were well on our way to a full-blown staring contest when Nic interrupted.

"I do wish you'd take more care with yourself," he said, wiping a handkerchief over his glasses and resettling them on his face. "I swear you'll forget your name one of these days, Penny."

It was a variation on the theme he'd played since the implant, seeing ominous shadows in every passing rain cloud. Fresh frown lines pinched the bridge of his nose. His eyes, once as merry as my own, were dark and somber.

"Thankfully, you'll always be there to remind me of it." I reached out and gave his arm a squeeze, trying to convey through layers of cotton and wool that I was stronger than he thought.

Before I could offer further reassurances, six men entered the study, guns raised.

THREE

In Which Hazards Appear Around Every Hedge

"Stand down!" Marcus barked at them. Under the command was steel. Steel, and layers of reinforced Chytin body armor.

They immediately lowered their weapons.

"The rest of the house is clear," the tallest of them said. "Save for rooms on the top floor we couldn't access."

I let go of a breath I hadn't known I was holding and explained. "The bedrooms have combination locks on the doors. There's no way to access them without chopping a hole in the wall."

The soldier spared me a nod. "No other breaches or signs of forced entry at the back or side doors. And no sign of any of the staff."

"We've only a chatelaine, and today's market day," Nic said. "She wouldn't have been here, thank goodness."

When Marcus reached into his pocket, the charcoal wool fell back far enough from his waist to reveal a holstered Magnetic Acceleration Gun. The MAG's metallic inlays and soldered joints tempted my professional curiosity, but I knew better than to try to reach for it without his permission.

Rather than draw the weapon, he flipped open a leather-bound notebook and assessed the room with a keen glance. "You never answered me before. Where are your parents?"

I hesitated to voice my suspicions. Perhaps it had something to do with Marcus's swift arrival here on one of the most important days in Bazalgate's judicial history. Or it was the way he studied the mess of papers on Papa's desk that warned me I ought to keep my suspicions to myself. Never mind that there was always the possibility that my father had simply forgotten his watch this morning.

I'll look a right fool if Mama and Papa turn up in time for tea.

"Your guess is as good as mine," I answered. "I sent my mother a RiPA message, but she hasn't answered it yet."

"I have a unit down at the factory questioning your supervisor, but is there anything you can tell me? Anything out of the ordinary you noticed before the blast?" Marcus looked at Nic, who shook his head.

"One minute I was gathering my things, the next I was on the floor."

"What about here?" Marcus scanned the room again. "I know the damage makes it difficult to tell, but does anything appear to be missing?"

"We won't know until we put the house back in order." I gave him a well-practiced smile of dismissal. "We'll be sure to file a full report once we've a list, but we don't want to keep you any longer. You're needed at the courthouse."

He automatically glanced at the military-encoded RiPA he wore on his left wrist. "I'm expecting a quarter-hour report any minute now. They should be close to announcing the verdict."

"You ought to be there when that happens," I said. "Perhaps there'll be a riot." I didn't want to think about such a possibility.

Neither did Marcus, it seemed. His gaze flickered about the room, monitoring the waning threat level. "You need a safety detail. I can spare two or three soldiers to man the doors."

I flapped a hand at him, doing my best impression of Grandmother Pendleton, who did not suffer the advice of others. "Nonsense. I'll have the locksmith around within the hour. Once Dreadnaught returns, she'll make short work of the mess."

Undeterred, Marcus peered hard into my face, as though trying to peel back the layers of lies and read the truth in my eyes. Whatever he lacked in battle instincts, that look of his burned me all the way down to my boots.

Sixteen years of swapping whoppers with my twin hadn't been for nothing. I met Marcus's gaze with my most guileless expression. "We'll be fine."

"Are you certain?" he asked.

"I am," I said. "We are grateful for your prompt response." He might have six inches and fifty pounds on me, but there was no need to shove him out the door. I lowered my voice to a stage whisper. "Don't fret, Mister Kingsley. I won't tell anyone that I laid you out flat in my entryway. I'm sure that would be bad for business."

Blotches of red reappeared on his cheeks, like I'd slapped him. He turned and ordered his men out with a clipped, "We're done here."

We watched the soldiers depart in shared silence. Violet still had her arms about Nic's waist, the brilliant spikes of her hair standing out in stark contrast to his bloody shirtfront. Her iridescent blue fingernails glittered when she trailed them over the holes in the cotton.

"You should go to the hospital," she said to him.

"We've bigger problems than a little blood."

"You're lucky to have escaped with only a couple of scratches to show for it." Sebastian's expression took a turn for the serious. "Are you in pain? If you need something to take the edge off, I have these lovely little purple pills I picked up on my last trip to Bhaskara." Taking a silver case out of his pocket, he offered it to Nic.

My twin smiled and shook his head. "I've told you that your habit of collecting foreign medications is a bad one, yes?"

"At least a dozen times. But you've no need of pills, foreign or otherwise, if you can survive an explosion and live to lecture me," Sebastian said easily, opening the case and shaking out a tablet for himself. "I felt the tremor in my office halfway across town. Looked out the window to see smoke plumes and emergency vehicles headed your way. The broadsheet sellers are already squawking, but I like to get my information straight from the source—"

He was interrupted by a startled shriek that emanated from the kitchen. Seconds later, Dreadnaught entered the room. Her eyes were wide with horror, and she had her hand pressed to her mouth. If I was the "First of the Augmented!" (as dubbed by the press), then she was the less-heralded second. After reading about my surgery in the broadsheets, Dreadnaught arrived on our doorstep with her right arm half-twisted out of the socket, the appendage rendered limp and useless by a factory accident. As soon as my father could get clearance from the medical board at Currey Hospital, a team of research surgeons Augmented everything from the shoulder down. Only the brass glint between her sleeve and a black glove betrayed her.

"The kitchen is chaos. The goose I was roasting is blackened, vegetables are all over the floor, half the good china is smashed . . . Did a bomb go off while I was at the market?" While each of us struggled to formulate an answer that would placate her, she contemplated us over the sea of ruin. "Would one of you explain what transpired here?"

Nic found his voice first. "Someone broke into the house while we were gone. Fortunately you weren't here when it happened."

While the housekeeper surveyed the mess in her hall with pursed lips, I couldn't help but think it was the burglars who were fortunate they'd already made their escape. Dreadnaught removed her neat straw going-out hat, turned up the gas lamps and then her sleeves. Moving with the grace and speed of a hummingbird, she cleared the worst of the broken glass as we straightened the rugs and righted the tables.

She retrieved her hat and moved to the door. "I'll fetch some refreshments."

"Yes, please." I was suddenly ravenous. When she returned, not only did I finish a cup of tea, but drank two more, consumed a plateful of sandwiches, and topped that off with a slice of lemon cake. The others watched me, no doubt fearing I might collapse face-first into the cart at any second, but I felt marvelous.

"Her appetite seems good," Sebastian said with great diplomacy as he bypassed the tea service and headed for the liquor cabinet.

"I've seen horses eat less in one sitting," was Violet's way of putting it. "Now tell me what happened at the factory."

In between bites, the morning's events came out in a rush. When I described the explosion, Violet lost her appetite and passed me her untouched slice of cake. Hand hovering over the Gentian Amaros, Sebastian blinked twice and moved straight from herbal aperitifs to hard liquor. I finished with the Vitesse ride across town, finding the house upturned, and Marcus's arrival on the scene. Had the carriage clock not been smashed, I'm certain I would have heard it ticking in the utter silence that followed my narrative.

Violet commenced cracking her knuckles, just as she always did when perturbed. "Do you have any idea who'd want to break in?" she asked, working her way through the letters in BAKE.

I should have been stuffed with cake and tea, but lemon sponge couldn't fill the dreadful hole in my stomach. Shaking my head, I tapped out yet another message on my RiPA. "We should have heard from my parents by now."

"If you're feeling well enough, we ought to drive down to the courthouse to meet them." Sebastian finished his drink and set his glass down on the tray.

Before I could agree or Nic could offer an argument, the pipes in the wall set up such a rattling that we all cringed. Rising from the chaise, I made my way to the vintage Calliope in the corner. It hadn't been used with any regularity since Papa installed the PaperTape machine, but it still had the capacity to send and deliver message cylinders all over the city via pneumatic tubes. It was a great gleaming thing, thanks to Dreadnaught's many hours of polishing. As a child, I'd been fascinated by the receiving tray that looked exactly like an enormous lion's head.

The message cylinder arrived with the clatter of metal against metal. When I reached into the feline's mouth, a sharp tooth grazed my skin. The scratch was a line of red crimstones in the gaslight. Blood dribbled between my fingers and onto the message cylinder. Cold and smooth against my hand, it bore none of the usual decorative etchings and lacked a maker's mark to identify it. Rolling it over, I noted the grooves in the brass, tested its weight, and examined the clasp. Not locked, thank goodness. Lacking a key, I'd require a combination of three explosives to get this open, two of which are illegal within Bazalgate city limits and the third rumored never to have existed at all.

"Open it, Penny." Nic's command was softly voiced.

"Do. I'm always in the mood for a good mystery," Sebastian said.

Flicking the clasp, I extracted the typed missive within.

Master and Miss Farthing:

We politely asked your parents for the notes and the diagrams pertaining to the more complicated Augmentation procedures, but they declined to relinquish them. Your parents are now residing with us, having graciously accepted our invitation to reconsider the matter. We suggest most firmly that if you care to see your mother and father again, you will locate the items they refused us. You have until noon tomorrow, when we will deliver your next set of instructions.

By the time I finished reading, I'd gripped the paper so hard that it was crumpled along both edges.

"How did they sign it?" Sebastian wanted to know.

"They didn't." I read the note over again, seeking out some clue that would tell us who'd sent it. Without warning, the paper spontaneously burst into flames and disappeared into a cloud of cough-inducing smoke. Yelping, I danced back.

Nic rushed to check my hands. "Are you badly burned?"

I shook my head and held them up. "Not even singed. What *was* that?"

Sebastian offered an answer. "It's high-security stationery. Only meant to be read once before combusting."

"Just how do you know that?" Violet asked.

"Remember my moving-picture project?" Realizing his tie was crooked, Sebastian straightened the bit of silk. "A sample of 'spy-paper' came with my orders for the nitrocellulose film we're using to shoot the first movie. Fun to play with, but damned dangerous stuff to have hanging about the place."

Violet went to pour a generous lemon and Fizz. "Don't you think the Edoceon must be responsible for this? They've been pushing for an Augmentation ban since Warwick was arrested."

"They were protesting at the Heart of the Star this morning," I said, the memory cracking open like the bottle under the Vitesse's wheel. "They shouted threats at me. One of them said the tables were turning."

"There you have it." Violet dispensed a second drink, sloshing out sparkling wine and citrus syrup in a fashion that made Sebastian shudder. Elbowing him aside, she handed the glass to Nic. "It's not 'reeducating the public' when they destroy personal property and kidnap civilians. You need to file a report right now. The Ferrum Viriae can have the Edoceon under lock and key in less than a day."

"I don't think it's that simple." Much as I would like the mystery solved so swiftly, a different suspicion tickled the back of my mind again. "What if Marcus is the one who broke into the house?"

The rest of them stared at me, their faces painted in varying shades of confusion and dismay.

"You can't think he would actually do such a thing," Nic said. He was the spitting image of our father at his most worried; it was an expression the two of them perfected over countless doctors' visits and overseas excursions to specialists. "He's duty bound to serve Industria."

"Precisely my reasoning," I countered. "The kidnappers want the Augmentation schematics. For all we know, Kingsley wants to use that information to build an army of Augmented soldiers. His men could have been dragging our parents out the back door even as I took the Pixii to him."

"Don't tell me you felled the great Marcus Kingsley with that pocket zinger of yours?" Sebastian asked. When I nodded, he looked amused and annoyed all at once. "Dash it all, I would have paid good money to see that! Other people would have done the same. We could have sold tickets." He finished his drink and set the glass down on the occasional table.

"It was about as satisfying as you might expect," I conceded, "but it doesn't change the fact that I can't call him back here. We can't bring in the Ferrum Viriae. If Marcus is involved, we might be the next to disappear."

"So if we aren't ringing the police, what are we doing?" Violet asked.

"I have to find the Augmentation papers before the kidnappers contact us again." I made my way to my father's desk and started to sift through the mess.

"You don't mean to give them the research!" Nic protested. "That belongs to Warwick."

"And Mama and Papa," I corrected, sorting through legal documents: our parents' Last Will and Testament, the deed to Glasshouse, passports, four birth certificates, and two death certificates: Dimitria Beryl Farthing, Age: 18. Cygna Garnet Farthing, Age: One day.

Both were killed by "myocardial infarction with genetic complications"—fancy words to explain a condition that afflicted only my sisters and me, not Nic.

I set the certificates aside with trembling fingers. "I've no intention of giving them anything except a jail sentence, but you can't catch a rat without cheese."

"That's a good way to get your fingers caught in a trap," Sebastian observed, joining me at the desk.

"Come, come, Mister Stirling, don't tell me your soul quails at a bit of subterfuge and espionage." I lifted the will to my ear to confirm that the Mechanical Movement Seal still ticked, then held it up to the light. At the proper angle, the seal produced the three-dimensional image of Industria's landmass overlaid with the Farthing emblem of a six-petal rose. "Still working. No one's tampered with any of these."

"Look through the rest of it," Nic urged. "If we're lucky, the kidnappers left a fingerprint on this." He gestured to the message cylinder on the desk.

Below the legal papers, my father's ledger contained notes on various projects, diagrams, blueprints, but there was absolutely nothing of a medical nature found within. The requested Augmentation notes, including the diagram for my clockwork ventriculator, were conspicuous only in their absence. "They're not here."

Sebastian's nimble fingers sorted through everything again. "Maybe you missed something."

"Or I'm looking in the wrong place." I knelt next to Papa's desk. Intricately carved out of redwood, it was honeycombed with hidey-holes. When I was young, my father used to secret chocolate bars and toys in it for me to find.

But this was no mere treasure hunt. Alternately using a penknife and a hairpin, I opened the first false-bottomed drawer and revealed a dog-eared copy of *Concise Remarks upon the Surgical Mechanization of the Human Anatomy*.

Violet's nostrils flared with distaste. "Why does he own that piece of utter rubbish?"

"I very much doubt he was reading it for pleasure." I turned the pamphlet over in my hands. Originally published under the title *Unvarnished Truths*, it had been surreptitiously distributed in the months preceding Warwick's very public trial and anonymously justified the risks of his experiments and the deaths of those involved. After he was arraigned on twenty counts of murder, he publicly claimed authorship of the manifesto, and the treatise went into second, third, and fourth printings within a month. I'd read part of it, but Mama caught me and burned it in the hearth.

Opening Papa's copy, I saw it was inscribed with an ink scrawl.

Perhaps this will help broker an understanding between us.

Though it was unsigned, I knew who'd sent it.

I set the pamphlet aside to wrestle with the desk's other hidden compartments and decorative panels. Within minutes, I'd amassed a collection of letters, all of them from Warwick. The earliest one dated back to the week after Dimitria's death.

Dear Sir:

It is my sincere hope that together we can avert further tragedy.

That one contained a rough pencil sketch in the margin: an early diagram of my Ticker. The newer missives, written on the thin, cheap paper provided by Gannet Penitentiary, were decorated with angry ink blots where Warwick pressed his pen too long or too hard upon the page.

You are not the only one to doubt me, but you are the only one whom I called "friend."

The final note I discovered had my name upon it. "This one is for me."

"Do you want me to read it for you?" Nic asked.

I shook my head. The broken wax seal on the back indicated my father had opened it already.

Dear Penny:

You are too young to understand yet, but it is my sincerest wish that someday soon we will speak and I will be able to explain everything to you. At the heart of the matter, I am both guilty and innocent. And I would do it all over again to save you. It is what your sister wanted.

"Lies. Dimitria never would have wanted him to kill in my name." With a shudder, I shoved all the notes into a pile and pushed away from the desk. "What we need isn't here. We have to get to the Bibliothèca."

"Whatever for?" Violet asked, forehead scrunched up.

"Papa kept copies of important information on Eidolachometer punch cards," I explained. "We need to retrieve them from our vault before the thieves realize that's an option."

Unable to stop himself, Nic raised a protest. "Downtown is going to be utter chaos. Everyone is waiting for the verdict. There are Edoceon everywhere. Never mind that you shouldn't go running about after what happened in the hall."

"I can, and I shall." I started to stand and felt the floor tilt under my feet. "But a few more minutes to gather my thoughts and another piece of cake wouldn't come amiss."

Violet laughed and handed me the last slice as Sebastian whistled, long and low.

“Little did I know when I woke up this morning that I would be knee-deep in Gordian knots by the lunch hour,” he said with a sardonic glance at my brother.

“Enjoy the ride,” Nic muttered. “If I know Penny, we’ll be up to our eyeballs in trouble by teatime.”

FOUR

In Which Silence Is More Than Golden

It was a ridiculous thing to have to stop and consider my clothes. Ripped in countless places and dotted with Nic's blood, my sadly maligned morning suit was now as inappropriate for a rescue excursion as Violet's SugarWerks uniform. I hurried as fast as I dared up the stairs, with everyone following close behind. The terrible knowledge that Mama and Papa were in certain peril pursued us to the third floor.

"I think my aubergine dress will fit you," I said to Violet, "if you can avoid tripping over the skirts."

"I'll loop them up about my neck if I have to," she promised as we reached my bedroom.

None of us commented on the door just down the hallway that was shrouded in mourning gloom. To my knowledge, no one in the family save Mama had entered Dimitria's room in the year since she'd died. There were times in the quiet, dark hours when I thought I could sense my sister moving across the floor with her careful footsteps, winding up the Cylindrella machine and playing her favorite recordings.

Try as I might to keep the door closed on the memories, they crept toward me with strains of remembered music. Though Dimitria played no instrument herself, she was always humming something under her breath, half the time not even realizing she did so. She also loved gardens and studied floriography.

"There's a hidden meaning in every flower, Penny," she'd told me once, touching her fingertips to a newly arrived bouquet of tulips. "The pink ones are for caring, and yellow is for good cheer."

"And the red?" I'd asked. Missives had been arriving with alarming regularity: messages via the Calliope, paper-wrapped parcels in the mail. Gifts, I had realized with a start, from my sister's as-yet-unnamed boyfriend. "Red flowers are for love, aren't they?"

Her answer had been a blush that put the tulips to shame, but any hope that her romance would bloom died with her, and along with it the hope that any Farthing girl could survive the condition that plagued us. She'd been the healthiest of us, while I'd been the invalid, and Cygna given no chance at all by fate. Warwick checked my older sister every month but only caught a vague, irregular heartbeat on occasion—certainly nothing that indicated her time left upon this earth should have been measured in minutes rather than years.

Sebastian nudged me out of the past with a gentle elbow as he headed into my brother's room. "Tend to your ablutions, Miss Farthing. You strongly resemble a chimney sweep."

Turning back to my own door, I lined up the letters for my password on a rotating copper permutation lock.

M-E-T-A-L-M-A-R-K

It was the common name for the *Voltinia dramba* Butterfly and the newest addition to my collection. Letters properly aligned, I pulled the activation lever. Gears behind wood and plaster whirred and clanked, then granted us permission to enter.

I stepped into the room, turning up the lamps and taking a mental inventory of the contents, starting with the chocolate-brown velvet eiderdown and the Bhaskarian rug in shades of coffee and cream. A warm glow danced over walls that shimmered with the movement of dozens of mechanical Butterflies. I'd dusted their shadow boxes that very morning, all the better to see the diamanté stickpins that held each specimen against black velvet. The constant tick-tick-tick of infinitesimal inner workings caused their wings to flutter up and down, and I automatically sought out my favorites: the Silver-studded Blue (*Plebeius argus*) winking next to the Geranium Bronze (*Cacyreus marshalli*).

Heeding Sebastian's suggestion, I also checked the nearest mirror. The morning had certainly taken its toll. There was dirt and worse on my face. Escaping its pins, my hair straggled over my shoulders in unruly copper curls. Wide hazel eyes stared back at me.

"Ever-changing Twindicators," Dimitria had teased, because the color of our eyes shifted from brown to amber to green depending on the light, the fabrics Nic and I wore, and whatever mood we might be in.

Knowing the wash water would take time to heat, I turned the spigot over the corner basin to "Scalding." The radiator hissed and clanked in protest, so I gave its cast-iron ribs a swift kick with my boot.

"I know just how you feel," Violet said, but I didn't know if she was speaking to me or the radiator.

"You go first," I told her when the copper water pipes rattled against the wall behind me, "while the towels are still relatively clean."

She obliged, stripping down to her underthings. I detached the RiPA from my garter, but hesitated to set it down on the desk, which was in its perpetual state of chaos. At the moment, the shiny innards of a pocket watch littered the scarred surface of the wood, and teetering towers of account ledgers sat under the magnificent stained-glass window known as the "Papilionoidea."

The RiPA in my hand began to clack and clatter. The message was from Ambrose Farnsworth.

BACK INSIDE THE FACTORY - STOP - DAMAGE LESS THAN ORIGINALLY ESTIMATED - STOP - SOME STOCK AS YET UNACCOUNTED FOR - STOP

Pursing my lips, I tapped out a response.

DESTROYED IN THE EXPLOSION - QUERY MARK

His answer was as troubling as it was puzzling.

CRATES EARMARKED FOR CURREY HOSPITAL ARE MISSING - STOP - DID YOU AUTHORIZE REMOVAL - QUERY MARK

I hadn't, but at this point in time, a few missing packing cases were the least of our worries.

I DID NOT - STOP - CHECK TO SEE IF THEY WERE PICKED UP IN THE COMMOTION - STOP

A soft knock at the door signaled Dreadnaught's arrival with more clean linen. "Can I assist with your toilettes, ladies?"

"I'm all right." I pulled off my shirtwaist and considered the damage. Before the chatelaine took up residency at Glasshouse, the majority of my wardrobe had been cobbled together with pins, liquid adhesive, and rivets purloined from the factory. Though I couldn't sew a tidy buttonhole to save my life, I was a crack hand at mending tears and holes. "I'll just get my stapler and fix this."

"You will *not*," Dreadnaught said. Only two degrees removed from a garment district stitch-counter, she was beyond horrified by the very suggestion. "Surely you have something more suitable."

I unfastened the hooks on my skirt and stepped out of my bustle without tripping and killing myself. Only that morning, I'd read that one in ten young ladies become entrapped in the wire cages. The claim was made by the founder of the Center for Fashionable Reform, but I didn't feel compelled to desert my own "dress-enhancing death trap" until official documentation linked it to fatality or dismemberment. "Define 'suitable.'"

"There's only one outfit fit to be seen right now." Dreadnaught crossed to the wardrobe and extracted a walking dress of dove foulard. I raised an eyebrow at the elaborately draped overskirt, the rosettes, and the broad box pleats of navy silk. From Kashenkerry's Atelier (Fine Garments & Ready To Wear) and a gift from my Grandmother Pendleton, it had hung in the wardrobe for a month like the shy miss at a cotillion. "Scrub everything from the waist up or you'll leave smudge marks," the chatelaine added.

Under her keen-eyed supervision, I washed the grit and grime of the factory explosion from my arms and face, scrubbing at my skin with a washcloth until I was the color of a boiled Meridian lobster. Aided by the chatelaine, both Violet and I were dressed, coiffed, and sensibly accessorized in due time.

Just not hastily enough for my taste. With every passing moment, my anxiety about my parents grew. It was one thing to watch them retreat into their own worlds after the deaths of my sisters and quite another to think that I might never see them again. "Everything that's happened has been my fault, Vi."

"Piffle," she retorted, adjusting her borrowed skirts. "It's not your fault you were born with a heart defect, or that your parents care enough for you to move the stars to see you healed and well."

"Maybe. But it's my fault they are goodness-knows-where. That Warwick tried to develop a better Ticker."

That he went mad and killed people in the attempt.

I wouldn't think about that just now. Defiant in the face of my fears, I marched from the room and made my way downstairs via a slide down the banister. Difficult to do when wearing a bustle skirt.

Difficult, but not impossible.

"Never mind waiting for your Ticker to give out, Penny. You're going to break your neck," Violet said for the second time that morning, following me down the more customary way. The ends of her ribbons flapped to match the cadence of her feet on the stairs. With lace mitts covering her tattoos and her gearring removed, she looked every inch the demure lass, save for her amethyst hair and her great stompy boots peeping out from under my skirts.

While we waited for Nic and Sebastian to finish refreshing their linen, I ducked briefly into the study to close the wall safe and retrieve my father's watch. Violet passed the time striding up and down the hall. After a particularly loud about-face, she caught sight of the chatelaine and tilted her head to one side.

"Perhaps you ought to come with us, Miss Dreadnaught. You shouldn't remain here alone. What if the thieves come back?"

“They wouldn’t catch me unaware,” was the chatelaine’s grim response. “I shall stay here to protect the house from further attack. There’s also a great deal of work to be done.”

“If I didn’t know better,” I said, closing the study door behind me and reaching for my bag, “I’d think you’re almost looking forward to a cleanup of this magnitude.”

“It will be quite satisfying to set everything to rights,” she admitted, seeing us to the door.

Just outside, a messenger boy stood on the stoop, one finger outstretched toward the doorbell. He had a pack slung over his shoulder and a winning, gap-toothed smile at the ready.

“Delivery for Miss Farthing,” he said with a tip of his cap.

Dreadnaught traded a handful of coppers for the letter, then passed it to me. The card stock was produced locally by the Featherweight Mill, watermarked with the Ferrum Viriae’s crest, and needlessly expensive, but then Marcus probably scribbled his grocery list on fine linen when it suited him.

“A bit soon for a summons from the good Mister Kingsley, isn’t it?” I murmured, not bothering with a letter opener.

But the paper within didn’t remind me of the stern Legatus. It reeked of sandalwood, and for an instant, I was transported to a silken tent on a Bhaskarian desert. I unfolded it with a frown and squinted at the spider-thin handwriting.

Dear Miss Farthing,

Your sister sent word this morning through my otherworldly envoy that you are in grave danger. She wishes you to proceed with utmost caution, though she also added that you are (and I hope you’ll forgive the direct quote) “more likely to run headlong into danger with bells on.” In any case, I wished to pass the message to you.

Yours in light and love,
Philomena de Mesmer
Professional Clairaudience and Trance, by appointment only

P.S. Dimitria also cautions you to mind the third step from the bottom. According to her, "it's a bit tricky."

Feeling ill-used and grimy again, I handed the letter over to Violet without comment. My older sister's passing had changed all of us and not for the better. While Papa often fell asleep in his chair after imbibing a full bottle of Gentian Amaros, Mama sought solace from every charlatan psychic in town. Encouraged by crystal-gazing swindlers from here to Helvetica, she spent a small fortune trying to contact Cygna and Dimitria "beyond the veil." Dragged to countless séances, I witnessed enough table rapping, crystal gazing, and phantom manifestations to last me through this life and the next. Mama might have been desperate enough to believe in it, but I had no use at all for that sort of sideshow.

"What a load of rubbish," Violet said, crumpling the paper in her fist, "claiming to have spoken with Dimitria!"

"It doesn't take a psychic to understand that there's money to be harvested from grieving families," I said. "Still, it does beg the question as to why a professional charlatan is writing to me on Ferrum Viriae stationery, doesn't it?"

"Or not," Violet suggested as the boys joined us. "Do you feel well enough to go?"

"I do," I said firmly, opening the front door and leading the way down the stairs. The morning's clouds had called in reinforcements, and thick fog crept toward us with an assassin's stealth.

Though it was only early afternoon, the sky was completely blotted out. The cold that snaked down my spine, however, wasn't a reaction to the change in the weather.

"We'll take my car," Sebastian said. Pulling out his driving goggles, he cut in front of me and indicated the Combustible at the curb. "Unless Penny thinks she can balance us all on her handlebars."

"Not in this outfit, I can't." Remembering my forsaken steed, I rushed to retrieve the Vitesse and move it out of the street. By the time I reached the car, Nic had claimed the spot next to Sebastian, leaving me to the backseat with Violet. I crammed my skirts in next to hers as best I could and adjusted the lap belt as we took off down the street.

"Still no news from the courthouse," my brother said after a short RiPA message clacked in on his wrist.

"We have more pressing concerns at the moment." I never thought something would eclipse the verdict, but right now there was nothing more important than locating those Augmentation papers. Fiddling about with Papa's watch, I clicked open the case and snapped it shut until Violet covered my hand with her own. We stayed like that in silence for the rest of the drive across town.

Leaving the Combustible parked at the curb, we climbed the stone staircase leading up to the Bibliothèca. A large and noisy group was gathered outside the doors, and I faltered, uncertain if I ought to take another step.

"It's the Edoceon."

"They're protesting here as well," Nic murmured. With a subtle shift of his body, he screened me from their view with his shoulders.

"Vultures," Violet said, closing in on my other side. Though I could usually see clear over the top of her head, the purple feathered hat she wore served as a brilliantly plumed shield.

"That's not the same group that threw a bottle at me this morning," I noted, peeking between her borrowed frills and bows.

"Let's not give them an opportunity to change that," Sebastian said. With debonair grace, he strolled forth, cane swinging, and began making inquiries about their "good cause, in which I am most passionately interested."

The rest of us hastened inside. The Bibliothèca structure was the oldest in Bazalgate, dating back almost five hundred years. Mammoth marble columns supported an arched ceiling. Enormous windows set high into the wall normally amplified the incoming sunshine. Today, colossal iron chandeliers compensated for the lack of natural illumination.

Even more intimidating than the architecture, thousands of mechanical *Xestobium rufovillosum* perched on the walls. The Death Watch Beetles monitored noise levels, and if an unlucky patron progressed beyond a whisper, the twitches of their mica wings summoned the Unseen librarians. Once charged with safeguarding the thousands of paper documents and illuminated manuscripts, the Unseen now tended the city's Eidolachometer Information Storage System. No one knew exactly where the librarians were trained or how they were recruited, but at least once or twice a month, a researcher's limp body was removed from the building and transferred to Currey Hospital for observation. It took anywhere from three days to a week for the patient to wake up, another month or more to recover his or her powers of speech.

Accordingly, I dropped my voice below a whisper when Sebastian caught up with us at the first intersection. "This way."

Private Eidolachometer cards were separated from the publicly accessible ones by a series of corridors and locking gates. The others followed me down the hall marked "Personal Archives." Numbered doors opened off either side of the hall.

"Six three six," I murmured. "*Tempus est clavis.* Time is key."

But an unexpected swarm of people barricaded the hallway. Each of the men and women wore the charcoal wool and iron bracelets of the Ferrum Viriae. Towering over them, Marcus Kingsley supervised the removal of brass and gold Eidolachometer cards from one of the vaults. With very little effort, I could guess which one it was.

I hadn't prepared myself to see him again so soon, hadn't braced myself against who he was and how I was drawn to him, yet I bounded the last few steps that separated us without hesitation. Employing my considerable bustle, I blocked the entrance to the Farthing family alcove, though it was a bit like closing the stable door after all the mechanical horses have rusted. "Stop! That's private property!"

Marcus's hand clamped down over my mouth before I could say another word, and just like that, he was touching me again. Overhead, a hundred waiting Beetles stirred, dislodging dust and glitter-flecks of stone; no doubt they could hear the beating of the Ticker in my chest.

Fingers still pressed to my lips, Marcus waited a long moment before whispering, "Indeed it is your property, but half the vault's contents were stolen just a few minutes ago. There's been another break-in. I advise you to go home at once."

I stared at him, trying to process everything without focusing too much on the fact that I was essentially kissing his palm. Reaching up, I pried his hand from my mouth. "Counting

Glasshouse, that makes two in one day, with you arriving on the scene mere seconds afterward. Quite the coincidence, is it not?"

"And just what are you implying?" he asked, gaze narrowing.

It was all I could do not to lunge at the same soldiers who'd helped clear Glasshouse. One by one, they sidled past us carrying boxes of hastily gathered Eidolachometer cards.

"I object to the confiscation of our property," I hissed.

Marcus glanced up at the Beetles before speaking again. "We're not confiscating it, Miss Farthing; we're following procedure. We need to catalog it against an inventory list."

Struggling to keep my voice down, I eyeballed the sheaf of papers in his hands, each bearing one of the Bibliothèca's Official Mechanical Seals. "And just why do you care about my parents' paperwork, Mister Kingsley?"

The pause before he answered set off every one of my internal alarms. "I don't, but whoever pulled this heist somehow stole a sizable amount of property and vacated the premises in less than three minutes, all without alerting the Unseen. Their only mistake was to trip one of the silent alarms in passing. Whatever's missing might give us some indication as to who these people are and what they want."

That might be the truth, but I doubted it was the whole truth. "I don't care about your lists or your timeline right now," I said, reaching for the last of the boxes. "I demand you release the remainder of my property to me at once."

"Here now," the soldier responded, trying to shake my hand off. "Leave off of that!"

Trying to evade me, he lost his grip on the wooden crate, and it fell to the floor with a terrific crash. The Beetles on the ceiling and walls began to dance, creating a living tapestry on the stones. A mighty rush of air surrounded us, gathering all the loosened bits of stone and dirt and flinging them at us. I kept my eyes tightly shut, trying to prepare myself for whatever the Unseen might do to me as punishment.

And what will the kidnappers do with Mama and Papa in the meantime?

As suddenly as it had arrived, the wind evaporated. The soldier who'd dropped the crate lay prone upon the floor, eyes rolling into the back of his head and mouth hanging slack. My breath caught in my throat as the ruffles of my overskirts settled back into place, and I pressed my own gloved hand to my mouth this time.

In complete silence, Marcus called back enough men to carry out their fallen comrade. The look he gave me before leaving would have felled a lesser person; I returned it in kind and added one perfectly arched eyebrow. Neither of us, it seemed, would offer the other a "farewell" or a "good day" in parting; at least he wouldn't be able to lord my lack of manners over me when next we met.

After he disappeared around the far corner, the space seemed to echo just a bit more. The stone walls and floors exuded a bit more dark and dank. The Beetles hovered overhead, ready to summon the Unseen back from their unknown lair. I shuddered and turned to the others, who looked as troubled as I felt.

"We needed those cards," Nic said, careful to keep his voice low. "What will happen to Mama and Papa if we can't track down the thieves?"

My brain performed a Knight's Maneuver. One square on the chessboard to: *The Great Mister Kingsley doesn't think the burglars had much time to escape.*

Another square to: *Perhaps they* didn't *have time to escape.*

And a final sidestep to: *That might mean they're still in the building somewhere!*

"I think the Legatus might have been right," I said.

"About us going home at once?" Nic's tone indicated he didn't harbor a single hope that would actually be the plan. Just as he always did when nervous, he pulled his glasses off and checked them for nonexistent spots.

"Hardly," I retorted. "You heard what Marcus said. The alarm went off, and the Ferrum Viriae arrived on the scene within minutes. The thieves have to be hiding somewhere nearby."

"With the stolen property," Sebastian said. An accomplished cardsharp, he had no tells that we'd ever discovered, and thus betrayed neither reticence nor enthusiasm when he asked, "But where could they have gone that Marcus's soldiers would have missed?"

"That is indeed the question."

An unexpected noise that strongly reminded me of a falcon's cry echoed off the stones. The Beetles overhead twitched in response. My Ticker thudded oddly in my chest as I stepped closer to Violet.

"What was that?" she whispered.

"I don't know." When I turned to Nic and Sebastian, both shook their heads with matching bewilderment. The mystery noise came a second time, causing my Ticker to skip a beat. The Beetles began their agitated dance; with the third and loudest of the bird cries, they seized up and began dropping down upon our heads. We ran for the nearest archway to take shelter from the unusual rain, clockwork corpses twitching all around us. To our right, circular stone stairs twisted down into the darkness. Once a repository for the bones of leaders and dignitaries, the area under the Bibliothèca now contained the dead tree files rendered obsolete by the invention of the Eidolachometer. Less interested in paper than my pulse, I wondered if that was where the Unseen cloistered. "We need to go into the catacombs."

“That isn’t funny, Penny,” Nic said, dislodging brass carapaces from his jacket with an impatient hitch of his shoulders.

Even Sebastian looked disconcerted by the idea of venturing downstairs. “Wasn’t that enough dead things to satisfy you?”

“I’ve no intention of joining them.” Reaching into my messenger bag, I pulled out a Watt’s Handheld Incandescent Lamp and the Pixii. “I’ll go first.”

“I’ll be right behind you,” Violet said.

Sebastian swung his walking stick so that it whistled slightly, then pulled a previously concealed short sword from its wooden sheath. “Old Reliable didn’t realize she might get to come out and play today. I really ought to spend more time with the three of you. It’s been quite the adventure thus far.”

Another bird cry traveled up from the bottom of the stairwell and echoed in my chest.

“Down we go,” I told the others.

“Remember what I said about teatime?” Nic said to Sebastian. “Up to our eyeballs in trouble, didn’t you say?”

“Indeed.”

FIVE

In Which Our Heroine Seizes an Opportunity and Is Left Holding the Bag

---

Wall sconces lit the way down the stone stairs and along another cold corridor. Once we reached a twisted iron staircase, modern blue phosphorescence yielded to vintage oil lamps. I could feel Nic's wary gaze shift from our surroundings to me every so often, though he didn't give further voice to his worries. Inwardly, I agreed this would be a most inopportune time and place to suffer an attack and issued my Ticker a severe warning.

Just in time, too, as I reached the third stair from the bottom and it gave way under my weight, unceremoniously dumping me into the lower corridor. Terrified that the least bit of noise would summon the Unseen, I did my best to muffle my squeak of alarm.

"Are you all right?" Nic asked as he picked me up off the floor.

I nodded, but I'd scraped the flesh on both palms, and pain radiated from both knees. My flashlight had rolled a few feet away; only when we recovered it did we notice that the lanterns along the next wall had been smashed. The Beetles in this corridor had been deactivated as well. They littered the floor, some of them crushed by boot heels, leaving smears of copperslip oil on the stones. The one nearest my shoe struggled to rise on shaky legs. With a flick of his wings, he began walking in erratic circles.

I carefully stepped over him and dimmed the flashlight to its lowest setting. The resultant darkness was an inky cloak, forcing us to make our way in a single-file procession, with each of us holding on to the person in front and behind. By the time we reached the end of the hallway, a hundred or more Beetles climbed the walls, scuttling with bent legs and broken antennae to their programmed stone quadrant. One ill-timed sneeze, and the Unseen would reappear.

Luckily enough, the final gate I encountered was no longer fastened. The lock had been forced, the iron lattice roughly pushed to one side. I squeezed Nic's hand, using the same series of dots and dashes that I would with the RiPA.

THEY ARE HERE - PROCEED WITH CAUTION

Nic relayed the message to Sebastian who, in turn, passed it to Violet. The catacombs were as still as a tomb, but if I'd been expecting cobwebs, a fetid stench, or a skeleton rattling his bones, I was disappointed. Invisible heating vents pumped clean air into the room, maintaining the appropriate temperature and humidity for preserving paper documentation. Set few and far between, ox-eye windows transmitted the meager aboveground light, transforming it into something curious and thin and green. Throughout the room, papers and ledgers filled bookcases, cabinets, and tables. The knowledge of generations surrounded us, seeping into the stones and brushing over our skin so that the hairs on the back of my neck prickled up.

The dead were with us, even if their bones resided elsewhere.

NIC AND I GO LEFT - V AND S GO RIGHT

We separated, picking careful paths and sticking to the shadows. My eyes adjusted to the lack of light, but I still thought with longing of the Starshine goggles sitting on my desk at home. Of course, a MAG wouldn't come amiss now either, especially when I recognized the outline of a man's head just before me. I knew by the way that Nic tensed up that he'd seen him as well. Pixii charged, I crept up behind our quarry. With a leap, I discharged everything I had into his neck with a burst of light and the accompanying muffled pop!

Except the Pixii wasn't designed to work on marble, so the bust of Malachi Baynard, one of Industria's founding scientists, wasn't at all perturbed by such an attack. I had no chance to recover my wits before a scuffle broke out to our right. Someone shoved Violet aside, and multiple dark figures suddenly dipped and ducked between the stacks. We gave chase, though pursued and pursuers alike moved in near silence. Papers took to the air like geese leaving a mill pond and then fell with whispers. A shelf started to fall, and Nic rushed to stabilize it. A thick ledger toppled off a podium, but I caught it before it could hit the floor. When I turned around, Sebastian had one of the burglars cornered, the tip of his short sword pressed to the soft skin of his opponent's throat. Violet sat upon the back of another, twisting his arms behind him until he whimpered. That left a third for Nic and me: the one scaling a ladder set into the wall. A heavy satchel swung in his grip. In his haste, he missed a rung and slid halfway down the wall, cursing all the way.

The Beetles commenced their twitching dance. I froze, but my prey accessed a glowing device strapped to his wrist. When he depressed a button, the bird cry we heard earlier bounced off every stone, every pane of glass. As one, the mechanical bugs seized and fell. The burglar immediately resumed climbing, and I vaulted over a stack of ledgers, charging the Pixii as I ran. Arriving at the ladder, I had to put the device between my teeth before starting up the rungs, nimble as a monkey.

"I'm right behind you—" Nic stopped suddenly, and I twisted about to see a fourth thief catch my brother about the neck and pull him back to the floor.

Nic plowed three quick blows into the thief's midsection. "Go!" he panted between punches. "Catch the one with the cards!"

I hesitated, as surprised by the swiftness and violence of my brother's attack as I was by the dark expression on his face. By the time I resumed climbing, the burglar had reached the top of the ladder and disappeared through a narrow opening. Doubling my speed, it took me less than a minute to gain the crawl space with a heave and grunt; it was another matter entirely to scramble forward with yards of dove-colored foulard trailing behind me. On hands and knees, I moved through complete darkness, choking on dust, eyes struggling to make out anything at all.

Ahead of me was a dragging noise, the scrape of heavy fabric and metal on stone, then my right hand encountered the rough burlap sack containing the Eidolachometer cards. I tightened my grip upon it just in time for the burglar to pull both the sack and me into an alleyway. I lost my grip on the Pixii, and it skittered across the stones, disappearing into the thick fog that swirled about us.

"Leave off!" the thief growled, trying to shake me free of the bag. I refused to let go, though I was at a distinct disadvantage in both size and weaponry. He stood a head taller than I and wielded a short, wicked blade. He didn't hesitate to swing it in my direction, either. "Troublesome little snip—"

My boot connected with his wrist. His knife went spinning down the alleyway. I lowered my head and charged, my skull connecting with his midsection, and the two of us went down in a tangle of limbs and a torrent of swearing.

All the colorful language coming out of my opponent nearly muffled the sound of approaching sirens and the hissing pops of a hundred activated *Lampyridae mechanika*. Falling like shooting stars, the Fireflies careened overhead in a blur of mica wings, exposed clockwork mechanisms, and blue phosphorescent abdomens. By their light, I could just make out the bandit's face.

"Air support's on its way," I said. Not even a bluff, because the distinctive whirring noise of rappelling wires signaled incoming Araneae.

"The only one who's going to get caught blazing is you." The thief shoved the burlap sack at me.

Thrown back by the weight of it, I hit the side of the brick building hard enough to jar everything from my Ticker to my toes. The impact forced my eyes closed—only for half a second, but that was long enough for my attacker to disappear into the shadows. The next moment, a dozen Araneae landed in the alley with the silent precision of spiders on silk lines. Six of the specially trained Ferrum Viriae unclipped from their harnesses and pursued the burglar. The rest swiftly surrounded me.

"Well timed," I said, scorn my only defense.

The tallest of them stepped forward like a jungle cat, with eyes that could obviously see far better in the dark than mine. Boots that should have made a heavy footfall on the cobblestones moved with uncanny silence.

"Of course it would be *you*," Marcus said, removing his face shield.

"Did you miss me?" Even breathless, I infused the words with a surprising amount of sarcasm. Ill-advised, I'm sure, but the remaining vestiges of fear and adrenaline needed some outlet.

"I've no polite answer for that question, Miss Farthing, and so I'll refrain from saying anything." Such formality made him sound older, but the exasperation behind the words betrayed him as he reached for the bag of Eidolachometer cards.

I considered resisting and then thought better of it. Despite my irritation, some traitorous part of me was reassured by his presence. "You're welcome."

"For what?" Marcus asked, never taking his gaze off me.

"For retrieving the stolen property." I scanned the alley until I spotted my Pixii in a heap of unidentifiable refuse. I retrieved it, wrinkling my nose and wiping off the device with my handkerchief. Depressing the resistance switch, I was gratified to see it still worked. "Isn't that supposed to be your job? Shall I send you a bill?"

"Not unless you want to explain to a judge why you undermined a covert operation." Marcus closed the distance between us; another man would have done it in ten steps, but he did it in five. "I knew the thieves were in the catacombs. We were trying to catch the gang red-handed, but thanks to you, one seems to have escaped."

Startled by the note of anger, I looked up until my entire world consisted of dark wool and his broad shoulders. "I was only doing what was necessary—"

"Wrong," he said, interrupting me. "We've met three times today, Miss Farthing, and thrice your reactions have put me or one of my soldiers in jeopardy. I can't guess how you'll behave in any given situation, except I can bet money that you'll conduct yourself poorly, and that makes you a liability."

"You certainly know how to turn a girl's head with compliments, Mister Kingsley." Cold fury iced over my Ticker, and slick silver needles coursed through my veins in place of blood. "Are you quite finished?"

"Not even close. You're going to have to explain to my satisfaction why every site of destruction and mayhem today has centered around your family and property." Marcus tapped out a message on his RiPA.

Violet emerged from the crawl space with Sebastian just behind.

"Can the interrogation wait a few minutes?" Sebastian queried calmly. "We have three criminals tied up in the catacombs. It wouldn't have taken us so long to meet up with you, but there's precious little rope down there, and we had to improvise. Nic is sitting on them right now."

Marcus dispatched two officers with a flick of his finger just as a silver SkyDart landed a few feet away. Designed for swift transport to and from the Flying Fortress, the aircrafts were too new and too expensive for civilian ownership and certainly not yet for hire by the hour. I'd never actually seen one of them up close and tried not to stare at the sleek lines that reminded me of a crossbow bolt, the open cockpit, the tendrils of luminous smoke created by the air-breathing engines.

"Just what is that thing for?" I asked.

"That thing, Miss Farthing, is your ride. I'm taking you in for more questioning."

I took a step back and found myself up against the wall for the second time in as many minutes. "I'm not going anywhere with you, Marcus Kingsley. I won't be treated like a criminal."

"I merely require a place of relative safety where I can offer you all due hospitality." When Marcus took me by the elbow, my choice was to walk or be dragged.

I chose the former, but not by a wide margin. "While you torture me within an inch of my life?"

"While I take down your statement of this day's events." He unfolded the SkyDart's metal stairs.

Though I liked it not a whit, I knew I had to go with him. Marcus was in possession of the Eidolachometer cards, and they might be the only way to get my parents back. The short exchange of words with the burglar had planted seeds of ice and fear in my midsection.

Caught up in my worries, I paused at the foot of the stairs. "I should wait for Nic."

Marcus twisted about to address our somewhat dumbfounded audience. "Mister Stirling, would you please advise your friend on the gravity of the situation?"

Sebastian's face was pale under his fashionable mustache. "Get in the SkyDart, Penny."

Just because I had to go didn't mean I had to be polite about it. I cast a deliberate glance at the burnished oxblood leather. "I never agreed to air travel. I'll be sick all over your very expensive upholstery."

"This should take care of it." Marcus reached under the front seat and extracted a bottle of Doctor Westerley's Vitamin-Fortified Liquid Courage.

I rolled it over in my hand.

A TONIC OF CONCENTRATED CURATIVE POWER
& A MOST EFFECTIVE TINCTURE
CONCOCTED FROM FENNEL SEED, PEPPERMINT,
WILD LICORICE, AND GINGER.
GUARANTEED TO REGULATE AND STRENGTHEN
THE DIGESTIVE SYSTEM!
WILL ALSO ADDRESS SYMPTOMS OF THE COMMON COLD
AND EASE ACHING JOINTS.
50 PROOF

But I wasn't done arguing. "This only has room for two. Where are the others going to sit?"

"The others are going to follow in a second transport as soon as we retrieve your brother," Marcus said, impatience clipping his consonants. "Now, will you please take your seat?"

When I continued to hesitate, I thought he might pick me up and toss me in. Instead, he reached for my hand and gave me the bag of Eidolachometer cards.

"I'll entrust this to you for the duration of the flight."

A moment passed, with something more exchanged than just the bag of purloined and recovered goods. Energy crackled between us until I felt an unexpected kinship with Tesla coils. Marcus looked as though he very much wanted to say something, his eyes the same somber gray as his uniform, a bit of bristle standing out on his cheeks and chin. I wondered if it felt as sandpaper rough as it looked, but wouldn't have dared remove my glove to touch his face.

Except to administer a right good slap.

I climbed in and tucked my hands firmly at my sides.

Marcus's features shifted from searching to stern as he followed. "Please do me the favor of fastening your safety belt, Miss

Farthing. It's a long way to the ground." He propped one foot against the door and made a great show of fastening his own lap belt. "Although every air transport must, by law, be outfitted with as many parachutes as there are seats, I wouldn't care to test such devices unless it was a dire necessity."

Reaching for the heavy safety belt, I fastened the connectors. "I would quite enjoy parachuting."

"Have you ever parachuted?"

"I've read the manuals."

"Theory and experience are two different things."

"The last time I read a manual, I immediately climbed aboard a Vitesse and drove it all the way around the Heart of the Star." I didn't mention that shortly thereafter I'd taken a header over the handlebars and landed without ceremony in a hay cart.

Marcus handed me a pair of ornate aviator goggles. "This will be a bit farther to fall than off your cycle."

The moment his hands returned to the controls, the flyer rocketed into the sky. I admit that I made an undignified noise that might have been a half-swallowed squeak. Torn free from its combs, my hair whipped about my face and shoulders, and I pulled on the goggles both to protect my eyes and relieve my squint. Soon, Bazalgate was no more than a collection of miniature rooftops and streets. The fog crept off the River Aire, and gas lamps the size of wax tapers burned bright.

Whatever I might have thought about Marcus as a conversational partner or a soldier, he was damned good behind the controls. His shoulders even relaxed a small measure while dealing with instrument panels and levers.

As opposed to people.

"This is marvelous!" I shouted over the mighty cacophony of the rushing wind and the engine. Remembering too late to whom

I was speaking, I hastily downgraded my enthusiasm by adding, "If ostentatious. Hardly inconspicuous, either. Certainly not made for stealth."

"The fog helps." Marcus's mouth quirked, though with irritation or amusement I couldn't be certain. "When people can't see the hand waving before their face, they don't look to the sky."

"Aren't you afraid of crashing into the Carillon Bell Tower?" Dedicated to the city's founders, it was Bazalgate's tallest landmark and the most impressive.

"There are a thousand and one instruments in here, at least half of them navigational."

"Naturally." I would have traded my eyeteeth for just five minutes at the controls.

Though I couldn't have leaned forward more than an inch, Marcus noticed. "Perhaps another time, when I'm quite certain my insurance premiums are up to date."

Any rejoinder I might have made evaporated with the clouds as the Flying Fortress came into view. Sunlight glinted off white columns and sleek glass architecture. Smaller satellite buildings clustered around a singularly imposing main structure, like chicks to a mother hen. Under it all, turbines produced the necessary amount of thrust to keep everything aloft. I hadn't any idea what the power source might be, nor could I fathom how Marcus's engineers achieved a nearly clean burn, but the utter lack of emissions meant that the air around the Fortress was cold water sipped from a crystal goblet, a far cry from Bazalgate's soot-smudged tankard. I adjusted my goggles and leaned as far out of the SkyDart as my lap belt allowed.

"Miss Farthing, please sit back so I might land without distraction," Marcus requested as we cruised nearer to the landing platform. Blinking red lanterns lit the circle's perimeter, though the sun subdued their brilliance. At night or in inclement weather, however, they'd be a veritable beacon of hope.

Marcus landed us with a gentle bump, no more than the basket of a hot-air balloon touching down in a grassy field. I remembered with a jolt that this was no mere pleasure jaunt, and all the fears I'd been holding at bay rushed back to weigh me down. Fumbling with the sack of cards, I released my belt and was halfway out of my seat before Marcus cut the engine.

"You have an Eidolachometer machine here, so we can read these?" I asked.

"I've sent for one." Determined to maintain some semblance of authority, Marcus tossed his goggles onto a seat, opened the door of the speeder, and leapt down. "Allow me."

Before he could unfold the filigree stairs, I gathered my skirts in one hand, vaulted over the railing, and landed next to him. Reaching back inside, I extracted the bag of cards and hoisted them over my shoulder. "Lead the way."

"Patience is a virtue, Miss Farthing." He turned on his heel and headed for a waiting elevator.

There was no way of asking him to hurry without explaining why, so, for once, I remained silent. The interior of the elevator was a capsule of elegance, with brass rails, etched mirrors, and thick Bhaskarian carpeting. Marcus operated the various levers with the same quiet assurance that he'd demonstrated in the SkyDart. A pulley system activated, and we glided downward. There was no floor indicator; it was only by counting off the seconds that I knew we'd descended at least three stories below the landing platform by the time the doors slid open.

The hall beyond was decorated with potted palm trees, jewel-toned rugs, and an extensive collection of curios alongside tattered leather-bound books, rolled maps, and globes of polished stone. Overhead, a system of bands and wheels rotated dozens of woven-straw fans. Formally dressed soldiers saluted as we passed. Plainly clad servitors carried silver trays set with message cylinders, ledgers, and other missives of importance. When the foot traffic cleared, a young woman sat in a chair opposite the elevator.

"There you are, Legatus." Though the unfamiliar woman wore the drab gray of the Ferrum Viriae, it was cut in the newest of fashions and embroidered collar to hem with metallic silver stars. Dangling green esmeraude earrings grazed her shoulders. Waist-length black braids cascaded down her back, and a Logodædaly Multilinguistic Translator dangled from her belt.

Marcus drew up short. "What have you done to your uniform?"

The newcomer looked down at her clothes with the air of one surprised to be wearing any. "This? A few minor alterations only." A dozen bangles jangled on her arms alongside her iron bracelets when she turned her gaze upon me. "And you have the famous Miss Farthing with you, just as I knew you would."

I returned her keen look and raised an eyebrow. "I'm sorry, have we been introduced?"

"Not in this lifetime," was her cryptic response.

Marcus located his tongue and his manners. "Penelope Farthing, I am pleased to introduce to you Philomena de Mesmer, recently appointed psychic consultant to the Ferrum Viriae."

A professional medium in Marcus's employ? I'd have been less shocked by a monkey hanging from the rafters. "I beg your pardon?"

Philomena cut in before he could respond. "I sent you a message, Miss Farthing. I hope you received it in time."

"I . . . did receive it, in fact."

Mind the third step from the bottom. It's a bit tricky.

And then I'd fallen on that precise stair at the Bibliothèca.

Coincidence, surely . . .

"I hope the information proved useful to you." Her forehead puckered in the tiniest of frowns. "Messages from the Great Beyond are often subject to interpretation."

Now it was Marcus's turn to be confused. "You sent Miss Farthing a note?"

"Little more than an hour ago," Philomena confirmed. "A personal correspondence, so perhaps I shouldn't have used official stationery. My apologies, Legatus." She set off down the hallway at a brisk clip. "I was headed to your office to deliver my report, then realized I could meet you at the elevator."

"Another premonition?" The words slipped out before I could stop them.

"That, and the announcement over the loudspeakers." Philomena tossed the words over her shoulder as she walked, leaving us to catch them and catch up.

I glanced at Marcus. "The Ferrum Viriae subscribe to a belief in the occult?"

He kept his gaze fixed forward. "We're conducting research in all branches of science and technology."

"Science and technology? You can't mean to tell me you're counterweighing some of the greatest advances of this century with a belief in such jiggery-pokery. Parlor tricks? Smoke and mirrors?"

A muscle in his jaw jumped at the accusation. "I've seen enough things in my lifetime to contemplate the possibilities of the next, Miss Farthing."

"As have I, and yet I refrain from such nonsense. As both an engineer and a person of science, I am absolutely appalled." I had more to say on the subject, but Philomena whirled about to face us.

"Come on then, we haven't all day." She strode backward with the confidence of one unconcerned with crashing into a large potted fern.

I suppose psychic energy is good for more than just forecasting and fortune-telling. She wouldn't need Starshine goggles to make her way through a dark room.

"Received a portent of doom, have you?"

"Oh, I receive all sorts of correspondence." Philomena paused outside a carved door bearing Marcus's name and rank etched in silver. "As I said in my note, your sister delivered another message to me this morning. Dimitria has been trying to reach you for some time."

"Don't." I sucked in a breath and struggled to calm myself. "Don't you dare drag my sister's name into your crystal-gazing hocus-pocus."

"Ordinarily I'd let you believe what you like, Miss Farthing, but your sister has been clogging up my communications with the Great Beyond to the point where I haven't been able to meet with my other contacts at all." The more Philomena explained, the more irritated she grew, until she prickled all over like a disgruntled porcupine. "I've important work to do here, and I don't appreciate the distraction, to be honest."

I leveled a freezing stare at the woman, the sort that Grandmother Pendleton would use on an impertinent lady's maid. "Miss de Mesmer, my mother visited every clairvoyant in the city limits and most in Meridia. They bilked her out of quite a sum, promising her they could contact my sister, and I can see that you are in the same sort of business. Good day to you." I turned to Marcus, who looked like he was struggling to decide which of us to admonish first. "I'll be inside, Legatus. If you wish to speak with me at all, you will do so alone."

Sweeping into his office, I dropped the bag of Eidolachometer cards in an empty chair. Curling in my fingers, I dug my nails into my palms and fought the tears that threatened.

Dimitria.

Thoughts of her were wrapped in fine linen, ribbon decorations, hushed whispers, Mama's tears. Striving to put the here and now before the memories, I concentrated on my surroundings: the Ferrum Viriae shield hanging over the mantelpiece, the fireplace surround carved with images of the Twelve Engineers, the elaborate machines whirring away on marble pedestals. On the wall hung several pictures, a set of framed medals under glass, and an article from *The Examiner*, dated six months past.

FUNERAL CONDUCTED FOR HEIR TO INDUSTRIA'S LARGEST PRIVATE ARMY

By Orville Accardo

A memorial service was held Saturday for Viktor Augustus Kingsley. Heir to the Ferrum Viriae empire, the twenty-two-year-old was killed during a training exercise gone badly wrong. Mister Kingsley was commanding a twelve-squadron live-fire exercise when an interruption in service to the secure RiPA lines put the young man in the wrong field position. Formal inquiries found no wrongdoing by any of the instructors nor the other soldiers involved.

Like everyone else in the country, I'd read this in the broadsheets, but I'd forgotten until this moment that I wasn't the only one suffering a loss.

A noise sent me scurrying back to my chair, then Marcus entered alone. Standing just inside the door, he studied my face like it was an illuminated manuscript, with all the answers he needed written upon my features. Certain I had smudges of dirt upon my nose, I did my best not to squirm under his gaze. There was no way to guess what his heart was doing, but the Ticker's pace had accelerated enough to flush my neck and warm my cheeks. And I didn't need a crystal ball to guess what he was thinking: we each needed information in the other's possession.

With deliberate steps, he moved behind the marble-topped behemoth of a desk and reached for the intercom. Turning the side crank produced a series of hisses and clicks, then there was a muffled, "Yes, sir?"

"Tea and brandy, please." Marcus put a hand over the mouthpiece to inquire, "Are you hungry?"

Luncheon seemed a distant memory after the excitement in the alleyway—not good for my blood sugar or the Ticker. As much as I would have liked to answer, "No, thank you, you may stuff your sandwiches somewhere most inconvenient," I was forced to nod.

"And a light repast," he added into the brass bell speaker. Clicking off the device, he pulled out several files and placed them on the desk. "Do you know what these are?"

"Lists of my many perceived shortcomings, alphabetized and arranged in descending order?" I volunteered.

"No, Miss Farthing, they're intelligence files. On you, your brother, your parents, and Calvin Warwick."

"How lovely." The thought that someone followed me about the city and snooped in our rubbish bins should have disturbed me, but in comparison to the other revelations of the day, this was merely irritating. "I suppose, then, you know what sort of tooth powder I use and how Nic likes his trousers tailored." The tirade was cut short by a knock at the door, indicating the swift arrival of food and drinks.

Then Marcus had a different query for me. "Cream or sugar?"

"Both, please. Two lumps." Seeing an opening, I used his courtesy as an opportunity to put him on the defense. "So are you going to share the real reason you turned up at Glasshouse this morning?"

Marcus stilled, silver tongs hovering over my cup. "I beg your pardon?"

"Legatus, you have half the city convened at the courthouse and face the possibility of rioting in the streets when the verdict is announced, yet you thought it important to answer a call about a break-in?" Though I sounded amused, my palms had started to sweat.

"I think you ought to let me ask the questions, Miss Farthing." He set my tea before me with a thump.

"You can ask." I stripped off my gloves and selected a cheese bun from the platter. If I were to spar with him, it wouldn't be on an empty stomach. "That doesn't mean I will answer."

He circled the desk with his own cup and unnerved me by taking the chair adjacent mine. "All right, then. Your mother is working as an independent contractor for the Ferrum Viriae, and she's in possession of some important schematics. When the break-in occurred, I wanted to make certain she was safe and then secure the blueprints."

I gaped at him. "My mother is working for you? How long has this been going on?"

"Approximately six months."

"What's the project?"

"I can't answer that question." Marcus spoke slowly, measuring out the precise amount of information he was willing to share with me and not another word more. “There are people who want the Augmentation technology Warwick developed. Dangerous people. We intercepted dozens of underground communications over the last few months, and that number spiked this week.”

“Is that why the city officials raised the alert level?” I asked. “You think something might happen when the verdict is read?”

“That was my suspicion, yes. Now I think it was just a distraction. As was the explosion at the factory.” Marcus gave me another searching look as he added, “It was a bomb.”

“A bomb?!” I sloshed tea over the lip of my cup and into the saucer. “Are you certain?”

“The preliminary tests came back positive for accelerant. That’s the quick and dirty way of confirming it.” Far from looking discomfited, there was a warrior’s readiness about the way he sat next to me. “What else can you tell me about the break-in at Glasshouse? Perhaps something valuable was taken?” The fire had time to hiss and pop before he spoke again. “Information is my best weapon, Miss Farthing. The more informed I am, the better prepared I can be.”

His honesty did ungodly things to me, and I found myself wanting to tell him. Dear Cogs! There was something so earnest about his face, about the way the words now poured out of him, but still I hesitated. “You have to understand . . . I’ve no reason to trust anyone right now.”

Marcus leaned forward a bit more, starting to reach for me. At the last moment, he reconsidered and retreated. “I am the proprietor and leader of the largest, most powerful private military in Industria. I have a network of informants larger than the number of workers at your factory—”

“None of whom can tell you what happened at Glasshouse, it would seem,” I countered softly. “So here’s the arrangement

I am willing to make: if I disclose what I know, you will tell me exactly what machine my mother was working on. You'll also give me access to your intelligence files and the messages you've intercepted."

Now it was his turn to pause. "You're not cleared for that information."

I willed myself not to flush or stutter. "I guess that's where it will come in handy, what with these being *your* files and *your* decision as to who should be able to view them. Now, do we have an agreement? My information for yours?"

Several seconds passed. Then, instead of answering, he went behind the desk and rummaged in a drawer. Withdrawing two circular bands, he approached me, went down on one knee, and took my hand in his. His skin was work roughened, marked by combat, and the Ticker gave a curious flutter.

"Marcus . . ." My voice trailed off when he kept his hands on mine. If there was anything to this—

And by *this* I meant *us*—

And the thudding of my clockwork ventriculator told me *this* was indeed *something*—

Then we'd gone about it all wrong. So many things should have happened before bare skin met bare skin.

The moment ended when he snapped an iron bracelet around my left wrist. Before I had a chance to process what he was doing, I wore a matching metal circlet on my other arm.

"I hereby swear you into unenlisted service in the Ferrum Viriae," he pronounced, the words as solemn as his gray eyes. "And I assign you the rank of Tesseraria."

I was startled by his use of the title; it was an old one given to the person responsible for safeguarding watchwords and delivering them to the commander on duty. A keeper and protector of classified information.

Marcus rose, brushing nonexistent dust from the knee of his pants as he addressed me. "Now, Tesseraria Farthing, we have an agreement. And more importantly, you have clearance."

I looked down at my new jewelry, momentarily distracted by the way the embedded diamanté refracted the lamplight. Minutely etched white lines formed a three-dimensional image within the stone: the Ferrum Viriae crest surrounded by laurel leaves. "This has been, in all possible ways, a most curious day." Looking up at Marcus, I felt compelled to add, "Don't think I'm going to address you as sir."

"Tesseraria," he said, lifting his cup of tea to his mouth and frowning when he found it cold, "I dared not even dream of such things."

SIX

In Which Various Events Shake Our Heroine to the Foundation (Not Garments)

Reconsidering his beverage, Marcus put down his tea and reached for the brandy. He held the cut-glass decanter up to the firelight, sending dancing flames through liquid amber. "I think I need some of this. You?"

"Strong spirits and my implant aren't ever a good combination, but I'll take a lemon and Fizz if you can manage it." Anything to calm my racing pulse, which felt like the galloping of horses through my veins. "And I'll continue to partake of the food, if you don't mind."

I'd eaten another currant bun by the time he handed me a tall glass filled with lemon concentrate and Effervescence. He followed that up with a substantial stack of papers.

"Here are the intelligence files on your family."

It was a most disconcerting feeling, opening the thick uppermost folder to see my name typed alongside a copy of my passport photograph. I splayed my fingers over my own face and winced. "This is truly a terrible picture."

"Hardly my top concern when gathering intelligence." Brandy snifter in hand, Marcus watched me keenly, making no pretense of his interest in my reaction.

Under my picture, stamped out in black on white, was everything anyone might want to know about me, from the names of my private tutors to the sums of money the family owed assorted creditors. Oddly enough, the Ferrum Viriae's reconnaissance also included a list of young men who escorted me to last season's social functions, cross-referenced by age and income, with notations of gifts that included "box of cream caramels, imported" and "bouquet of lilies of the valley tied with a pink ribbon." An entry about my mechanical Butterfly collection was underlined, and I wondered why Marcus had thought it important. When I glanced up at him, I found him intently studying a selection of cakes. With great nonchalance, he settled on a cream slice studded with fruit before handing me the plate.

"Take one. They're from SugarWerks, flown in daily."

Fruit and cream were all well and good, but under these circumstances, only chocolate would do. I finished the first tart in two bites and selected a second before asking, "What sort of machine was my mother building for you?"

The RiPA on his wrist fired to life. Watching his frown deepen, I swallowed just in time for him to meet my gaze.

"The verdict is in," he said.

"And?" I couldn't have swallowed again if I tried.

"Guilty," Marcus said with uncharacteristic gentleness. "Warwick is to hang on the morrow."

Every siren in the building wailed. Dropping the dessert tray, I clapped my hands over my ears.

"What's happening?" I shouted at him over the tidal wave of noise.

"Get to the archway!" Marcus didn't wait for me to move, instead catching me by the hand and towing me into an alcove.

Crowding me into the half-circle under a monogrammed medallion, Marcus lifted one of his bracelets and waved it under a Geodesic Spectrophotometer. Pressed up against one another, we stood there for what seemed an eternity until the device recognized and acknowledged his clearance. There was a flash of bright light, a sound like a gong, and then the floor twisted underfoot one hundred and eighty degrees. Beyond a screen of copper latticework, silk-blindfold darkness blanketed the view.

"Hold tight," Marcus advised. He braced me with his own body a second before the platform plummeted like a lift with its cables cut.

My scream chased us all the way to the bottom. Twisting my fingers in Marcus's sleeves, I could feel my skirts billowing around my knees and my hair whipping me wildly in the face. A few seconds later, our descent decelerated until our arrival was as dainty as a well-born lady alighting from a carriage. Somewhere overhead, a bell pinged like an oven timer.

"The cakes are done," I said, noting the internal lurch and resettling of the Ticker's balance wheels. Trying to keep a bellyful of sandwiches and chocolate where they belonged, I extracted myself from his grip and gasped, "Where are we going?"

"The Communications Center." Marcus folded back the gate.

"Do you know what's happening?" I asked. Golden emergency lighting revealed other soldiers arriving via similar transport, the parade of well-muscled bodies only slightly less intimidating than the architecture of the barrel-vaulted hallway.

"So many messages are coming in my RiPA that I can't make heads or tails of it," Marcus said, using his bracelet again to unlock the door at the far end of the hall. "Whatever occurred, it exceeded my preparations for the verdict. Damage control is going to be necessary."

Displeasure was evident in his tone, his expression, and his agitated gait as we entered the next chamber. With pops and flares, lights flickered on at intervals, allowing the vast space to unfold around us. Every possible means of delivering information lined the walls, including a few engineering marvels as yet unfamiliar to a civilian like myself.

"Confirm incoming bulletins!" Marcus demanded. "Someone tell me what is happening down there!"

One of the officers standing by the Aethergraph Station jerked on a set of headphones. "There's been an explosion at the courthouse!"

Still numb from the news of the verdict, I thought for a moment that I'd misheard him. Trained soldiers gasped and swore. Horrified murmurs raced around the room. I didn't join in, too caught up in my own thoughts to give them voice. Gripping the railing and skipping every other stair in his haste to ascend, Marcus climbed to a circular platform in the center of the room.

I gave chase as best I could. "Where are Nic and the others? They were supposed to be right behind us in the second SkyDart!"

"They're on the landing platform." He spared me only half a glance before barking out, "Get me the city plans!"

Detailed maps hung on the walls: the port city of Meridia, Industria and her surrounding coastlines, the empire in its entirety. Etched upon thin sheets of metal, deliberate green oxidation marked the land masses and a delicate blue-gray patina the rivers, lakes, and oceans. The map of Bazalgate slid forward on a set of rails. As new messages arrived, miniature incandescent lights activated all over the city.

"The Third, Fourth, and Eighth boroughs have checked in!" someone relayed.

Marcus lowered a brass trumpet that projected his orders to the farthest reaches of the room. Though the others couldn't see it, his knuckles were white from gripping the mouthpiece. "Get the rest of the districts on the wires."

"Yes, sir!" a soldier responded.

"Numbers coming in from the scene, Legatus!" another shouted. "A dozen injured and one death reported so far."

"Get me a list of everyone taken to Currey Hospital, and I want the names of the dead as they are located." Marcus pivoted on his heel. "What's the damage to the courthouse?"

The thrumming of the communications machines filled the long pause before someone answered, "The soldiers clearing the site found undetonated explosives in the rubble, and Calvin Warwick has gone missing in the chaos, sir."

Suddenly, there wasn't enough air in the room.

"All the media outlets in the city have received a statement!" shouted the officer presiding over the PaperTape machines. "We have an incoming message."

"Pull it up on the Solaris." Marcus turned to face the massive display, which was larger than the SugarWerks menu board and far more technologically advanced. Where Violet still chalked the day's specials onto slate tiles and slid them into brass grooves, the Solaris was an advanced magnetomechanical device that could receive and display Aethergraph messages up to one hundred and forty-four characters long.

Painted flaps whirred, revealing one letter at a time.

AN OPEN MESSAGE TO ALL CITIZENS OF INDUSTRIA:

I RESPECTFULLY REJECT THE JUDGMENT AGAINST ME.

FOR THE GOOD OF ALL, I MUST CONTINUE MY WORK.

When the machine finished translating, an oppressive silence descended over the room. The PaperTape machines paused for just a moment. The Aethergraph Station went eerily still. I could feel the pressure of the words bear down upon my neck, my shoulders, my back. I refused to bow my head, though I had to grip the railing enclosing the platform as hard as I could.

The Solaris whirred to life again with a message to replace the previous one.

PLEASE DO NOT ATTEMPT TO LOCATE ME.
IN THIS MATTER I WILL NOT BE DISSUADED.

"Get a communication back to him," Marcus shouted. "He can either turn himself in or be hunted down." An incoming RiPA message diverted his attention, but this next bit of news was welcome. "Your brother and the others are upstairs. I'll have someone take you to meet them."

I could see Marcus's mettle tested by everything that had gone awry and all the soldiers looking to him for leadership. Responsible for their well-being and the safety of all the citizens of Industria, he was bending under the weight. Bending, but not breaking. It was a lot to ask of someone his age, but sometimes age had precious little to do with maturity or capability.

And he has all three of those in spades.

I followed the escort, watching as Marcus spoke with the members of his staff, checked the PaperTape messages, and consulted with the operations expert. When the door to the Communications Center swung closed between us, I forced my thoughts away from Mister Kingsley.

Three corridors and an elevator ride later, my escort led me to a private alcove and offered me a crisp salute. "There you go, Tesseraria. Ring if you need anything."

"My thanks," I murmured, ducking inside.

"Penny!" Nic ceased pacing before a fireplace and leapt at me. I caught a fleeting glimpse of his face, pale with worry, before he enveloped me in a hug.

Reveling in the embrace, I wished it would never end, but Violet interrupted, "Is your RiPA turned off? I sent you half a dozen messages!" The ride in the SkyDart had painted her cheeks pink.

I unstrapped the device from my leg garter; sure enough, one of the switches was bent at a ninety-degree angle. I handed it to Nic with a weary, "Must have happened in the catacombs."

"The verdict came in," he said. "They found Warwick guilty, then there was some sort of explosion."

"Quite the jolt it caused, too. The noise of it was certainly impressive." Removing a glove, Sebastian made a great show of tugging at his ear.

"I know. I heard the reports coming in afterward." I couldn't help but picture it: the courthouse exploding, the city descending into chaos. "Warwick claimed responsibility for it."

Pulling me to the nearest chaise, Nic forced me to sit. I expected harsh words from him, but he slipped an arm about me and let me rest my head on his shoulder. In my recollection, five minutes was the longest we'd gone without arguing since Dimitria died.

"Apparently," I said softly, "all it takes for us to get along is two explosions and a double kidnapping." We'd already lost two members of our family, and the prospect of losing another two sickened me. As hastily as I could, I told the others about Mama's work with the Ferrum Viriae. "But Marcus didn't have a chance to explain what sort of machine it is."

"I suspected she had a new project," Nic said.

"I didn't," I said with a large serving of guilt. "I just assumed all those appointments were with more psychics."

When Nic squeezed my hands in unspoken sympathy, his thumbs brushed over my iron bracelets. He scrutinized them by firelight. "What the blanketed codfish are these?"

I repressed the urge to salute. "Tesseraria Farthing, reporting for duty."

"We left you alone for a half an hour and you enlisted?" Intrigued, Sebastian peered at my wrists. "If you wanted a new bit of jewelry, Penny, all you needed to do was ask."

"It's not what it looks like," I started to argue, before realizing it was exactly what it looked like.

"I need a cup of tea," Violet said, pinching the bridge of her nose. "You just put a crease on my brain."

"I don't think there's enough tea in the world to fix this," I said.

"I'm not taking any sass off you, Penelope Farthing," Violet snapped back. "If I'd known where a box of sticky buns was leading me today, I never would have messaged you this morning."

"If you hadn't, I would have been on time to pick up Nic, and he wouldn't have been caught in the factory explosion," I countered with an equal amount of heat.

Perhaps as a result of sparring with twelve siblings, Violet's hands curled into fists when she answered, "I won't be blamed for that. You'd have been late anyway."

As we glared at each other, Sebastian strolled over to the refreshments cart, poured a cup of tea for Violet, and thrust it into her hands as a distraction. "My lady." He then poured several fingers of brandy into a cut-glass tumbler for himself and took the conversation around an abrupt but welcome corner. "Just where were you when the courthouse bomb went off, Tesseraria?"

"In Marcus's office, in the middle of a mutual interrogation, and don't call me that." I fiddled with the bracelets, unused to the feel of them upon my wrists. They seemed to contain all the weight of my worry, dragging at my arms, a constant reminder of Mama and Papa and their precarious situation. "He took me down to the Communications Center. There's news coming in from all over the city. People got hurt. They're still counting the number of injured . . . and the dead."

"The verdict is ridiculous," Nic said with raw vehemence. Head bowed, he attacked my broken RiPA with a series of jerks, bending bits back into place and tightening screws with the set of microscopic tools he always carried in his breast pocket. "That judge is an idiot."

Still bristling from our exchange, Violet wasn't letting that observation pass without comment. "I know Warwick was a friend of the family, Nic, but don't let that skew the matter. The man is a murderer—"

"The man is a genius," Nic interrupted, "and anyone who says different is a fool."

My mouth fell open, and I wondered if his ride in the SkyDart had addled his senses. Violet and Sebastian wore similar expressions of surprise.

Violet recovered first. "Then I'm the greatest sort of fool," she said, as tart as one of her lemon pies. With deliberation, she went to stand next to Sebastian. Her hand trembled a bit when she lifted her cup from its saucer.

I was torn, wishing I could explain one to the other but unable to find the words. Nic wouldn't have listened anyway, not in this dark mood.

"That ought to do it." He flicked the RiPA switch to "On" and sent out a test message. Seconds later, Sebastian's RiPA clicked out the relayed sentence.

I COULD DO WITH A DRINK MYSELF - STOP

Sebastian attended to Nic's request as I flicked the RiPA to "Receiving." Old messages were lost to the aether, but I didn't want to miss a communication from Mama, Papa, or Dreadnaught.

"Send me something," I demanded, "so we can confirm this still functions properly."

Violet obliged, tapping out a series of dashes and dots. With a sputter, my RiPA relayed her message.

YOU WERE RIGHT - STOP - YOUR BROTHER IS AN IDIOT - STOP

When her terse observation was done, the RiPA continued to clack and clatter. Soon enough, we realized the new message wasn't from anyone in this room.

DEAREST PENNY - STOP - PLEASE LOCATE THE AUGMENTATION PAPERS BY NOON TOMORROW - STOP - IT IS OF THE UTMOST IMPORTANCE - STOP - WARWICK

Warwick. He wanted the Augmentation papers. *He* must have arranged for the break-in and our parents' kidnapping. Not the Edoceon. Certainly not the Ferrum Viriae. I immediately flicked the machine over to "Outgoing" and pounded out a response.

WHAT HAVE YOU DONE WITH OUR MOTHER AND FATHER - QUERY MARK - IF YOU HURT THEM THERE IS NO PLACE YOU WILL BE ABLE TO HIDE - STOP

Jolted from his black cloud, Nic squeezed my shoulder in solidarity. We waited several breathless seconds before Warwick responded.

SAVE YOUR ENERGY FOR THE SEARCH - STOP - LIVES DEPEND UPON IT - STOP

The line went silent just as the elevator alcove behind us rotated open. Marcus stepped out with a slip of paper in his hand. Taking great measured breaths, he handed it to me without comment. Puzzled, I looked down to see it was a transcript of Warwick's first RiPA message.

"Has he sent another?" Marcus carefully modulated his words even as a bead of sweat trickled down the side of his face.

I realized he must have run flat out from the Communications Center to arrive so quickly. "Only to tell us to save our energy for the hunt. How—"

"Our surveillance machines intercept anything sent on personal communications devices." After another deep breath, he straightened his shoulders. "I didn't have a chance to brief you on security measures. Now, would you care to explain just what Warwick meant by that message, Tesseraria?" Reaching out, Marcus looked as though he would take my hand, but settled instead for touching a finger to one of my bracelets.

He needn't have invoked them; I was more than eager to tell him everything now. "It wasn't just a break-in at Glasshouse—it was a kidnapping. Someone acting on Warwick's orders took my parents hostage." Remembering the bodies the surgeon left in his wake put a razor-edge on my words. "We need to get them back before something terrible happens."

Marcus wore an expression of grim resignation. "So that's the missing puzzle piece. I thought as much when I saw the house, but you didn't say anything."

"I didn't know whom I should trust just then," I said. "Obviously circumstances have changed. Any more news from the Communications Center?"

"Two more dead, and the list of the wounded is growing by the second," he answered. "The Araneae team apprehended the other suspect fleeing from the Bibliothèca. He made it all the way to the courthouse and might have been involved in the bombing there. All four suspects are in holding cells, awaiting questioning."

"I'll help," I said, "especially if thumbscrews are involved."

"So will I," Violet added. "And I won't need thumbscrews."

"We've trained professionals for this sort of thing," our host protested, but she held up a hand.

"Mister Kingsley, I have *twelve* older brothers and sisters. I am as experienced as anyone on your staff in the art of extracting delicate information." The row with Nic had put Violet in quite the stubborn mood. She folded her arms over her chest and jutted her chin at him. I knew that expression well, even if Marcus Kingsley didn't, and he'd already lost the argument. "Indelicate information is my specialty. You'd be ten sorts of foolish to refuse my help."

When he hesitated, I jumped in with, "She can start with the scoundrel you caught at the courthouse."

Marcus looked to Sebastian and Nic, who simultaneously shrugged.

"If you've an hour to spare, you can try to dissuade them," Sebastian added. "You'll get better results pounding your head into the nearest brick wall."

"I have enough of a headache without adding to it in such a fashion," Marcus said. "Very well. Everyone who's with me, fall in."

I was first in line behind him, followed closely by Violet and the boys. Unable to stop toying with the bracelets around my wrists, I noticed in a vague way when carpet yielded to bare floor, wood paneling to plaster, soft gaslight to harsh white luminescence. Through two sets of locking gates and down a stairwell, we descended deeper into the Fortress. I couldn't help but be reminded of our sojourn into the catacombs, except there were no shadows permitted here. The bright light pouring from the electrified sconces nearly burned my eyes to ash. Not even the darkest part of a villain's soul would go unlit in this place.

I winced at the glare. "By all the Bells, have you ever seen anything like that?"

"Imported white-light technology from Glacia," Marcus said over his shoulder. "The expeditions north have turned up quite a few discoveries."

"You mean besides the white maritime bears at the Square Park Zoo?" Violet asked. "This is useful, at least."

"And a profitable side venture," Sebastian observed from the back of the line. "Would you like a partner?"

"I've spoken with several interested parties," Marcus said, pausing outside a door, "but I won't entertain offers until matters of national security are settled."

"With luck, the stiffest of my competition was removed in the explosion."

As one, we paused to stare at him; though Sebastian had the reputation of a fierce businessman, this was the first time I'd witnessed such ruthlessness.

Realizing his mistake, he mustered the faintest of laughs. "You're right, though. Never get into bed with anyone in the middle of a crisis."

Wearing various shades of discomfited and disgruntled, we entered the interrogation room. A man sat behind the table, his effects spread out before him: a few copper coins, cigarette papers and tobacco, but no identification of any sort.

"What is all this?" he demanded. "A tea party?"

The moment he spoke, I knew it was the burglar I'd chased into the alleyway. Tired of fighting with my friends, I dragged a chair to the table and focused all my ill wishes and energies upon a new foe. "Why? Do you fancy some tea?"

"Something stronger wouldn't come amiss."

"What happened to the metal cuff you were wearing?" I demanded. "The one you used to disable the Beetles."

"I haven't the foggiest notion what you're talking about, love." In a show of bravado, the captive started measuring out tobacco. He tucked a mean, skinny cigarette into his mouth and winked at me. "Give us a light."

I wanted to slap it from his ugly mouth, but I very much doubted that was proper interrogation technique. "Though you don't look it, you must have been smart enough to get rid of the device. Tossed it in a rubbish bin. Threw it in the river."

"What device is this?" Marcus asked, his notebook in his hand.

"He was wearing it in the Bibliothèca," I explained as Sebastian produced a gold lighter and passed it across the table. "It emitted a noise that deactivated the mechanical surveillance. Just the sort of thing Calvin Warwick could build." I twisted back to confront the thief. "How long have you been working for him?"

Just taking a puff off his cigarette, the prisoner choked and sputtered. "The mad butcher what's been in all the papers? I never!"

"Just so you understand the situation, I have three of your comrades-in-arms in custody." Marcus stood just behind me. "Only the first to speak will be considered useful to us. Only the first to speak will receive any sort of immunity from prosecution."

"I don't have any comrades-in-arms," our captive said, slippery as a bar of greased soap. "Everyone hired for the Bibliothèca job was freelance."

"Hired by Calvin Warwick." Marcus leaned past me, putting his hands on the table. I wanted to glance over at him, but I kept my eyes trained upon the prisoner, noting every twitch of his facial muscles, every flicker of his eyelids. The smallest reactions were oftentimes the most telling.

The captive licked his lips with the dart of a very nervous garden snake. "It weren't him. Not in person, anyway. The money, the details of the job, everything came via message cylinder."

"Where did you receive the cylinder?" Violet asked. Still angry with Nic, the edge to her voice suggested she could have the prisoner's arms twisted behind his back and his pants filled with leeches if he didn't start cooperating soon.

"It was delivered to me aboard the *Palmipède*." He plucked his cigarette from his mouth and knocked off the ash.

I shifted my gaze to Sebastian, who was standing against the wall as though determined to hold it up at all costs. He didn't so much as blink, but I knew that if anyone had frequented the waterborne gambling vessel, it was he. Rumored to sail constantly on the River Aire to avoid raids, the paddleboat was renowned for its illegal gambling tables. Official reports from city council meetings always detailed plans to shut it down due to tax evasion and inadequate licensing, but every attempt to locate the *Palmipède* had come to naught. The broadsheets conjectured it was because too many of the city's notables enjoyed its vices, so they never let a raid come to fruition. All of this had to be a thumb in Marcus's eye.

The Legatus must have been thinking something similar, because he made an exasperated noise. "I should have known that den of iniquity would play into this somehow. Could you pick your contact out of a lineup?"

Our captive shook his head. "He wore a mask and used a Vocal Distorter."

"None of this is very helpful," Sebastian murmured to Marcus, perfectly pitched to be overheard. "Perhaps Gannet Penitentiary is the appropriate place for our friend here."

Another puff off his cigarette, another nervous cloud of smoke. "I'm not that sort of criminal. Thief, maybe, but murderer? No, sir."

"I beg to differ," Violet jumped in with another well-timed flash of temper. "You and your co-conspirators killed innocent civilians today. You are, in fact, a murderer. One who has declared war on the city."

"And a kidnapper," I threw in for good measure.

"What? No!" The captive looked to Marcus for clemency. "Whatever is she on about?"

"Two citizens were taken from their home this morning," he clarified, tapping a pen against his notebook.

"I didn't have a thing to do with that, but I can give you names of men in that line of work," our prisoner hastened to assure us. "Addresses. Just give me your pen and a piece of paper."

Marcus handed him the requested items. "A full confession as well, if you please."

The man hastened to comply, tongue darting about his mouth as he struggled to put down the words. Marcus ushered us back into the hallway, though I could see Violet would have cheerfully remained to box the captive's ears every time he paused in his transcription.

"That was well done," Marcus said. "We certainly got more out of him than I expected."

"Not enough," I said with a shake of my head. "He didn't know anything about my parents."

"Names," Nic reminded me. "He said he could give names."

"Names are well and good, but I think we need to go straight to the source for information." Stepping over to Sebastian, I slipped my arm through his before he could make polite excuses and disappear in a puff of gentlemanly smoke. "If anyone knows where a fog-chasing, illicit-gambling riverboat is to be found, it's you, my dear Mister Stirling. My guess is you've been on board dozens of times."

"I have," Sebastian admitted. Though he automatically reached down to pat my hand, I could tell by the way he eyed the nearby doors that he was contemplating exit strategies. "But I don't think you should go anywhere near her. It's a rough sort of place, for all its crystal chandeliers and Effervescence fountains."

"You'd have to bind my hands and stuff me in the coalhole to leave me behind," I fired back.

"I never said we were going," he replied, though the sigh that followed meant I'd already won. "I'd argue, but we both know that if I thwarted you, I'd get a broken nose for my troubles. I'm inordinately fond of my nose just as it is."

In no mood for his palaver, I pinched the appendage in question with enough firmness to suggest a very real threat. "Then there's nothing for you to do but say 'Yes, Penny, shall we adjourn to the gaming tables?'"

Airway constricted, Sebastian's voice sounded a tad less dignified than usual. "Very well, I'll do my best to gain the group's admittance." The moment I let go of his nose, he dropped his arm around my waist.

Full up with worry for my parents, I didn't swat him away. "There's still the small matter of locating Warwick's papers."

Walking under the harsh light of the wall sconces, Violet shrank into herself; even with a dozen tattoos and piercings, she looked small and lost. "I suppose we ought to check the Eidolachometer cards now."

"I'll have them sent to a room for you," Marcus said.

Nic sidled closer to Violet, but she gave him a freezing glare and marched ahead, stomping her boots more loudly than usual. Nic followed in her wake, hands stuffed in his pockets.

"Signal the boat now, Sebastian," I demanded. "The sooner we locate the man making all the arrangements, the sooner we find my parents."

Instead of reaching for his RiPA, Sebastian attempted to lighten the mood. Grasping me by the hand, he forced me into a waltzing trouble step with a turn at the end. "I don't doubt you could dance the night away, my lovely, but there are rules. It's past time for setting up a rendezvous. We'll have to wait until tomorrow night."

We passed Marcus and Violet with a gay promenade. When next Sebastian whirled me around, I could see that the good Legatus didn't like to see his hallway turned into a ballroom.

However, all he said was, "It's a complicated matter, arranging the pickups?"

"Ah, ah, ah," Sebastian said, wagging a finger at him. "Unlike my charming dance partner, I received no jewelry, so I've no information to trade with you yet."

I made the mistake of catching Marcus's eye on the next turn. There was something desolate about his posture, something about the way he quietly excluded himself from our group that cut me to the core.

Extracting myself from Sebastian's grip, I moved alongside Marcus. "Another question for you, Legatus."

To his credit, he didn't sigh at me. "Yes?"

"We never got around to discussing just what sort of machine my mother is engineering for you."

"That's true. We were a bit distracted by the explosion, if I recall correctly." His pace picked up when he admitted, "It's a device that will allow us to lift the veil."

"Lift the veil?" I hurried to keep up with him, both mentally and physically. "You mean a machine that speaks with the dead?"

"The original prototype was built by Malachi Baynard," he explained. "We discovered it in an overseas vault, but it's too antiquated to be of much use once a corpse has gone cold."

"Corpse . . . meaning you actually use the machine *on* the dead?" Trying to rid myself of the mental image was like trying to stamp out a wildfire with my boots.

"It only works in conjunction with Philomena de Mesmer. She's the actual conduit."

Such a project certainly would have captured my mother's interest. "Mama never said a word about it to anyone."

"She couldn't, not without breaking the confidentiality agreements she signed." Marcus glanced at me. "The larger version of the machine—the Grand Design—isn't finished. Your mother had the schematics with her when she disappeared."

"I understand your concern," I said, biting my lip.

"Duty comes before anything I might want for myself, Tesseraria, and the blueprints are the least of my worries now that your mother's absence is a matter of national security." Before I could remark on such a sacrifice, he straightened his shoulders, shifted his gaze away from my face, and tapped out a message on his RiPA. "I'll arrange for supper and a change of clothes for everyone."

"You don't mean we ought to stay here for the night?" I asked.

Violet's half-closed eyes flew open. "I need to go home. My family will be sick with worry, and I'm in desperate need of a bath." She considered the grubby state of her arms and my dress with regret. "Again."

"You can message your families and tell them where you are." Marcus's words walked the fine line between offer and order. "I'll put you in the guest barracks."

"This is all your fault, Tesseraria Farthing," Nic muttered. When our escort arrived, my brother and Sebastian followed the newcomer as Marcus excused himself with a curt nod.

Violet looped her arm through mine so neither of us had to walk alone; it seemed she'd forgiven me for our earlier spat, even if she had yet to do the same for my brother. "At least we know that Marcus is on our side," she said.

"Small comfort," I lied, thinking of his hands on my wrists. I could only hope that the iron bracelets I now wore wouldn't reveal themselves to be shackles.

SEVEN

In Which Midnight Feasts Do Not Go Unpunished

Nic and I had only Dreadnaught to contact, Sebastian no one at all, given that his parents were out of the country at the moment. But Violet had to send almost twenty messages before she could get her siblings to calm down and agree to cover her work shifts. It took the rest of the afternoon to inventory and catalog the Eidolachometer cards, but eventually all were accounted for, and none contained the information we needed to ransom my parents. Over supper, little was eaten and even less was said. With Nic and Violet refusing to converse with each other, it was a relief to retreat to a hot bath in the most new-fashioned lavatory this side of the Exhibition Hall of Modern Conveniences. Only the chill of the water could have driven me from the tub to dry off and accept my military-issued flannel nightgown.

Perhaps if everyone had been on good speaking terms, we would have found the accommodations in the guest barracks something of a pleasant surprise. Spare without being sparse, the narrow beds boasted thick gray-and-white striped coverlets and down pillows. The rug was a splash of crimson against the stone floor, and the fire in the hearth radiated enough heat to make a palatable piece of toast. Indeed, the best amenity by far was the tray of thick-sliced bread, accompanied by jam, butter, and chocolate nut spread.

Violet marched past the offering as though it, too, had offended her. Taking one of the top bunks, she curled up like a Meridian shrimp and turned her back to us. Sebastian quickly gave up being charming and fell asleep in a chair, head lolling and mouth hanging ajar. The occasional snore punctuated the half-dark as I turned down the gas globes and joined Nic.

Agitation had driven him to fiddling, so he'd extracted the Pixii from my messenger bag and neatly disemboweled it upon the rug. Adjustments made to his satisfaction, he returned each switch and screw to its proper place.

"Our destiny has altered over the course of this day," he said, careful to keep his voice low as he snapped one of the brass faceplates back on, "but our guiding star still points to breadstuffs and jam pots."

After all that had happened, it was incredibly surreal to sit there with him, fed, warm, and safe. Hard to have a normal conversation, though, with Mama and Papa missing. I forced myself to breathe, to remember the trick of a toasting fork, to hold another piece of bread over the flames. "This is like being back in the nursery."

"That seems like a very long time ago." With a wayward lock of hair hanging in his eyes, Nic reminded me of the boy who'd played romp and tussle games upon the hearth rug despite our nanny's strictest orders, the brother who'd walked three miles to the nearest shop to fetch me a bag of sweets when I was confined to bed.

"Remember smuggling the bread upstairs?" I said after taking a sip of tea. "I hid it under my pinafore while you carried off a pot of marmalade in your trouser pocket."

"We thought we were so stealthy." He shook his head at the memory of our exploits, and his hand slid into mine, just like when we were little and scared of something. Thunderstorms, the imagined creatures under the beds . . .

Death.

Because it was the best way to distract him, I switched the subject to science. "What do you remember from our lessons about Malachi Baynard?"

Nic squinted at me. "One of Industria's founding scientists Malachi Baynard?"

"No, random passerby Malachi Baynard. Yes, dummy, him."

"He was the one obsessed with the occult. He thought that life and death were merely multiple planes of the same existence." A suspicious note crept into Nic's voice. "Why?"

That left me to explain about Mama's work with Marcus and the Grand Design. By the end of it, Nic had taken off his glasses and cleaned the lenses with his handkerchief at least twice.

"Malachi was brilliant but had enough near-death engineering experiences to turn every hair on his head white," he said. "He was actually pronounced dead twice and resuscitated. He designed and built that machine to try to communicate with the Great Beyond."

"A place he actually thought he'd been," I said. "What did he say it was like? Stars and comets and fluffy white clouds?"

"That was the really odd part," Nic admitted. "All he wrote about it in a journal entry was that it was like 'going home.'" When I opened my mouth to ask another question, he shook his hand at me. "Seriously, Penny, that's all I remember."

"Allow me to change the subject then." I jerked my thumb at the bunk where Violet was a lump under the coverlet. "Don't you think you should apologize?"

Nic flushed up to the tips of his ears, pulled away from me, and sent a furtive glance in Violet's direction. "It takes two to argue," he said, "and I'll thank you to keep your nose out of that particular book."

I thought about all the times this past year that he'd spoken his mind or expressed his concern for me. Now was the time to return the favor. "You can't try to control the people you care about, not even to keep them safe. You'll only push her away."

"Like I've pushed you." Worry filled his eyes, and the barely healed scratches on his face looked somehow worse by firelight: darker, deeper, with the promise of blood and bone beneath them. "How are you feeling?"

I left the toast upon my fork to scorch as I contemplated the pattern on the rug, pretending to find it very interesting. "Fine. Why do you ask?"

"Don't play that game with me, Penny," he cautioned. "Your Ticker stopped today and you nearly died. *Again.*"

"I'm still here," I said, trying to reassure both of us. "Still breathing. That's enough for now, isn't it?"

"It's not, no." Though his voice was low, urgency roughened up the words. "You know what needs to be done, don't you?"

Pulling the charred bit of bread off the fork, I flung it to the flames and reached for another slice. "I won't lie abed like some invalid."

"That's what our parents would have you do," Nic said with impatience. "You need to see Warwick."

The very idea was preposterous. "The man is a criminal. A murderer."

My twin bent closer in his eagerness to explain. "He's also the only one who can save you. Papa and I have worked with the surgeons since his arrest, trying to perfect the new implant, but they're no match for him. And he wants to help."

"How could you possibly know that?" The words came very slowly, because I wasn't sure I wanted to hear the answer.

The silence spun out between us like cooked sugar from Violet's fairy-floss machine and then broke. "Because he told me when I went to see him."

"By all the Bells, Nic, have you lost your mind?" I abandoned the toast completely, dropping the fork on the hearth. Disturbed by the clatter, Violet and Sebastian shifted and resettled, so I lowered my voice. "You went to the prison? When?"

"Months ago." It seemed Nic didn't have a look to spare for me now, and perhaps that was just as well. "That weekend you thought I went with Sebastian to Carteblanche."

"Mama and Papa—"

"Didn't know. Not until afterward." My brother scowled with the memory of it. "In this matter, our parents are acting the fools."

"You really think so? You think them fools to be wary of a man who kidnapped people and experimented on them?" The muscles in my chest tightened like strings on a violin. I'd seen the pictures in the papers, faces that would haunt me for a lifetime. "The last girl, Nic . . . the last victim was only ten years old. What excuse could he give for that?"

"He did it for you, Penny." Nic kept his voice calm, but an echo of Warwick's mad passion bled through. "All he ever wanted to do was help you. He told me he just needs the original diagrams and a bit of time to finish your new Ticker."

Despite sitting so close to the fire, I felt the cold creeping up my legs and arms. A spreading frost reached for my clockwork heart with icy fingers. "Did you know any of this was going to happen? The jailbreak? The kidnapping?"

"No!" Nic's jaw clenched. "He never said a word to me, but I can't say that I'm surprised. Or sorry he escaped."

"Nic, people *died* in that explosion!"

Now his hands were balled up into fists. "You died in my arms!"

"This morning was just a fainting spell!"

"You know damn well that's not what I meant!"

Yes, I knew what he meant. The memory of that particular day was stitched into the scars on my chest, relived with each faint tick-tock inside me. We'd been picnicking at Sebastian's country estate. Carteblanche rested its elbows on thousands of acres of rolling lawns, ancient oak trees, and streams. The house itself was the epitome of a country manor: vaguely drafty, enormous, echoing. Thick plaster coated the walls, and the gauze hangings obscured wooden shutters. Nic and I spent a considerable number of our leisure and holiday hours there, perhaps because adult supervision was such a rarity.

On that day, though, my parents had accompanied us. It had been a scant month since Dimitria had died, and we were all clad in a cloud of mourning black. The shadows under Mama's eyes were the purple-blue of a bruise, and her reddened nose suggested nights of weeping. Papa wore the bleary look of an owl coaxed into the daylight, blinking in surprise at the glowing orb of the sun hanging in a brilliant blue sky. I half expected him to hoot and hurry back to the car; instead he retreated into a bottle of Gentian Amaros.

Warwick had been persuaded to come along with us. He looked ragged about the edges, unkempt and uncared for, as if he'd been sleeping in his suit because it was the last thing Dimitria had touched. Perhaps it was, but I was too afraid to ask. Afraid that if I offered him any words, any comfort, the dam I'd used to shore up my own tears would break.

Hoping to escape the others and my own feelings of guilt, I had gone out into the fields with Sebastian, Violet, and Nic. After reveling in a few moments of freedom and the sun's warmth on my upturned face, I consulted my pocket copy of *Felix Bertram's Field Guide to Lepidoptera Mechanika, Second Edition*. At the ready was a new net of my own devising, one capable of stunning a captured Butterfly with a small electrical discharge.

"The elusive Brimstone shall be mine, by any means fair or foul," I called to the others, though I would have traded a hundred of the rare and coveted *Gonepteryx rhamni*—nay, my whole collection of Butterflies—just to have my older sister back.

"I don't think you ought to be chasing about after mechanical insects," Mama said, fretting when we returned to the blankets, nets empty, for glasses of lemonade and sandwiches.

Over the previous four weeks, her manner of parenting had shifted from devoted to smothering. When she wasn't reading tarot cards or dragging me to a séance, she monitored my pulse, my color, every breath drawn, and every mouthful eaten. Nothing was ever good enough to set her mind at ease; her fears were like the lions prowling behind the bars at the Square Park Zoo. She even went so far as to withdraw me from school and had forbidden me from riding cycles and horses both.

Mama's forehead puckered like the row of pinch pleats in her bustle skirt. "Isn't her color a bit high, Emery?"

Papa was already snoring, having consumed his bottle, so it was Nic who answered.

"She was walking in the sun for an hour, Mama. Note the freckles on her nose, a sure sign of good health." With the eye she couldn't see, my twin winked at me before clapping Warwick on the shoulder. "How much longer are you going to fiddle with that thing?"

Startled, the surgeon peered up from the clockwork innards of the original Ticker prototype. "It's almost done. Not as refined as I would like, though, and the pumping mechanism sticks every so often. The next one will be more sophisticated. Then . . ."

He paused, inevitably thinking of the surgery I'd need to keep me alive.

I didn't want to reflect on it any more than he did. "I'm going for another walk. Would anyone else care to join me?"

Ever willing to play the knight in shining armor to a needful lord or lady, Sebastian volunteered. "I have a new project in development I'd like you to take a look at."

Before Mama could protest, I had found my feet. With Violet and Nic trailing behind, Sebastian led us to the Carteblanche stables. Inside, the scents of warm metal, saddle soap, and hay tickled my nostrils. Mellow sunshine slanted in through the chinks in the wooden slats and bounced off the gleaming surfaces of a prototype ThoroughBred. Seventeen hands of slender, copper-plated equine rose above us. Its forelock, withers, and hooves already showed signs of blue-green oxidation, but the patina only added to her charm.

"I give you Her Royal Highness, the Princess Andromeda!" Sebastian said with a grand flourish.

"Better to have named her Bucket of Bolts and a Prayer," Nic said, "because that's what you'll need for her to complete one jump, much less an entire course."

"Never mind him," I said to the metallic mount, reaching for a bridle and reins. "You're gorgeous."

"She's hot-blooded," Sebastian said with barely suppressed pride. "I modeled her after the Bhaskarian racers."

The winding key had stuck at first, but he forced it around. Andromeda's shuttered eyes slid open, the amber fire in their depths growing brighter as her inner gears picked up speed. *Whiiiiir-clang! Whiiiiir-clang!* She lifted one dainty foot, then the other, following him out of the barn.

Nic's professional curiosity soon got the better of him. "I suppose the jumps knock her balance wheels loose?"

"The mechanics spend more time realigning her innards than they do riding her," Sebastian admitted with a laugh.

I had no idea what came over me in that moment. Perhaps it was the desire to call my fate my own. The need to take control of my life. Or it could have been the thought of Dimitria dropping dead without warning and the knowledge that the very same thing could happen to me at any time.

"There's no better diagnostic than putting her through her paces," I announced, abruptly grasping Andromeda's reins.

"By all the Cogs of the Carillon," Nic said the moment he regained his wits and his tongue, "you're going to kill yourself! And then Mama is going to kill *me*!"

Though I'd always cherished my twin's good opinion of me, I was beyond tired of being bossed about. "You can weep for me when I'm gone and not a moment sooner!"

The words cut deep; I saw it on Nic's face.

Conscience already pricking me, I gathered my skirts in my fist. "Give me a hand, Sebastian."

He looked from his pristine gray gloves to my muddied boots, then, with a long-suffering sigh, helped me to clamber up. "The things I endure for you, my dear Penelope."

"Your devotion is noted along with your sacrifice." I stroked Andromeda's glowing copper coat. Then, squeezing with my knees and holding on for dear life, I shouted, "Tally-ho!"

She had leapt forward, racing down the road. My perch was precarious, but the pace was exhilarating. I lost my hat, shedding hairpins until my curls tangled over my shoulders in wild streamers. It might have been a few weeks since I last rode, but I hadn't forgotten the way of it. The mechanical steed was a bit tricky to master, with an occasionally hitching gait that necessitated adjustments of balance and posture.

Determined to take at least one jump, I had aimed her for a low stone wall. Behind me, I heard a faint cry from Nic.

"Penny, take care!"

"I'm trying, but there's only so much care I can manage right now!" I braced myself for the jump.

It had felt like we were airborne forever. The forest blurred into shifting draperies of moss-green velvet. The sun crystallized like a drop of honey on a plate of robin's-egg blue. Then we landed, and several things happened simultaneously:

I held my breath.

Andromeda's innards made a terrible noise.

My heart seized up.

With a gasp and a cry, I had let go of the reins and clutched at my chest. My nails scrabbled ineffectually against the black mourning dress, but even if I'd been able to tear the cloth aside, there was nothing I could do to turn back the tide of pain. The world cartwheeled around me as I slid off Andromeda and landed in the mud. Unable to breathe, unable to think, I stared up at the sky as it darkened to midnight taffeta shot through with brilliant silver shooting stars.

Death wears a ball gown.

Nic had reached me first. He scooped me up and carried me back to the house at a flat run, calling for help, for our parents, and, in between gasps, he begged me not to die. My head bounced off his chest with every hasty step, but I hadn't the breath to protest. It hurt. It hurt, but I clung to the pain with tenacious fingers, welcoming it. As long as I could feel anything at all, I was still alive.

But not for long, I feared.

I heard Violet sobbing, my mother screaming my name, Warwick's shout of "Get her into the house!"

Then we had entered the kitchen; all cold white tile and shining metal surfaces, it served as an excellent stand-in for a hospital. Nic set me down on the table near the fire, and Warwick turned up his sleeves.

"Compress her chest with your hands," he ordered my brother. "Keep her blood moving."

Someone must have fetched his medicine bag from the car. The next thing I knew, gentle hands clamped a cotton rag reeking of ether over my nose and mouth. I tried to pull it away as everything began to fade. Nic leaned over me, and his hazel eyes looked into mine.

That was the moment he broke; I saw it happen as clearly as if he'd cracked in half.

After that, there was nothing. Nothing until I woke with a bit of clockwork machinery lodged in my chest. A piece of technology I was never meant to test. Ticktock was the reminder it gave me with every passing second.

Looking at my brother now, I knew I wasn't the only one with scars. After a year of shadowboxing, it seemed only willpower and the quiet determination to keep me alive kept *him* going.

"Every time you die, it breaks something inside me." Nic let out a harsh breath. "What if I can't get your Ticker restarted the next time your balance wheels go off-kilter?"

"Cygna was only a day old when she passed. Dimitria made it to eighteen." I drew my knees up, wrapping my arms about them and resting my chin atop. "The Farthing women tend to leave the party without notice."

"Don't say that." He swallowed so hard that I could see the knot in his throat bob down and up again. "You can't leave me here by myself. The only Farthing boy. The only one without a death sentence hanging over my heart. Mama and Papa already look through me, trying to see where you are, what you're doing, how you're faring. If you die, they'll never see me properly again."

I would have argued, but I felt much the same after Dimitria died, like I was the ghost haunting the house. "I won't go quietly, Nic. To my last breath, I'll be kicking and screaming and fighting to take another."

"With Warwick's help, you wouldn't have to," he said softly.

"He took our parents, Nic. How can you trust him?"

"I . . . I guess I can sympathize. Always trying to do the right thing, even when loved ones fight you every step of the way." Reaching past me, he snagged my messenger bag. A quick rummage produced Papa's watch. "Mind if I hold onto this for a bit?"

I leaned against his shoulder. "A sundial isn't going to be of much use by firelight."

"True." Nic snapped it open and lifted the metal dial into place. "But maybe it will keep me from wandering too far afield in my dreams." Pressing the briefest of kisses to my forehead, he made his way to one of the unoccupied beds and climbed in.

I also retired, though I didn't think I'd sleep at all. Staring at the top bunk, I listened to the soft, even breathing of the others. The fire was mere embers by the time I relaxed enough to drift off. Swirling in my head like fog off the River Aire, the events of the day largely featured the honorable Marcus Kingsley and the expression on his face when he'd placed the iron bracelets on my wrists. Recalling him there, on bended knee and looking up at me so earnestly, did very odd things to my Ticker.

I rolled over and put the pillow atop my head.

"Penny?" A gentle hand on my shoulder roused me.

"I can fetch a bucket of water," said someone decidedly masculine.

My brain skipped about, leaping to the realization that Sebastian and Violet stood over me, that I wasn't in my own four-poster bed, that this wasn't Glasshouse at all, and that my hair must look a fright.

Being a layabout isn't one of my countless faults, and I can go from asleep to awake faster than Sebastian's Combustible can charge down a thoroughfare. "What time is it?"

"Rise-and-shine time." Violet was already dressed in a gown of navy silk twill, expensive for all its lack of frills and fussing. It was strange to see her so somberly dressed, but she'd made it her own with an acid-green sash and a matching ribbon tied about her head.

I squinted at the clock on the mantelpiece. "Did I miss breakfast?"

"Perhaps that's where he went," Sebastian said, turning to stir up the fire in the hearth. He wore a suit that was not his. Though it lacked the impeccable tailoring that was his calling card, he looked affably rakish, as usual.

"Where who went?" I stretched to remove the kinks from my spine.

"Nic was gone by the time we woke up," he clarified.

Violet sniffed to indicate that my brother's whereabouts were of no interest to her. I, however, sat up and cracked my head on the wooden slats of the bunk above.

"He's not here?"

"I checked the lavatories already," Sebastian said, clearly puzzled by my reaction. "But not the dining hall."

An uncomfortable tingling took up residence in my spine and tickled at the back of my brain, like I needed to sneeze but couldn't quite manage it.

Damn it, Nic, I was worried enough about Mama and Papa. Now I have to worry about you as well?

I could easily imagine his retort of "Turnabout is fair play."

Hastening from the bed, I ran my fingers through the snarled mess that was my hair and cast about for something to wear. "Why didn't you wake me earlier?"

"You still have circles under your eyes from yesterday, and we thought you could use an extra hour." Violet had approximately four hundred and seventy-three frowns in her repertoire, which ranged from "The Biscuits Went Flat" to "You're Being Dreadfully Annoying." Just now, still peeved with my brother, she wore "Don't You Use That Tone of Voice on Me."

"There's an hour, and then there's an hour," was my response as I twitched aside the collar of my nightdress. Inserting the key into the Ticker's faceplate, I turned it for the first of a hundred clicks with a wince; the touch of the cold metal was like splashing ice water over my face. "I assume there's a dress for me?"

"There is." When I was done with the winding, Violet handed me a skirt and bodice of bottle green, then flapped her hands at Sebastian. "Turn your back, please."

"And here I thought I would be allowed to witness that mystery of mysteries, a lady's toilette," he said as he obliged.

She slapped his shoulder anyway. "Don't be pert."

Fingers flying, I dressed in record time. Dreadnaught would have marveled at the sight of it. "Despite his other shortcomings, Marcus Kingsley has decent taste in clothing."

"Impressive how he got your measurements so close to perfect," Sebastian said, peeking over his shoulder with a wicked grin.

Violet forced me to sit long enough for her to plait my hair and coil it at the nape of my neck. "We'll probably have to take one of those SkyDarts back to the city," she said, her words muffled by a mouthful of pins. "No need to look a right mess when we arrive."

"Breakfast first." Sebastian checked his pocket watch as he led the way to the door. "I warn you, I'll start nibbling the draperies if I have to wait much longer."

The commissary was a shifting sea of gray wool, so Nic would be easy to pick out. Indeed, the dresses Violet and I wore, plain as they were in contrast to our usual attire, drew a bit of attention. In his midnight black three-piece suit, Sebastian enjoyed himself thoroughly, strolling like a gentleman taking the air, greeting every enlisted man and woman, officer and private alike, with his dimples on full display.

"Stop that," Violet hissed at him as she slid into a chair. "You're making an utter ass of yourself."

"I can't seem to help myself," Sebastian said without taking his eyes off the group sitting adjacent us. "Life is short, so I'm going to have dessert whenever possible."

The morning papers were stacked on the sturdy oak tables. Although filled with coverage of the courthouse blast, they contained precious little information beyond the ugliest of details:

"The damage to the structure is worse than originally reported." "Twenty-seven people were rushed to Currey Hospital." "Eleven Dead!"

More people had died as a result of their injuries, then. I glanced over the worst of the headlines, my stomach sinking further with each typeset word. By the time I finished, I had no appetite, though I had to eat or suffer the consequences later. The military's idea of a simple repast meant that the rolls were plain instead of braided and the butter wasn't carved into rosettes. Brawn and galantines quivered alongside fish kedgeree and crinkled strips of bacon. Homely stewed prunes occupied the space next to a platter of fresh apricots and strawberries. I studiously avoided the foods that wobbled, making my way through a plate of bread and fruit.

"Where's the tea?"

I'd barely finished the request when an arm reached past me and delivered a pot to the table. I twisted about to thank the server and found myself looking up at Marcus Kingsley instead. I instantaneously realized I had half a dozen hairs out of place and shadows under my eyes from staying up too late. Everyone else shot to attention and didn't relax until he'd taken a seat just to my right.

"I hope you all slept well," he said by way of greeting. Sebastian and Violet murmured their thanks for the comfortable beds and clean linen. When they returned their attention to the food, Marcus moved an inch closer to me and lowered his voice. "You're uncharacteristically quiet this morning, Tesseraria. Are you feeling well?"

"I've a bit of a headache."

And that headache is my twin.

"Rest easy that I will not add to it." Marcus poured out a cup of tea and passed it to me. "I've given myself a strict lecture about what's important, and my top priority is locating Warwick and your parents."

As I tried to find a way to explain that we might need to add Nic to that list, Marcus passed me the cream and sugar bowl.

"I'd also like to offer an apology," he continued. "I'm not enormously fond of surprises, and I'm afraid I blamed you for much of the chaos yesterday. I do my best to plan against the worst possible scenario, but you make that a bit difficult." With a crooked smile, he took a plate and spooned out a heap of scrambled eggs. "Have you eaten yet? Or are you one of those people who can't stomach food first thing in the morning?"

Forgetting her grievances with the world, Violet smiled into her teacup. Sebastian outright choked on a mouthful of bacon.

"You have no idea with whom you are dealing," he finally said when he'd cleared his airway. "I've seen Penny reduce an entire cake to crumbs."

I glared at him. "It was a very small cake."

"But of course," Marcus said. "And just what the table is missing. I forget, sometimes, that civilians enjoy more varied fare." He went to signal a passing waiter, but I caught his hand in mine.

"Please don't trouble yourself." Thinking of the danger my brother might be swimming in by now, my fingers clenched Marcus's. "Have you seen Nic anywhere about the Fortress this morning?"

"I was just going to remark upon his absence," Marcus said, studying my hand before continuing. "We're not in the habit of pulling guests from their beds in the night, if that's what you're implying."

I wrestled with my conscience and my sense of family loyalty. If Nic had gone back to the house and found the Augmentation papers, Marcus needed to know about it. There were also the bracelets to consider; I owed him the truth and was honor-bound to share whatever information I had. It was the only way to see the complete puzzle for what it was. "Is there any way he could have gotten back to the city this morning?"

Though Marcus didn't move, every line of his body suddenly indicated we were in the presence of the Legatus legionus. "Why would he leave you behind?"

Softly worded, but still an interrogation. Though I'd never smoked a day in my life, I almost wished for a cigarette to better play the part. "He's operating under the misguided notion that I need to be rescued from myself. I think he's gone back to look for the Augmentation papers."

"Why didn't he say something to us first?" Violet set down her spoon with a clatter, her expression quickly shifting from peevish to puzzled to a level of worry that almost matched my own.

"He wants to turn the papers over to Warwick." It hurt me to admit such things; I wasn't accustomed to the role of Vile Betrayer, and there was a desperate edge to my words, an unspoken plea not to judge my brother. "Warwick claims he can upgrade my Ticker if he can only get a look at the original diagrams."

The onslaught of information caused Marcus to fumble, putting his teacup down with a *clack!* on the table. He recovered quickly, though, tapping out several inquiries on his RiPA.

"One would almost think," Sebastian murmured into his napkin, "the good Legatus is growing accustomed to the perpetual chaos that surrounds you and yours, Penny."

I kicked him under the table. Only a moment later, the answers to Marcus's inquiries came in, and he relayed them to us.

"None of the SkyDarts went out, but two larger transports left this morning. He could have slipped aboard one of those." Marcus was up and moving before I could push away from the table. Violet, Sebastian, and I had to run to catch up.

"I might be mistaken," I offered, trying to tamp down my fear that we were already too late.

"I'm more inclined to trust your instincts." Despite the brisk clip he maintained all the way out to the landing platform, Marcus continued to send RiPA messages with military precision. "Head for the end of the row."

"All of us this time?" Sebastian asked. "Or did you want another moment alone with Miss . . . er, I beg your pardon, *Tesseraria* Farthing?"

"Get in the damned SkyDart, Stirling, before I have you charged with war crimes."

This time, there was no conversation, no explanation of lap belts or offers of antinausea medication. Marcus went through his preflight checklist with rapid-fire accuracy, settled into his seat, and slipped on a metal earpiece to request clearance for takeoff. He got the answer he wanted within seconds, and the SkyDart rocketed into the sky.

"We'll land at the airfield," he told us. "I don't dare draw attention to the house by putting down in the street."

I leaned forward to shout into his ear. "If Nic's headed back to Glasshouse, we haven't time for stealth!"

"Everyone's on tenterhooks as it is, Penny!" The winds ripped away all formalities as Marcus banked to the right. Though he was very much in control of the aircraft, his maneuvers were more abrupt than on yesterday's flight, his style more aggressive. "With Warwick at large, I've had to recall every one of my deployments to Bhaskara and Aígyptos for security details. Work has stalled out on the Grand Design with your mother and the blueprints missing. And now I find myself chasing down your brother in the hopes that he hasn't yet handed sensitive medical information over to a terrorist."

That comment rankled as much as it worried me. "It's our family's research and information, I'll kindly remind you. It's not a crime, what he's doing."

"Aiding and abetting a fugitive?" Our descent became unnecessarily bumpy when Marcus turned toward me. "That most certainly is a crime, by every definition of the word."

He was like an Eidolachometer machine: reading the situation like a punch card, making every decision based on plans and patterns with no margin for error. The reaction vexed me greatly, and I sat back in my seat with a sharp "Keep your eyes on the runway, if you please!"

The SkyDart glided to a halt near a hangar where heavily armed Ferrum Viriae waited with two new-model Combustibles. Frederick Carmichael was among the guards, but not as the jovial traffic officer I knew. Stern jawed and serious eyed, he presented his bracelets for inspection.

Satisfied, Marcus turned and reached for my arm. "Let's go, Penny."

Equal measures angry and afraid, I clambered into the car under my own power. "Might I remind you that my position in the Ferrum Viriae is an honorary one? I don't take orders from you or anyone else."

"Which is fine, just so long as you understand I'm not about to let your brother conspire against the empire." He turned over the engine and roared off the airfield at top speed.

The security team followed us in the second vehicle. I was surprised by the depth of reassurance I felt in their presence as we barreled down the ash-strewn streets toward Glasshouse, but I wouldn't have admitted it for all the dessert in SugarWerks.

Sitting in the front seat, Sebastian glanced over his shoulder at me. "You do realize that you're arguing with one of our few allies."

"Mind your own business, sir." I tilted my chin toward the window and studied my worried reflection.

Never one to let a dormant hedgehog alone, the indomitable gentleman nudged Marcus with his elbow. "You know you ought to kiss her and patch things up before the rent cannot be darned, Kingsley."

Heat rushed to my face. The myriad of rearview mirrors along the dash reflected Marcus's similar expression as he glowered at Sebastian.

"You keep your ridiculous whiskers out of this, Stirling," he added.

"Ridiculous you say?" Sebastian traced his thin moustache with a contemplative finger. "If you liked me better clean-shaven, you ought to have said so."

Without preamble, Marcus swerved right with a sudden squealing of tires. Glass shards rained over us as swift-flying projectiles shattered the Combustible's rear window. Silver fléchettes riddled the upholstery and dashboard.

Someone had been lying in wait for us: more of Warwick's mercenaries, or I missed my guess. I twisted about to get a better look in time to see them run our secondary unit off the road.

"Marcus!" I shouted, but he'd seen it in his mirrors.

"It's all right," he said, though that seemed far from the truth. "I planned for a contingency like this. Trade places with me, Stirling."

Sebastian blanched. "Not for a million aureii—"

"Now!"

"All right, all right!" Somehow, Sebastian slid over while Marcus climbed into the other seat.

"Drive as fast as you can," Marcus instructed, fastening his safety belt. "Evasive maneuvers only if necessary. I don't want us to end up in the gutter with a broken axle." He reached under the front seat and extracted a long case of polished wood before he turned his attention to Violet and me. "The metal panels of the car are reinforced, so stay low."

We obeyed without question. With my cheek pressed to the floor, I could feel the engine strain as Sebastian jammed his foot down on the accelerator.

"Care to explain what in the Cogs' names you are doing?" Sebastian swung the car to the right and immediately corrected for the gravel alongside the road. Apparently evasive maneuvers *were* necessary.

"Going up and out," Marcus said, pulling on a pair of tinted goggles and kicking loose the latch on a counterweighted wheel. The roof over his head slid back on brass tracks, and his seat clanked up to fill the open square.

"Marcus!" I twisted out of Violet's grasp, flying iron nails be damned.

Protected by the overlapping metal plates of the turret chair, he already had a very large and ominous-looking weapon braced against his shoulder. "Get down, Penny!"

Violet caught me by the back of my skirts just as Marcus fired. Muzzle flare, then the deafening thunderclap of the shot reverberated through my bones before I was once more on the floor of the car. There was the whistle of the projectile, and no one could have missed the sudden, groundshaking explosion that followed, nor the screech of tires and the rending of metal.

The turret chair descended into the car with a shudder and a rattle. Marcus put down the shoulder cannon and pulled off his goggles.

"What did you do?" I popped up again like a demented jack-in-the-box and saw the enemy's rear bumper protruding from a large, smoking crater a hundred yards back.

"I blew a hole in the road," Marcus replied, calmer now that he'd coped with the worst of the threat. "The first course of action for the Ferrum Viriae is to discourage criminal behavior."

"What if they'd swerved around the pit?" I demanded.

"Step two is disarm."

"And step three?"

"If they'd been foolhardy enough to give me three opportunities to shoot at them, they wouldn't have lived to see a fourth," Marcus said, picking up a handset and ringing the Communications Center. "This is the Legatus. The suspects gave pursuit on Second Etoile Road. We're en route to Glasshouse. Send backup."

"The Pixii is no good as a long-distance weapon," I said the moment he was done. "Do you have another gun in here?"

"Under your seat," he answered.

I stuck my hand under the leather cushion and extracted a metal case. Releasing twin latches and opening the lid, I revealed two service revolvers. Heavily engraved along the barrels, they had polished wooden grips and held six black-powder rounds each. I checked both cylinders to make certain they were loaded before handing one to Violet.

"What about the men who ended up in the crater?" she asked. "Do you need to double back and arrest them?"

Pulling out his MAG, Marcus checked the charger and the safety switch before answering her. "Responding units will be on the scene in minutes. They'll take care of the hostiles. After an impact like that, they won't be fleeing the scene."

Sebastian maintained a near breakneck speed. "In case everyone failed to notice, they're jumping the deadline. Noon, they said.

Something must have spooked them." He clipped the raised side-walk when he swung the car onto Trinovantes Avenue.

Marcus braced himself against the door. "Watch out!"

Another hail of bullets ricocheted off the car. Slamming on the brakes, Sebastian steered into the turn. By luck or by grace, he swung the Combustible around outside Glasshouse. We collided violently with the curb just before the front stairs, and Violet and I were thrown to the floorboards again.

"There are mercenaries at three, six, and nine o'clock!" Already reloading the shoulder cannon, Marcus passed Sebastian his MAG. "Do your best to hold them off until backup arrives!"

All the doors hung partially ajar, and Violet was the first to lean out and get off a shot. It was one thing to shoot a handgun in an open meadow at a target pinned to a roll of summer hay, and quite another to pull the trigger in a confined space. All the Carillon bells seemed to swing in the space between my ears, and I shook my head to clear it.

I shouldn't have bothered. A second later, Marcus fired the shoulder cannon and Sebastian let loose with a barrage of fléchettes from the MAG. Answering gunfire whistled around us, clipping the mirrors, riddling the seats. Glass shattered and fell out of the windows of nearby houses. Distraught neighbors screamed and incoming sirens wailed. I knew we should wait for backup, but it was possible Nic was inside. I had to stop him from doing something foolhardy. Something we'd all regret.

"Cover me," I told Marcus as I ducked out of the car and ran for the stairs.

"Penny!" His panicked shout was lost in another volley of gun-fire, and brickwork around me exploded in puffs of gray and white powder. Moving with lightning speed, Marcus turned and lobbed two Less-Than-Lethal grenades at the enemy—not part of his plan, perhaps, but effective nonetheless. Upon impact with the street, the grenades detonated, and one hundred spherical Bhaskarian-rubber projectiles pelted the mercenaries. They fell with shouted oaths and groans, bruised but not bleeding, as I took the stairs three at a time.

Though the locks had been changed, the knob still turned under my hand. Out of breath but otherwise unharmed, I peered around the front door. Violet held off an advance of six new men. Two more were creeping in from the left. I shot the first in the shoulder and missed the second when he ducked. Marcus hit him before I could get off another round.

"Get Nic," he yelled at me. "Don't let him leave with the papers!"

It was an order I didn't mind obeying. I ran down the hall and into my parents' study, half hoping I'd been wrong and Nic wouldn't be there. But my twin knelt on the floor, hurriedly packing leather notebooks into a rough-cloth satchel. At the back of the wall safe, a secondary compartment stood open.

My Ticker lurched and settled. "You found the Augmentation diagrams."

Nic slowly turned to face me. Everything he wore was slightly askew, as though large hands had rumpled him and set him back on his feet. His eyes were hard, his hair the bristled ruff on a brindled cur. "I played hide-and-seek with Papa, too. Took me most of the morning to realize he puzzle-boxed this wall the same as the desk. The compass flange on his watch matches the tooled metal on the inside of the safe. There's a slot at the back, so slim as to go almost undetected. *Almost.*"

"So the watch unlocked a hidden partition," I summed up as I sidled into the room, the revolver concealed by the folds in my skirt. "*Time is key*. That's a clever bit of clever. What about the blueprints for the Grand Design?"

"No sign of them. The Legatus will have to look elsewhere."

Outside, our friends exchanged another volley of shots and shouts with the mercenaries, but I didn't flinch. "How are you going to rendezvous with Warwick? You don't know where he is."

Nic held up a message cylinder, silver this time but similarly unmarked. "I have instructions. This arrived the same time I did."

"And just what are your instructions?" I stared at it, wishing I could see through the metal.

"I'm not saying just yet." He tucked the tube deep into his pocket. "I wanted to persuade you to come with me until all the men with guns showed up. Now I need to meet with Warwick first, to be certain it's safe. That he really does want to help you. I'll send word when I'm convinced. Until then, you need to stay with Marcus and the others."

Bad enough that he would sneak out this morning, but the idea of him entering the viper's nest alone chilled me. "You don't have to do this."

"You deserve to *live*, Penny, don't you understand that? That's why you snapped that day at Carteblanche and climbed up on Andromeda. Just existing isn't enough for you. Shouldn't be enough for you." Determination settled over his features, turning them to granite. "I won't hold you in my arms and watch you die, Penny. Not again."

I stood in the doorway, blocking his exit. "And I won't let you give those papers to that monster."

Nic didn't so much as flicker an eyelid before he charged. I had no time to raise the gun, not that I could have brought myself to use it, and it flew from my hand when he collided with me. Crashing through the set of doors, we stumbled across the hall-way and into a storage alcove under the stairs. I landed on a pile of winter boots, and before I could regain my footing, Nic exited and slammed the door shut. As I struggled to right myself and the crazy tangle of skirts billowing about me, I heard the key twist in the lock.

"You're going to do as you're told for once, and stay out of harm's way!" he shouted. "Do nothing unless I message you otherwise. And tell Violet that I'm sorry."

The finality in his voice raised every one of the hairs on my arms. I crawled forward on hands and knees. "Nic, don't!"

"Good-bye, Penny." My brother's voice went flat, all emotion ironed out of it as though by hot steel plates. Footsteps confirmed his retreat.

I pounded my fists against the sturdy wood until the key fell out of the lock and pinged against the floor. Putting an eye to the keyhole, I could only watch, helpless, as Nic grasped the satchel with all the medical documents and climbed nimbly out the window.

"Come back here," I shouted with impotent rage, "and open this—"

Without warning, the door obeyed. I fell into the hallway and at the feet of a startled Dreadnaught. The chatelaine brandished the key in one hand and a cast-iron poker in the other.

"Penny!" she gasped, putting a hand to her chest. "Whatever are you doing in the boot cupboard?"

Pulse thudding in my ears, I vaulted past her. In the study, I paused at the safe long enough to reach inside and pull out my father's pocket watch from the false door. Snapping it shut, I stuffed it down my bodice. "Nic's found the Augmentation files. He's taking them to Warwick."

Dreadnaught used a very naughty word that was altogether out of character for her. "And the gunfight in the street?"

"Mercenaries after Nic and the papers. Stay inside and away from the windows." Contradicting my own advice, I scrambled onto the ledge and slid down to the driveway. Nic was nowhere in sight.

Dreadnaught appeared overhead. "The Vitesse is in the coach house!"

I dashed to the outbuilding. There was no covert way to turn over the engine, so I gave it a flying start by running the bike down the length of the driveway and jumping on as it shot into the road. The sudden noise startled both the mercenaries and the Ferrum Viriae soldiers who had arrived in the interim. Marcus and the others called to me and signaled I should stop, but there was no time to make explanations or apologies as I rocketed through the worst of the fighting.

Besides which, I wasn't sorry. I was petrified. I had to catch up with Nic before anyone else did. Weaving between cars and buggies, I paid scant regard to their mirrors or my limbs in my haste to find my twin. To get just about anywhere in Bazalgate, he'd have to head for the Heart of the Star. As I scanned the crowded avenues for him, cinders from the secondary fires triggered by the courthouse explosion drifted down on me.

Almost at the roundabout, I caught a lucky glimpse of him hunched inside an open-air cab.

"Nic!" With one arm raised to wave at him, I was unprepared for the jolt of something slamming into the back of the Vitesse.

A dilapidated vehicle sped up alongside me, the occupants' faces contorted as the driver veered at me again. I didn't know if their plan was to run me off the road or pull me from the seat, and I didn't care. I swung abruptly into the roundabout behind Nic's cab and promptly lost control of my cycle.

My brother yelled something as the Vitesse crossed all eight lanes of traffic. I crashed into the raised stone pavers that encircled the Heart of the Star and took a header over the handlebars. For a split second, everything moved slowly and silently. Then I noted the crack of my elbow and the scrape of my cheek against the rough ground. The shrill blare of a police whistle. My brother shouting at me from a very great distance.

It was that day at Carteblanche all over again, except when Nic ran toward me, three blurry figures grabbed him. Tossing a sack over his head, they threw him into the back of the Combustible that ran me off the road.

I clung to consciousness as everything around me softened like ice custard melting in the sun. A scream built up inside me, but "Nic" was all I managed before darkness swallowed the word.

EIGHT

In Which the Language of Flowers Speaks Volumes

I was dead. That was the only explanation for the flowers that greeted me upon waking: flame-colored dahlias and jewel-toned chrysanthemums crowded next to dainty offerings of lavender asters and deeply purple pansies. Death wouldn't necessarily explain the candy, though. Striped boxes of caramel creams and apricot jellies were tied up with bows and set between the bouquets. A stuffed bear stood silent guard over a jar of Well-Wishes that brimmed over with calling cards.

Reaching out a trembling finger, I touched the coverlet and realized I was alive. But I didn't need a doctor to tell me I hadn't much time left. *That* was something I could feel, the way another person might intuit they'd broken a bone or twisted a ligament. The header over the Vitesse's handlebars had inflicted the last bit of damage the Ticker could take. With my eyes closed, breathing shallow and labored, I could travel in my mind's eye to the clockwork heart of me, see the mainsprings uncoiled, the wheels slightly off-balance. Instead of the precise cadence of marching soldiers, the device wobbled and faltered. A clockmaker would have stopped its hands. Put it out of its misery.

Voices in the corridor proved a welcome distraction, descending in volume as their owners went down the stairs.

"Thank you, Doctor Carmody. I appreciate you checking in on her." That one belonged to Dreadnaught.

The second was unfamiliar but somber. "I just wish the damage weren't so extensive. As it is, I'm not qualified to do any repairs to the ventriculator." The front door opened, and I could barely make out the next bit. "There's still the possibility of a concussion . . . keep an eye on her . . . any change in her condition, send for an ambulance."

With great effort, I pushed off the blankets and lifted myself from the heap of pillows. My head felt like a silk balloon, impossibly light, drifting with the wind. If I fell, I'd land with a gentle bump and then deflate, I was sure of it. No harm in getting up.

It took a single step to prove that notion wrong. Crossing the room might as well have been an excursion to Glacia via ice floe. The smallest of movements shot cold arrows of pain up my legs and down my arms. Arriving at the mirror, I took inventory of the rest of my injuries: stitches on my forehead, a purple-blue bruise on my jaw, and more scrapes than I could count with a tabulating machine. My skin felt raw, as though the barest of whispers would strip it from my bones.

But I was more ghost than skeleton, and even ghosts want company.

I forced one foot in front of the other, continuing the painful trek across the room, through the door, down the hall. I passed Nic's chamber, trailing my scraped hand over the wood paneling.

Though there was no one to deny me entry, I still tiptoed inside Dimitria's room.

Everything was just as she'd left it. A soft blue brocade quilt and a dozen tasseled pillows decorated the bed. Her desk was as neat as mine was messy: her fountain pen sat in the tray on the inkwell; a clear space was left for the stack of accounting ledgers she'd always brought home with her from the factory. Organized, punctual, and poised to work alongside Ambrose Farnsworth as factory supervisor, she had been a far more capable manager than I could ever hope to be.

As though drawn by invisible strings, I drifted to her Cylindrella. Hundreds of recordings occupied an adjacent cabinet. One yet sat on the turntable. The few rotations of the winding arm I could manage caused flares of pain in my shoulders, but that was nothing compared to the ache in my Ticker as music filled the room.

"Come to me, child of mine, rest your weary head," sang a soprano over faint hisses and pops. "No harm will come to you, child of mine, so long as I watch over you . . ."

I sat upon my sister's bed, already lost to the memories. She'd been getting ready for her eighteenth birthday party, humming happily as she dressed. A stunning bouquet of bloodred roses sat on her dressing table, richly glowing. We chattered about everything and nothing at all while I pulled on my stockings and adjusted my many ribbons. She laughed, stepped out of her dressing gown, and reached for her party frock.

That was the moment I'd seen it: the white-fire glint of diamanté.

I leapt at her, reaching for the chain hanging about her neck. "Demy, what is *that*?"

Blue eyes widening, she pulled away from me and clasped her robe to her throat as though hiding some terrible secret. "Oh, Tuppence!"

It was the silliest of nicknames, left over from our days in the nursery, but I wasn't about to be shoved back into pinafores. Not when there were secrets in the air. "When did all this happen?"

"A few months ago," she said after a moment, "at the lantern-light party. Do you remember the one?"

I did. The ice on the river had been all the colors of the aurora borealis. Warwick had been adorably awkward on his skates. Sebastian and Nic had bought bag after bag of hot chestnuts for us to warm our hands. Violet's nose had been redder than a cherry, and Dimitria had had snow in her eyelashes.

"Calvin kissed me behind the oak tree," she confessed.

There were certain things that sisters were obliged to discuss at great length, one of them being the exchange of affections, proper or improper. So, while I ought to have asked her how it came to pass and whether she enjoyed it, my unguarded response was "Ew!"

With a soft sigh, Dimitria sat upon the bed next to me. "Don't say that. It was lovely!"

She was embarking on a grand adventure, leaving me behind once again. "What's it like? Falling in love, I mean."

Dimitria slipped her hand into mine, and it was colder than expected though color splashed her cheeks. "Like my heart was an anchor dropped from the side of a boat. He's a very dear man. I knew that from the first day he came here and started tending to you. But he's so much more than the sum of his work—"

"I hope he at least asked your permission before he kissed you." When she started to answer, I tugged my hand away and plugged my fingers deep within my ears. "Never mind. I don't want to know any more of the sordid details!"

"Oh, I think you do." She lowered her dressing gown by inches until I could see that the glitter-glint I'd spotted earlier was no mere pendant, but a diamanté ring.

That could mean only one thing. "You're engaged?"

"We're going to tell everyone tonight at the party," she said, the radiant look on her face all the answer I needed. "At midnight, just after we have cake. Calvin is so nervous, but I bought him a pocket watch and set it according to the Carillon Bell Tower. He'll know the very second it's time to announce the news."

After that, there had been a flurry of hugging, a few tears shed, and much smothered nervous laughter as we finished dressing and hurried downstairs to the party. Mama had outdone herself with the decorations, and the dining room looked like a sort of fairyland. There were blue and gold banners with ribbon streamers, beeswax candles, bowls of fruit and flowers. I placed a tinsel crown on Dimitria's head. Nic escorted her to the birthday throne. The butler and ten liveried men delivered course after course to the dining room, each received with applause and appreciative appetites.

By the time we had reached the dessert course, I thought I might burst from all the food, but such qualms were stifled by the arrival of the SugarWerks Carry-Away Box. I caught Warwick surreptitiously glancing at his pocket watch and knew that in a few seconds, Dimitria would make her big announcement. I prepared myself for another round of hugging and happy tears.

"Happy be long years before you, skies a-gleam with sunshine o'er you," we sang as Mama set the box down before my sister with a smile. "The greatest of things have yet to be seen!"

The clock on the mantelpiece had ticked down to midnight. Dimitria and I exchanged a short, knowing look, and then her gaze shifted to Warwick. He smiled back at her with wonder and light in his eyes, and I felt like a trespasser upon their happiness.

"Ten . . . nine . . ."

Unseen gears within the Carry-Away Box whirred to life.

"Eight . . . seven . . . six . . ."

The vibration shuddered through the table.

"Five . . . four . . ."

The lid to the box slid back.

"Three . . . two . . . one."

The clocks around the house had begun to sound the first of twelve chimes. Sparklers ignited as they grated across the pyrolant rails inside the box. The cake spiraled up, spitting embers of gold and silver. The towering confection came to a standstill, and there was a hushed silence.

Mama pressed a kiss to Dimitria's cheek. "Make a wish, darling."

The greatest of things have yet to be seen.

In the midst of the cheers and clapping, Dimitria had turned very white. I saw the look upon her face. Felt it burn into my memory.

"Mama." My own heart seemed to block my throat, strangling the word. "Warwick . . ."

Before I could say anything more, my sister had slumped back in her chair and everything descended into chaos. Screaming. The table shoved aside, the cake forgotten, the gold pocket watch dropped on the rug. The servants scattered. I pressed myself against the far wall, watching Warwick trying to revive her with chest compressions and smelling salts.

"Don't leave me," he muttered, working furiously. "You can't."

It had seemed to work when Dimitria took the scantest of breaths and whispered something to him. He gathered her up in his arms, tears streaming down his face. I saw her hand reach for his, but it fell slack to the carpet before it found its mark. By the time the ambulance arrived, Dimitria's lips were blue. Papa pried Warwick away from my sister's body, but I was the one who dragged him into the hall.

"She can't die," he said again, even as the light faded from his eyes.

That night had claimed my older sister. Cygna had been torn from us long ago. And this week took Mama, Papa, and Nic from me.

It seemed as if I might be the only Farthing left.

Dreadnaught found me in Dimitria's room, holding one of her pillows to my cheek. Without a word, she carried me back to my own bed.

"They took Nic, Dreadnaught," I murmured as she thoroughly tucked me in. "They put a bag over his head and shoved him in a car." I couldn't stop seeing it.

The chatelaine wrung out a compress and pressed it to my sweaty forehead. "The Ferrum Viriae are still looking for him. Mister Kingsley was here, wanting to see you, but he had to leave before you woke up. He said to tell you he has every available unit tracking down the car that ran you off the road."

"It won't do any good." I averted my face from her sympathetic gaze. "Warwick has been a step ahead of us since the very beginning."

Dreadnaught retrieved a steaming cup from my night table. "Ginger tea," she said, quite unnecessarily as it filled the room with the aroma of spice cookies. Reassured that I could hold it without dousing the bedding, she went to fetch an invalid's fare: blancmange, softly white and wibbling on its plate. Dreadnaught subscribed to *Mrs. Chewitt's Household Guide*, and I could well imagine the chapter headed "For Delicate Stomachs and Those Recovering from Sickness."

"Start with that," she instructed. "If it stays down, we'll see about something heartier. You've only had broth spooned down your throat for the better part of three days." She hesitated then added, "I hope you'll forgive the impropriety, Miss Penny, but I also wound your Ticker for you every morning."

Three days. Three days I'd been unconscious. Three days Nic had been missing. Had he found his way to Warwick? Had he seen our parents?

"There's absolutely nothing to forgive, Dreadnaught. Thank you for caring for me." I summoned a smile as wobbly as the pudding. "I'm lucky to have you."

The chatelaine gently patted my hand. "If the pain gets to be too much, the doctor left some drops on the side table." She paused to note the jinglejangle of approaching zippers and buckles.

Violet appeared at the door to my room, wearing her battered brown leather "stealth" jacket, a miniature top hat, and a worried expression. The strap to a SugarWerks Carry-Away Box was looped over her shoulder. "I showed the guards at the door my clearance from Marcus, and they let me in. I hope you don't mind."

"Not at all," Dreadnaught trumpeted. "I'm going to recheck all the doors and windows. Make certain she drinks that," she ordered, pointing at the cup of ginger tea before hastening from the room.

Divested of coat, gloves, hat, and Carry-Away Box, Violet wrapped my hands about the cup and forced me to take a sip. Only when most of the tea was gone did she speak.

"They took him, didn't they?"

"Yes." I waited for the usual reassurances, that Nic was a fighter, that the Ferrum Viriae tracked them, even now. "He said . . . he said to tell you that he was sorry." Violet said nothing. When the silence stretched impossibly thin, I ventured to ask, "You love him, don't you?"

Not a moment's hesitation. "Yes. Are you upset?" A light shone in her eyes more wonderful and awful than tears.

"Upset? Not remotely." I sat up as best I could, undoing most of Dreadnaught's diligent tucking in.

Violet reached for my hand, the silver rings she wore only marginally colder than her fingers, her expression shifting to one of fierce determination. "We have to get him back, Penny."

"We will, Vi." It was a promise made, one heart to another.

Dreadnaught returned with a silver tray that held a full tea service and a smaller tray that offered up a crisp, clean calling card. "You have another visitor. The Legatus is back. He's most anxious to speak with you."

"Send him up, please."

Dreadnaught hesitated for the briefest of moments. "I'm not at all certain your parents would approve of a gentleman paying you a call in your bedroom, crisis or not."

I squirmed impatiently against the pillows. "I doubt anything untoward will happen, but should the romance of the situation overwhelm him and he attempt to ravish me before your very eyes, you may knock him out with a tray."

"I'm glad to see neither your spirits nor your powers of sarcasm were injured in your accident." Dreadnaught opened the doors to the clothes press and pulled out a foamy, frothing concoction of lace and ribbons.

Violet was startled into a hoot of laughter. "By all the Bells, what is that?"

"A bed jacket from my Grandmother Pendleton." I glowered my hardest despite the lance of pain such a mighty frown caused.

"The woman has both atrocious taste in gifts and medieval ideas as to what a young lady should wear."

"It's perfect," Dreadnaught said, handing it over to Violet and hurrying from the room.

"I'm allergic to fuss," I protested.

Violet tied the ribbons and fluffed the lace ruffles, enjoying herself far more than the situation warranted. "Don't be ridiculous. And you could do with a bit of fussing, in your delicate condition."

"Delicate my arse."

At that precise moment, Dreadnaught returned carrying yet another tray, this one laden with missives and parcels, with Marcus Kingsley right behind her.

He didn't appear at all taken aback by my ridiculous frills or my foul language; instead, he made a lovely bow, hat tucked under his arm. "Tesseraria."

"Legatus."

"I'm glad to see that you are well."

"If by 'well' you mean I look a right monkey," I said, "then verily, I am well."

"You have to admit she looks fetching, Marcus," Violet said.

"Far be it from me to pass judgment on a lady's attire," the clever man replied. A few stiff steps brought him within feet of the bed. "I'm glad you're going to recover. It was terrifying to watch you fly through the crossfire on the Vitesse. If I find a dozen gray hairs on my head, I'll know who to blame."

I studied the military-short haircut, ignoring the temptation to rub a hand over the closely cropped black curls. "Not a one."

"Yet," he added. "Give it time and a bit more of your reckless behavior."

"Without a doubt, driving through a gunfight was the most reckless thing I've ever done," I admitted. "And I've done quite a few reckless things in my life."

He reached for my hand. "I shouted to you when you shot out of the driveway and took off down the street."

"I heard you." I stared hard at the place where our fingers met, thinking it better to look there than into his eyes.

He didn't seem to care that we had an audience of two. "But you didn't stop."

Startled by the note of concern, I looked up. "I had to get to my brother."

Marcus's grip tightened to the point of impropriety. "You should have waited. I would have gone with you."

"You were a bit preoccupied at the time, what with all the bullets whizzing past you." I tried to extract my hand from his, but his gloves might as well have been coated in glue. "You were protecting Violet and Sebastian, too."

"I've never been more tempted to abandon a post." He let go of me, but only to reach into his jacket pocket to retrieve his notebook and pencil. "I need to know what happened when you went after Nic."

Without realizing it, I'd braced myself for a lecture. A tirade, even. Instead, he offered me a level of understanding so deep that it was like a gift. It took a moment to recover, another to start giving my report. Some of the details stood out as stark and clear as newspaper typeface. Others had been smudged by three days of sleep and whatever medications the doctors had given me. I described the car. The faces of those inside it. How they'd tried to pull me from the Vitesse. How they'd captured Nic, and what direction they'd fled.

Then it was my turn to pose a question. "Did you investigate the *Palmipède* while I was . . ."

"Out of commission?" Marcus finished for me. "I'm afraid the good Mister Stirling hasn't been able to procure a boarding yet."

Something about his tone suggested unvoiced suspicions. When Violet hitched in a breath, I knew I hadn't imagined it.

"And?" I prompted.

Marcus closed the notebook and changed the subject. "You'll be glad to hear we recovered the Vitesse from the scene of the accident."

"That's not at the top of my list of concerns," I said, unwilling to be distracted.

"It's parked in the carriage house," he persisted, accepting a cup of tea from Dreadnaught and studiously adding sugar. "Carmichael returned it personally after you were transported to the hospital."

"Give that man an extra set of bars." Suddenly tired, I fell back on my pillows and closed my eyes.

"Should we leave?" Violet asked. "You look dreadfully tired."

"More dreadful than tired, I'm certain." I forced my eyes open and focused my attention on the heap of mail at my elbow: notes from tailors and hatters, envelopes from various foreign medical universities. It would fall to me to pay them, to answer them, to make explanations.

Deepest apologies for the lateness of the payment, due to the fact that parties in question were kidnapped.

"This is also addressed to you, Miss." Dreadnaught handed me a thickly wrapped parcel and a penknife. "Careful. It's heavy and marked 'Fragile.'"

Puzzled, I cut the string and pushed aside several layers of brown paper. Inside, daguerreotype slides were neatly stacked and interleaved with thin silver tissue. There was a folded note atop everything, but it fluttered to the floor when I caught the image on the gleaming surface of the first glass.

"By all the Cogs," Marcus swore softly in my ear, but I couldn't summon a single word in reply.

The topmost daguerreotype showed Nic in some undisclosed and poorly lit location, propped up in an iron bed. Bandages were pulled back to reveal a surgeon's handiwork, stitches and swelling ringing the flesh about his eye sockets. The eyes themselves appeared untouched until I looked closer; within the depths of the pupils, there was a hard gleam that was wholly foreign and frightening. Looking at my twin, I felt trapped, a diamanté-headed pin through my clockwork heart.

"Unmistakably him, isn't it?" I said like a ventriloquist's dummy, my mouth moving and sound coming out without my say-so.

"What?" Violet placed her cup on the edge of the table. "What's happened?"

I set down the daguerreotypes and covered them with my hands, wishing I could erase the truth with my fingers. "Warwick Augmented Nic's eyes." Only when I said it aloud did my Ticker react, shuddering horribly in my chest.

"What?" Violet faltered.

Marcus leapt forward, catching her about the waist when her legs gave out. Left to my own devices, I clung to consciousness, gripping the coverlet until I nearly tore the fabric.

Don't you dare faint again, Penny Farthing. Don't. You. Dare.

The Ticker's balance wheels righted themselves, but only barely. Enduring the pain was better than the numbness.

"That poor, dear boy," Dreadnaught said between the fingers she had clasped over her mouth.

"I'm fine," Violet told Marcus, pushing away from him to stumble to the fire. I waited for the tears, for the screams. Goodness knows I could have shrieked loud and long for the both of us. Instead, an aura of calm settled over her. "I'll be fine." This time, the words rang with truth and fury both.

Marcus took two of the slides to the window, using the thin sunlight to study them further. "It's a wonder the procedure didn't kill him. These have to be the first ocular implants in the empire."

"What could Warwick have been thinking?" I breathed.

Dreadnaught retrieved the note from the floor next to the bed. "Perhaps this explains it."

I opened it with trembling hands, recognizing the surgeon's handwriting immediately.

Penny,

I wish there was some way to make you understand that all I've done was for you. That day at Carteblanche, I held your poor withered heart in my hands. I will spend the rest of my days correcting the weaknesses of the flesh. I hoped you would come to me, but I was able to start with Nic. He'll never need glasses again.

Please let me do the same for your ventriculator.

Your Devoted Servant,
Calvin Warwick

I tossed the paper away from me only seconds before it burst into flames. Marcus's shout of surprise took me aback; I'd forgotten he hadn't witnessed the self-destruction of the last note.

"Nitrocellulose," I explained. "Sebastian said it's highly flammable stuff that gets used in the making of moving pictures."

"That it is," Marcus said. "It's also the primary ingredient in black powder. It's possible Warwick has a connection to the mills just outside of town." He lifted his wrist and began tapping out commands on his RiPA. "I'll have a detachment check there and speak with the maintenance crew. If anyone's been lurking about or any property's gone missing, we'll know within the hour."

"Fast, but not fast enough," I said. "We need to get to Warwick. I don't think he's going to leave well enough alone."

"You think he'll keep operating on Master Copernicus?" Dreadnaught blanched even as she posed the question.

"He might. And for all we know, he's pulling people off the street again." I tried not to picture a row of beds like Nic's, each one containing a limp body—like dolls on a nursery floor, their arms and eyes and legs removed by a careless child. Averting my gaze from the daguerreotypes, I focused on the bedside table where another floral arrangement sat, a note tucked in the brilliant greenery. I pulled out the card, which was thickly ornamented with doves and roses, gilded along the scalloped edges, and stamped with silver lettering that read "Get Well Soon!"

No signature.

There's a hidden meaning in every flower.

"Dreadnaught, who delivered this bouquet?" I asked, turning to the chatelaine.

Discreetly wiping her eyes with a handkerchief, she paused to study it. "It arrived this morning by courier."

I eyed the arrangement again, searching for any clue it might yield. "I think it's also from Warwick."

Marcus peered closer at it, suddenly intent. "What makes you say that?"

"The flowers," I said, reaching out to touch each bloom in turn. "Gladioli symbolize sincerity and strength of character.

Purple hyacinths ask for forgiveness. White roses are for secrecy and silence. I can't think of anyone else who would have reason to speak to me of secrets."

Marcus pulled out a spotless pocket square. "Has anyone besides yourself and the delivery person touched this, Miss Dreadnaught?"

"No, Legatus."

He plucked the flowers from the vase and set them to one side, then poured the water into the wash basin. "It's been quite some time since I sent flowers to a young lady."

"You ought to study floriography before attempting it again," I said, telling myself I didn't care a whit if Marcus sent flowers to anyone, young lady or not. "You don't want to send the wrong message."

He made a thoughtful sort of noise far in the back of his throat. "Let's say I wanted something to serve as a reminder of new friendship. Hypothetically, of course. What sort of flowers should I select?"

Violet poured herself another cup of tea and answered his leading question when she saw I wouldn't. "I suggest blue periwinkle."

"That is certainly good to know. May I?" Marcus indicated my desk. Perplexed, I nodded, watching as he ground the tips of several lead pencils into fine powder between two pieces of paper. "What if I wanted to suggest the flower of friendship might be blooming into something greater?"

I knew he only wanted to distract me from the dreadful situation with Nic, and yet my suggestion was a faint, "Honeysuckle? For devoted affection."

"Or salvia," Violet added. "For thinking of you."

I hoped that would be the end of the conversation, but Marcus had other ideas. Taking the lead dust, he applied it to the vase with a horsehair brush.

"What if I wanted to tell a certain young lady that she was in possession of my most ardent affection?" he asked. "What ought I send her?"

"Roses," I said, praying my voice wouldn't crack under the strain of remaining detached. "Red ones."

When next Marcus spoke, it was as though he and I were the only people in the room. "I think I will study this language of flowers a bit further."

"Will you?" I met his gaze, refusing to play the coquette. "To what purpose?"

"So that when I send the girl of my heart a bouquet," he said, so softly that I had to strain my ears to the utmost, "it will tell her everything I want to say. But for now, Tesseraria, we will have to make do with hard evidence."

He held the vase so I could see the fingerprint plainly standing out on the surface.

"It might belong to the delivery person or the florist," I said, realizing why he'd gone through so much trouble.

"Either of whom might have some clue as to Warwick's whereabouts." Marcus passed the vase off to Dreadnaught. "Give that to one of the guards on duty and tell him to have it transported to the Flying Fortress for processing."

The chatelaine nodded and rushed from the room. Violet went to fiddle with the tea service, and I could have cheerfully strangled her for leaving the conversation. Alone with my frills, my bows, my worries, and Marcus, I stared with great determination at the coverlet. The clatter of his RiPA was a welcome distraction for us all, despite the message being encoded.

He listened thoughtfully before tapping out a brief response. "That was Sebastian. He's finally arranged a boarding on the *Palmipède*."

"You see?" I said. "And the very moment I awakened. Fortuitous timing."

"Fortuitous indeed," Marcus said with a rueful shake of his head. "Until you consider the fact that you have stitches and most likely a concussion."

"If you go to the *Palmipède*, I'm coming with you," I said. "I'm the one they want."

He exchanged a long look with Violet, then ventured, "Perhaps we'll see how you're feeling come this evening."

When I sat up, I set my lace flounces aflutter. "A clever dodge from someone wholly unfamiliar with my recuperative powers. What sort of firepower are we taking?"

"Everyone who is going," he said with a pointed look, "will do so with hopes for the best and prepared for the worst. In other words, armed to the teeth and carrying a few extra surprises."

"I want a gun," Violet announced, jerking on her gloves. "A big one. I'm going home to get a frock, and then I'll return. I expect you—" she jabbed a finger at Marcus, "to see to it that she—" her attention shifted to me, "eats the contents of that hamper." She slapped the Carry-Away Box. "Watch out for the salted caramel tarts, though. They're very sticky and won't do the bed linen a bit of good."

Marcus caught her at the door. "I've assigned a guard to escort you wherever you might go. Check in with us every hour. Don't take any unnecessary risks. We don't want anyone else disappearing."

Stompy boots made their way along the hall and down the stairs. Watching Violet go, Marcus didn't glance at me when he said, "She's very much in love with him."

"Yes."

"Does he love her in return?"

"Yes."

"Good. That will keep him fighting."

"He's a Farthing. We fight to our last breath and then defy logic to take another." Realizing we were alone, I suddenly gave thanks for my ridiculous bed jacket. "There's more tea on the table. And blancmange."

"You'll never get back your strength eating that." Opening the lid on the Carry-Away Box, Marcus pulled out the salted caramel tarts and several molten-middle chocolate cakes before he spoke again. "Penny?"

Some sort of electrical current ran up my spine when he used my name, but I wouldn't have let on for a million golden aureii. "Yes?"

"When you begin to plan something . . . and I know you will . . . I want to know what it is. Full disclosure."

"I haven't any plans yet." I pointed at the iron bracelets, sitting in a pool of light on my desk. "I will keep you abreast of any future plotting, though."

"So long as that plotting doesn't include handing yourself over to Warwick." Marcus took a napkin off the tea tray and settled it in my lap. "That wouldn't do either of us any favors, would it?"

I found it very hard to concentrate. My every thought was a Butterfly battering against my skull and wheeling about to fly in tipsy circles behind my eyes. "I don't know. It might be better for everyone if I did."

"Don't ever say that." Marcus issued the command and followed it by handing me a caramel tart. "Now eat this."

I smiled, relieved that I could focus my attention on anything other than his hands, his face. "Only if you take half." I broke it messily in two and gestured that he should sit down. My Ticker gave a lurch when he obliged, not in the adjacent armchair but next to me.

"Will Dreadnaught have a fit if she comes in here and sees me sitting on your bed?" he queried.

My stomach suddenly realized how long it had been since I'd eaten, and I eagerly bit into my half of the tart. Shortbread crust crumbled to sweet sand on my tongue, and the saltiness of the caramel coated the roof of my mouth. "Are you afraid of our chatelaine, Mister Kingsley?"

"Of all the threats I've faced this week, she does seem the most formidable." Remembering something, he pulled a paper-wrapped parcel from his other pocket and handed it to me. "This is for you."

"Handcuffs this time?" I guessed. "Surely you're going to arrest me for criminal stupidity, among other things."

"That can wait until you're able to walk on your own." When he fell silent, there was nothing for me to do but unwrap his gift.

String untied and paper removed, the bundle revealed itself to be a carved wooden display box. Under glass, the elusive Brimstone Butterfly fluttered sulfur-yellow wings at me with the whirring of tiny gears. It was one of the few missing from my collection, the very one I'd been determined to capture that day at Carteblanche. I could hardly believe Marcus had handed it to me like it was no more than a paper bag of Meridian taffy.

"I know you collect things of this nature." He paused. "This particular specimen is from my personal collection. I hope it pleases you."

I would have never imagined him hunting *Lepidoptera mechanika*; the good Legatus had taken me quite by surprise this time. "It's lovely. I don't know what to say."

"You don't have to say anything," he assured me.

"I oughtn't accept it," I said, splaying my fingers over the glass. "But I shall. It's a treasure, as well you know."

"I do." He reached up, trailing his fingers along my jawline before cupping my face in his hands. "But some treasures are more important than others."

Wishing I could trade my Ticker for a single kiss—*what good is a clockwork heart if I never give it to anyone?*—I closed my eyes and tilted my head back.

With a small, strangled noise, Marcus pulled away from me. My eyes flew open, and if I'd been pink with embarrassment before, now I was surely the color of the fire department's Combustible engines.

He saw the stricken look on my face and caught hold of my hands. "I want whatever this is, Penny. More than anything I've ever wanted before. But when I swore you into service, I promised there would be no secrets between us."

Something stuck sideways in my throat. "Yes?"

"There's a piece of information that wasn't in any of the files." Though Marcus spoke with visible reluctance, there was nothing cowardly about how he met my gaze. "Something you need to know before anything else happens."

The hole in my middle opened up again, dark and bottomless. "Do you know something more about Nic's condition?"

"No, not that," Marcus reassured me. "But I'm not certain you'll think this any better." He cleared his throat and stared at the ceiling, trying to find the words he wanted to use. "Calvin Warwick's illegal experiments were funded by a private investor."

The very idea caused my stomach to clench until I thought the bit of tart I'd eaten might come back up. "Someone knew what Warwick was doing and didn't stop him? Knew, and *paid* for it?"

"I had no idea that people were dying, Penny," Marcus said quietly. "I promise you."

Suddenly, there wasn't enough air in the room, enough space between us. I wanted to scramble away from him, but I was trapped by my broken flesh and his hands and the sick desire to understand why he'd done such a thing. "*You* paid for Warwick's research?"

Marcus stared at me as though facing a firing squad. "Yes. He came to me for investment capital. In exchange, he said he would develop battlefield Augmentations for the soldiers. I never had reason to believe he was doing anything else. Certainly not killing innocents he kidnapped off the streets."

Numbness spread from my head to my Ticker. "It never came out at the trial or in any of the papers. You hid it."

"I didn't. As soon as I realized what was happening, I notified the appropriate authorities. The Ferrum Viriae was cleared of any wrongdoing, and our involvement wasn't revealed at the trial, for public safety."

All this time, I had believed I was the one to blame for the carnage. For the lives of twenty people, most of them children, all of them dead at Warwick's hands. But the knowledge that I wasn't alone in my guilt didn't comfort me.

"I've done my best to make restitution to their families," Marcus added, eyes still trained upon me.

"No amount of money can bring loved ones back from the dead!"

"Don't think I haven't thought of that every day since the killings came to light," Marcus said, voice tight with regret. "I did it to protect the men and women serving this country. I did it for Viktor. If he'd been Augmented, he might have survived."

"Is there anything else you've kept from me?"

"No." There was a quiet plea in the single word.

In that moment, the connection between us was a sheet of glass. I had the choice: grip it and safeguard it with forgiveness, or let it fall. Full up with secrets, lies, betrayals, and unwelcome revelations, I made my choice. "Perhaps you ought to leave now."

His expression shifted, so the look of loss traveled all the way up to his eyes. "If that's what you want." Giving me the tersest of nods, Marcus gathered up the daguerreotypes.

I wanted to smack his hand away from the slides, but I was afraid one might get broken. "I suppose you're confiscating those as evidence?"

Carefully, delicately, he rewrapped them. "You don't need to sit here and stare at them all day. I'll have them analyzed for source of origin."

"You will not. They're my property, and I'll analyze them myself."

Ignoring my wishes, he tied a sturdy knot in the string and tucked them under his arm. "Tesseraria, I understand why you are angry with me, and I wish to take my leave before either of us says anything we might regret." With that, he exited the room.

Sliding out of bed, I hobbled after him and shouted, "Come back here and get your damned Brimstone!"

Finally losing his temper, Marcus bellowed from downstairs, "It was a gift! Keep it!" Then he slammed the front door to Glasshouse so hard that the windows rattled in their frames.

"I won't be ordered about." I would send for a courier and specify that delivery included ramming the box down his throat. Carrying it to the desk through a haze of pain and heartache, I stumbled over the tiniest of wrinkles in the rug and landed hard upon my knees. Flying from my hand, the box smashed against the decorative tiles of the hearth. A tinkle hung in the air for several seconds, followed by silence. I crawled over to inspect the damage and found the glass shattered and the box cracked along one side. The Brimstone dangled from its diamanté-headed pin, but it had escaped unscathed. I extracted the mechanical creature, watched it flutter in the palm of my hand, then crossed to the open window.

I'll not hold you captive.

I held out my hand, and the Brimstone took flight on the next gust of air, dipping and twirling like the autumn leaves that rained down from the trees. Soon their bare branches would be frosted over. The city would don the ice-sequined cape of winter. I could already feel the chill of it in my bones. But, for now, there were golden leaves and Butterflies winging their way free of the city.

I desperately wanted to crawl back into my bed and pull the covers over my head. Instead, I downed the entire bottle of pain-killer the doctor left upon the side table and tore off the bed cape, unwilling to suffer its frills a second longer. Stripping down to my bloomers and chemise, I pulled an ancient woolen sweater over my head, wincing as I jostled my bruises, then matched it with a belted uniform kilt in gray wool. So ironic that an unprecedented sale of Ferrum Viriae surplus garments had sparked a brief military fashion craze this spring! It meant that, for the first time, I looked the part of Tesseraria.

"Marcus wants a proper soldier?" I said, setting my hands on my hips. "Let's show the Legatus what kind of warrior a girl with a clockwork heart can be."

In his haste to depart, he had overlooked a daguerreotype half-hidden by my bedding. Handling it with the utmost care, I went to my desk and adjusted the lamp. There was something familiar about the glass, something that teased around the edges of my mind. I'd seen pictures like this before, but where? Try as I might, I couldn't bring the memory into focus.

Probably due to malnutrition.

I reached out and lowered the filigree mouthpiece that funneled my words downstairs. “Dreadnaught?”

On the wall above me, a wafer-thin speaker labeled “Kitchen” vibrated with the chatelaine’s reply. “Yes?”

“I think I’m ready for something more substantial than blancmange. And I need a frock to wear tonight aboard the *Palmipède*.”

NINE

In Which Our Heroine's Social Circle Makes a Study of Fluid Dynamics

---

If war were to be waged, it would be in fashionable style. By the time I finished the considerable contents of my dinner tray, Violet returned with her composure and her evening frock. I don't think either of us gave a china pig about our clothes, except as a disguise to aid in infiltrating enemy territory. The two of us prepared for battle standing before the mirrors in my room. Her wine-colored voile was caught up with small pinwheels of bronze and black, leaving a peep of striped silk stockings on display.

"Given half a chance," she told me, adjusting fingerless black lace gloves, "I'll strangle anyone who gets between us and Nic."

"Agreed." I studied myself in the looking glass. A careful application of actor's greasepaint and face powder concealed the worst of the bruising, and Dreadnaught's artful arrangement of my curls obscured the stitches on my forehead. Given a lack of options and time to send out for another gown, I'd donned one of my mother's dresses: cinnamon silk, trimmed with freshwater pearls and silk confetti fringe. Mama wore it only once, the night of Dimitria's birthday party. I felt like I'd raided a tomb to retrieve it from the trunk in the attic, but the scent of my mother's rose water raised my courage to new heights.

I was going to find my family. I was going to see Warwick brought to justice.

"We're very likely walking into a trap," I said.

"No doubt." Turning around, Violet looked at me. "But we'll have Sebastian with us, half a dozen covert Ferrum Viriae, and Marcus, of course."

"Of course." I needn't apply any rouge, not with the persistent flush that colored my face whenever I thought of him. "He left here in high dudgeon."

Violet arched an eyebrow at me the very moment someone rang the bell at the front door. "You picked a fight with him, I'm sure."

"If we were sparring, he threw only one punch." I hadn't told her about Marcus funding Warwick's research; perhaps I never would. Taking up my gloves, I did my best not to meet her eyes. "I can't seem to spend more than three seconds in his company without arguing with him."

"Or wishing you could kiss him?" There was a touch of sadness in the suggestion, reminding me that her last words to Nic before his kidnapping were angry ones. I started to say something, but she quickly added, "The young Legatus is quite dashing, especially in uniform."

"Shut up, Vi." I smoothed my gloves up over my elbows and buttoned them at the wrist. "The last thing I need right now is the distraction of an ill-fated love affair."

"Pity," Sebastian noted from the hallway, able to eavesdrop through the wide-open door. "And here I was working up the courage to ask for your hand in marriage."

"Sebastian!" We pronounced his name with varying numbers of syllables, all of them indignant.

"Just how long have you been standing there?" Violet added.

Assuming his best Lord of the Manor air, he lolled against the doorjamb and checked his pocket watch. "Long enough. Might I offer a bit of unsolicited advice?" He continued before either of us gave him permission. "In matters of love or otherwise, play your cards close to your vest."

With a last, fleeting glance at the mirror, Violet turned to ask, "Any other well-meaning counsel?"

After thinking it over a moment, Sebastian said, "Never hit on a seventeen. That, and you oughtn't keep Marcus waiting. He's in the foyer and wound tighter than a twenty-five hour clock."

"I think we could all use an extra hour about now." I put the Pixii in my beaded purse and closed the wardrobe. "But you arrived just in time to escort us downstairs. Make certain we don't trip in these wretched heels."

Marcus was indeed pacing the carpet. He'd traded his uniform and iron bracelets for a discreet fake moustache and evening dress far more colorful than anything I'd seen him wear before; maybe he'd consulted the good Mister Stirling in that department. The gaslight slid across the broad expanse of his shoulders and along the impressive *musculus biceps brachii* that even a topcoat with tails and a vividly striped vest couldn't disguise. When he caught sight of us descending the stairs, he paused in his foot-soldiering activities.

Sebastian offered down Violet first. "The lovely Miss Nesselrode."

Marcus put his heels together, letting his "kiss" linger an inch or so above her hand, lips never making contact with the lace. "You look resplendent."

"Thank you, Legatus." She stepped aside, and Sebastian handed me forward.

"And Miss Farthing."

"Tesseraria." The formality of the address was tempered by the note of warmth, an unspoken plea for understanding, and Marcus pressed his mouth to my glove.

I felt a tingle run all the way up my arm, as though he'd shocked me with my Pixii. It would have been easy to smile at him, to squeeze his hand in a gesture of clemency. Instead, I extracted myself from his grip. "I hope you brought suitable artillery."

His expression hardened, and he turned on his heel to lead us into the study where an arsenal was set out on the mahogany table. "The fingerprint on the vase was a match for the lead florist at Scent & Sentiment on High Street. The order was placed in person, but the only thing the clerks remember about the patron is that he was young and of medium build. The search at the gunpowder mills turned up nothing of importance. We're going into the *Palmipède* blind, and I want everyone carrying whatever arms they are comfortable using."

"No sense shooting oneself in the foot," Sebastian agreed.

He might tease, but the weekends at Carteblanche had been good preparation for this. Violet put the smaller revolvers in her velvet purse and tucked a throwing knife into her bodice. Sebastian had his cane sword and two MAGs slipped into a leather holster under his dress jacket. Already carrying his usual sidearms, Marcus secreted a dizzying array of small explosives on his person. I had the Pixii and chose twin black-powder pistols. Pulling back yards of copper fabric, I buckled on above-the-knee gun garters.

As warm as any hearth fire, Marcus's attention slid over me; I tried not to wonder if it was due to the exposure of my stocking-clad legs or concern about my borrowed weaponry. I fixed him with a look, a deliberate "Excuse you, sir" expression that caused his eyes to narrow, and he homed his gaze in upon me like he was sighting a target on a field.

But I'm no man's bull's-eye.

Letting my silk skirts ripple back into place, I took up my fan and purse. When Marcus offered me his elbow, I swept past him murmuring, "Hands to yourself, unless you want to get riddled with bullets."

—

Marcus's Combustible glided along the dusk-painted streets, the night air rushing past the windows. Bazalgate was in a rare mood tonight, poking finger holes through the fog to reveal flashes of a star-bedecked sky. Concentrating on the road didn't keep the good Legatus from lecturing us about his battle plan.

"We're only after information," he said. "If the mercenaries' contact is aboard, do not engage him in any way."

I felt his gaze upon me in the rearview mirror. "I have no intention of letting him slip through our fingers, even if that means tackling him over a gaming table."

"You're not going to help Nic or your parents if you get shot tonight, Penny," was his firm rejoinder. "Make no mistake, this is going to be risky, and any rash actions on your part could put everyone in danger."

"I'll be on my best behavior," I replied, wording it so that I wasn't making promises I couldn't keep.

"We'll be able to gather twice the information as two couples rather than a group of four," Sebastian suggested, firing off a series of aethergrams on his own encrypted RiPA, lack of light be damned.

I leaned forward to tap him on the shoulder. "Who are you messaging?"

He jumped as though I'd rammed a live wire into his tympanum. "Tesseraria, you just made me tell them we'd be there 'presemently.' Kindly cease your abuse upon my person. I'm making final arrangements for our boarding. Half a dozen plainclothes Ferrum Viriae should already be aboard, if all has gone according to plan."

"With any luck, we'll be able to get the information we need without too much fuss," Marcus said. "I don't want to cause citywide panic by letting things get messy."

"I think we bypassed messy when Warwick escaped." I held all feelings of helplessness at bay by trailing my fingers over the weapons concealed on my person. "If we're splitting into couples, I'm with Sebastian."

Marcus's shoulders stiffened for a brief moment, and his hands flexed on the steering wheel. "I prefer you stay with me."

Undeterred, I shook my head. "The *Palmipède* is Sebastian's territory, and people are more likely to speak to him than you, especially once they get a good look at that ridiculous mustache."

"Penny," Violet started to argue, but I looked daggers at her, and she subsided into perturbed silence.

"I must say, I'm flattered," Sebastian said, preening just a bit. "Do try to remember this later when we're all running for our lives." Returning his attention to the road, he indicated Marcus should turn at the next intersection. "Here we are."

"This is it?" Violet peered out the window as we pulled into a deserted and dismal area on the River Aire waterfront.

"It is." Turning up the collar of his coat, Sebastian added, "Best tuck under a blanket. Some time may pass before the *Palmipède* arrives, and it's about to get chilly."

True to his word, a damp mist swirled about the car within minutes. Violet and I shivered under the scratchy, woolen throw she unearthed, the boys huddled in their overcoats, and all of us retreated into an uneasy silence. I entertained glorious thoughts of rescuing everyone and seeing them safely home. Violet cracked her knuckles as she fretted for Nic. Marcus was probably making contingency plans for everything from fire to flood. And Sebastian?

Well, Sebastian's always up for an adventure.

The minutes ticked by on the various pocket watches until I could no longer feel the end of my nose.

"I could really use a h-h-h-ot toddy," Violet said, sounding more irked than pathetic, "and this damp cannot be good for Penny."

"I'm fine," I lied before Marcus could lodge a similar protest. A soft noise danced across the water, equal parts foghorn and steam whistle, and I peeked over Sebastian's shoulder. "What was that?"

"The boat is here," he said. "Mind where you put your feet. The cobblestones are slippery."

The moment I stepped down from the car, I spotted the ghostly apparition gliding toward us through the mist. Painted in shades of gray and palest yellow, the *Palmipède* was nearly indistinguishable from the fog. No lights illuminated the exterior of the vessel. The only sound to mark her progress was the gentle slosh-slap of water against her sides.

"It's not anything like I imagined." I shifted from one foot to the other, impatient to be aboard.

"What did you expect?" Sebastian retorted. "For her to glide out of the fog like a waterborne circus spectacular?"

If I didn't know him better, I would have thought he sounded nervous. "Strung stem to stern with colored lanterns, perhaps accompanied by flash trays and shooting stars?"

Sebastian tucked my hand in his elbow, a return to his usual gallantry. "We'll save that sort of thing for your next birthday celebration, all right?"

"If we make it to my next birthday."

The moment the vessel glided to a halt, silent workmen bridged the space between boat and dock with a short gangplank. We stepped aboard single file and followed Sebastian to a small door where he silently withdrew a hundred aureii from his pocket and paid our admission fee.

"Take this." He pressed a similar stack of coins into my gloved hand. "You're going to need pocket money."

"You know I haven't any talent for the cards." The hallway stretched out before us, its darkness tempered only by the dull red glow of a lantern hanging at the far end. One step, two, three . . . I bumped into Sebastian's back when he paused to open the inner door.

"Live without limits, my dear Penny," he advised, leading me inside.

Here was the circus. Light and color and noise exploded around me. Crystal chandeliers blazed overhead, causing jewels to wink from coiffures, slim throats, and white-gloved wrists. Polished wood gleamed against flocked velvet wallpaper that was darker than blood. Chance wheels were spun, cards shuffled, and dice thrown under the scented haze of expensive perfume and cigarette smoke. Waiters threaded through the assembled patrons with trays of brandies and imported cigars, and I very much hoped that Marcus's undercover officers could be counted among the men and women crowded into the room.

The boys shrugged off their outer coats, and we all handed our wraps to a servitor. Marcus drew us into the corner nearest the bar, identifying possible threats.

"I don't see any of the Ferrum Viriae aboard yet," he said. "We're not staying if we don't have backup."

"Perhaps they're just doing a better job blending in than you are," Sebastian said. "Do try to relax, there's a good chap. Your posture is a dead giveaway."

With a flicker of a scowl, Marcus loosened up his jaw and his shoulders. "That better?"

"Marginally," Sebastian said. "You still look as though you forgot to take the hanger out of your coat before putting it on. Think happy thoughts, if you please."

"Kittens." Violet undercut the suggestion with an assassin's gaze. None of us believed Nic would be concealed aboard the boat, but she looked as ready to wring information from someone as she had back in the interrogation room. The wicked smile that followed confirmed my suspicion. "Multicolored light refractions and double-horned narwhals."

"Madame, I will have you know I have never in my life entertained a single thought that included narwhals." Opening a slim silver case, Marcus extracted a cigarette. I'd never seen him smoke, but I had to admit, it did play into the part of debonair, devil-may-care gentleman.

Sebastian held out his monogrammed gold lighter before Marcus could locate his own. "There's no use standing about like a brace of pheasants asking for the shot. We need to mingle and see what information we can glean. What game will you have, Penny?"

Mama's dress felt a bit tight around my ribs when I tried to take a deep breath. "The wheel it is."

We stepped out, Sebastian at my right elbow and Marcus escorting Violet. Everyone was suspect in my eyes: the demoiselle in the peacock-blue gown settling into a card game, the group of five young men raucously knocking back liquor at the bar, the mutton-chopped servitor gliding ahead of us as we crossed to the felt-covered tables. Sorting out the wheat from the chaff would be a tricky business.

Swearing under my breath, I dropped a golden aureii on the felt. "White, please."

The attendant moved my money to a mother-of-pearl plate and spun the wheel. "Stakes, ladies and gentlemen. Place your final stakes."

Others dropped bills and coins on either the white square or the onyx black. The attendant dropped an ivory ball into the wheel and announced, "Bets closed."

Watching it spin in a sickening circle, I knew differently.

All bets are off.

The ball whirled around and around the wheel, dancing in and out of the black-and-white slots before finally settling into place.

"White," the attendant declared, returning my coin to me along with its twin.

I pressed both of them back into his hand and lowered my voice. "Perhaps you could help me locate someone? We're seeking a man with a talent for making discreet business arrangements."

The attendant kept the tip but answered my query with a blank stare. "My deepest apologies, Miss, but you'd do better to seek the help of a reputable employment agency. Would you care to place another bet?" He turned to the group and raised his voice. "Place your stakes, please."

I set my coin on black this time and addressed Sebastian behind my fan. "That was less helpful than I'd hoped."

"Only your first query. And it's early yet."

The ball landed on black; I'd won again. Far from pleased, I accepted my winnings with a curt nod of thanks and moved away from the table. "Time to circulate."

A quick glance put Marcus and Violet at the Speculations table, so we headed for the dice. I winced when someone jostled me on our way across the room.

Sebastian acted as human shield, guiding me to the far corner of the bar. "You're still hurting."

I didn't respond, taking a careful seat at the counter.

"I have something that ought to help." He held up a hand to signal a waiter. "A bottle of Effervescence, please."

It arrived within seconds, cork popped and glasses filled over low murmurs of "There you are, sir," and "If there's anything else you desire, please let me know." Sebastian waved him off with a practiced flick of fingers and extracted a vial from his pocket. Cobalt glass glinted in the light from the chandelier.

"What is it?" I had to inquire, seeing as how it lacked a label. "And where did you acquire it?"

"It's called Quick-Heal, and I discovered it on one of my many and varied adventures abroad. Experimental but effective." Unscrewing the lid, Sebastian added three drops of the dark tincture to my Effervescence. The medicine broke against the bubbles and twirled through the liquid like a clockwork ballerina dancing on copper tiptoes.

"Should it be mixed with alcohol?" I asked as he handed me the glass.

"That actually helps with delivery to the circulatory system," he said with a professional nod.

"Thank you, Doctor Stirling. Be certain to send me your bill." I raised the flute and toasted him before taking a hesitant sip. At first,

I could taste nothing save the sweet tang of the sparkling wine, but within seconds, I could imagine the grapes themselves, the vine on which they'd flourished, the sunshine and wind and rain and dirt in which they'd grown. My pulse sped up by my second sip; this time, I tasted oak aging barrels with the undertones of caramel and vanilla and smoke that my father had always described. Dazed, I closed my other hand around the bottle and slid the Quick-Heal into my reticule. "I'm going to keep the rest of this, if you don't mind. With the week I've been having, I'll probably need it."

Sebastian cheerfully clinked his crystal flute against mine. "In a few minutes, you ought to feel well enough to swim to Meridia."

A bit unsteadily, I crossed to the nearest gaming table. The smallest of details now loomed large in my eyes. Every whisper was a scream in my ear. The man to my left tossed the dice, and they rolled with a clatter to the far end. A loss, so the crowd groaned and money moved like partners changing in a waltz. I reached out and captured the dice before anyone else could claim them. My throw sent them dancing down the felt to a win.

A second toss, another win.

A third.

Somewhere between the fat stack of silver denarii pushed my way and the fourth throw, I finished my glass of sparkling Quick-Heal. Another toss of the dice and yet another win. It was as though Sebastian's beloved Lady Luck wished to make up for the chaos and heartache by lining my pockets, but the weight of the coins did nothing to fill the emptiness inside me. More people gathered about us, heads tilted back with laughter, garish silks and jewels on display. Leering gentlemen leaned over my shoulder to toss money onto the table. Looking around, I found myself trapped in a stained-glass window, locked inside the lurid colors, light pouring through me, all substance drained away.

"Steady there," Sebastian's voice was low in my ear, close enough to ruffle the curls on the back of my neck. "Don't forget why we're here."

"Right," I said slowly. When the attendant passed me yet another stack of coins, I left a golden aureii in his hand. "We wondered if there was someone we could speak to about a special hire."

The attendant glanced over at Sebastian and then nodded. "Might be. The boss occasionally arranges jobs of a delicate nature."

Luck was with us again, it seemed. "And is he aboard this evening?" I ventured.

"He is." When the attendant paused, I gave a second gold coin into his keeping. With the smallest of bows, he tilted his head at a hallway to our left and said, "Private Room Seven, the owner's suite. But you'll have to hurry. He usually leaves at midnight, and it's nearly that now."

A glance at the clock revealed there was only a minute or two until everything was pumpkins and lost glass slippers. Marcus and Violet were wholly absorbed in a conversation with the doorman. I had to decide: charge ahead without them or risk losing the fox in this hunt.

"Wait!" came Sebastian's strained protest from behind me, but the combination of adrenaline and Quick-Heal sent me skimming down the hallway as though my heels had wings. Rucking up my skirts as I ran, I pulled the pistols from their holsters. Closed doors alternated on either side, and it took me only seconds to reach Private Room Seven. Skipping over the nicety of knocking, I kicked it in and entered with arms extended, guns cocked and ready to fire.

The room was empty except for polished wood and expensive antiques. Moving carefully, I checked behind the bar and the larger pieces of furniture, but our quarry wasn't hiding in any of the corners. Disappointment spiraled through me.

"Damn all the Bells, that attendant lied to us." Lowering my guns, I exhaled through my nose and tried to slow my hammering pulse. "He's not here."

Sebastian closed the door behind him, slid a key into the lock, and turned it with a horrible finality. "Yes, he is."

I stared at him, trying to process what he was saying. That I was looking at the owner of the *Palmipède*. That I had indeed met up with the man responsible for hiring the sneak thieves, for arranging the break-ins at Glasshouse and the Bibliothèca. All the blood drained from my head, but I still lifted both pistols and aimed at his chest. The barrels wavered a bit because my hands shook, and I prayed he wouldn't reach for his own guns. "You should start explaining."

"You want answers," Sebastian said smoothly, taking a step toward me, "and I want you to put the weapons down. One must happen before the other, pony before the cart."

We exchanged a long look, my gaze trapped by the blinding blue of his eyes. Friend, companion, cohort—but what possible explanation could he make for his actions? I owed it to him to listen. I owed it to myself to proceed with the utmost caution. By inches, I lowered the pistols . . .

Just far enough to shoot him once in the leg. Trying to avoid any major arteries, I aimed so the bullet grazed his left thigh. Eyes widening with shock, Sebastian dropped his walking stick and reached into his coat for his guns, forcing me to fire again, this time at his knee. Crippled by pain, he crumpled to the ground.

In half a heartbeat, I stood over him, pressing the point of my shoe into the uppermost wound. "Pull out your MAGs, Sebastian, and give them over. If you so much as twitch a finger toward the trigger, I'll aim higher and shoot again."

Silently, he reached into his coat and pulled out both guns.

"Toss them aside," I ordered him. When he complied, I stepped back immediately, giving him tacit permission to clutch at his leg. "Now explain to me how you got caught up in this mess. When did you start working for Warwick?"

Groaning, Sebastian pressed his hands over the oozing bullet holes. "I'm going to bleed to death. You need to call for a doctor."

"They're flesh wounds. And luckily for you, I have a bottle of amazingly potent healing fluid in my reticule. You can have it, just as soon as you sing me a little song." Thinking about the blue glass bottle, I added, "You got the Quick-Heal from Warwick, didn't you?"

"He's been tweaking the formula for months," Sebastian admitted, his face pale. "To use when he swaps out your old Ticker for the new one."

"Have you been working for him all that time? Arranging for his escape? Setting up the burglaries at Glasshouse and the Bibliothèca? Nearly killing Nic in that damned explosion at the factory?" Remembering my brother lying in the ruins of his office, I found it difficult to keep my voice even. "Why would you do such a thing?"

"It was a distraction!" Words spurted from his mouth. "He wasn't supposed to be there. Warwick never wanted to hurt him."

"But he's hurt so many people. Why, Sebastian? Why would you help him?"

He gave a short laugh, one entirely lacking in mirth. "Do you have any idea how much money people would pay to live beyond their time? There's a fortune to be made in Augmentation, my dear.

You know I never let a profitable business opportunity pass me by." With great effort, he started to stand.

I leveled the pistols at his chest. "Don't move." He didn't stop. Every dragging step was a struggle, but still he came at me. "I mean it." I took another step back. "Damn it, I don't want to kill you, Sebastian!"

"That's the genius of it all." He gifted me with his lady-killer smile, except now it was the sort that strangled women and left them in alleyways. "You're not going to kill me, Penny." Giving me a wide berth, he made slow and terrible progress to the far wall. With the pull of a lever and a soft grunt of effort, he opened a hatch. A small rowboat was moored to the side of the *Palmipède*. Beyond that extended a black canvas unrelieved by lantern or lamplight. "You're going to get in the boat and let me take you to Warwick."

"Like hell I will."

"He's going to fix your Ticker. Nic and your parents are waiting for you."

I stepped toward Sebastian, but only so I could take better aim. "Where's he keeping them?"

"Get in the boat."

Finally losing my patience, I shouted, "Tell me where he's keeping them!"

Hands hammering at the door distracted us both, and the wood-muffled cry of "Penny!" came from the far side in two-part harmony.

"Stirling, what's going on in there?" Marcus shouted, following that with a vehement kick to the door.

Sebastian lunged for me. Had I fired then, at close range with the guns aimed at his chest, I surely would have killed him. But if I wouldn't pull the trigger, I wasn't going to let him turn the weapons on me either. I twisted in his grasp and threw them as hard as

I could out the open hatch. They hit the water with twin splashes. Looking out at the limitless darkness, I was momentarily tempted by Sebastian's insanity, by how comforting it would be to reunite with my family, to have my Ticker fixed, to see this come to an end.

Still trapped in the hallway, Marcus ceased pounding on the door. "I'm setting explosive charges," he warned through the wood. "Move back!"

"Get in the boat, Penny!" Sebastian urged again.

The wall behind us blew inward, showering everything with splinters. I could resist, or I could jump.

When I ducked under Sebastian's arm, his own forward momentum and my swift shove launched him out the escape hatch. I pulled the hatch shut with a heave and a gasp as Marcus and Violet emerged from a cloud of plaster dust, weapons raised.

"Where is he?" Marcus demanded.

"Learning the finer points of rowboat operation," I answered, pushing past him and heading back into the hall. "Have him followed. He's working for Warwick."

"I'll wring his highborn neck!" Then Violet let loose with a string of profanity the likes of which I hoped never to hear again.

Marcus only blinked once and muttered, "I was afraid of that," before relaying the information via his RiPA.

A loud and wrenching shudder rippled through the floorboards, and the ship slowly, inexorably tilted to one side, throwing everyone off-balance. I fell against the wall as the lights flickered. Back in the gaming room, shouts broke out.

Unperturbed, Marcus grasped me by the elbow and towed me down the hall in the opposite direction. "Step lively, Tesseraria. We're on contingency plan H already."

A second shudder was accompanied by the scream of iron against rock, and I winced. "What's happening?"

"Backup finally arrived, and they're running this ship aground," he answered.

"When we lost sight of you, Marcus messaged for reinforcements," Violet added.

By now, the *Palmipède* listed horribly to starboard, making it even more difficult to walk through the water pouring down the hall and swirling about our ankles.

"It seems the good Mister Stirling played merry havoc with our plans this evening," Marcus said as he hurried us along. "My soldiers didn't make it aboard until I called them in. They'll clear everyone out of the vessel, and I just sent a secondary unit out to the river to search for Sebastian." Striding through knee-deep currents now, he led us to a passageway that sloped unnaturally downward. At the bottom, he opened another door; beyond that was only gently sloshing darkness.

"Can you see him?" I asked, peering under Marcus's arm.

"Visibility is at zero, and perhaps that's for the best. If we can't see Sebastian, he can't see us." Marcus pulled a handheld water-surface propulsion vehicle off the wall. "Take one of these and swim for shore."

"Swim?" I repeated, wondering if the Quick-Heal had clouded my brain.

"With help." By the light of the lamp hanging on the wall, he gestured to a switch on the handlebars. "I've used these Skimmers in training exercises. This button activates the motor. Point it toward the opposite bank, keep your head above water, and stay close to each other."

"I'll go first." With a grim expression, Violet silently pulled off her petticoats, and I followed her example. There was only time enough for me to give her elbow a quick squeeze before she jumped.

Looping my purse over my wrist, I clutched the Skimmer's handlebars. Hitting the water was like falling chest-first onto a sheet of ice. My Ticker seized in shock.

Don't you dare, you piece of junk!

After a long moment, the Ticker righted itself, leaving me free to activate the Skimmer. Vibrating with barely restrained power, the apparatus slowly but surely towed me forward, the weight of my sodden skirts dragging at me all the while. Filtered by the fog, the warm blur of a streetlight gradually appeared. The dripping smudge under the post coalesced into Violet. By the time I felt the shore under my shoes, Marcus caught up with me and we exited the river together, leaving the Skimmers in the shallows.

Behind us, the *Palmipède* rested sadly on its side. The area around it was bedlam, with soldiers rounding up fleeing patrons and loading them into waiting boats. Marcus's RiPA sputtered, relaying half a message before it shorted out. He swore as he removed the frizzled device from his wrist, but a thunderous crackle interrupted the oath. I might have wanted flash trays and shooting stars, but this was no fireworks display. Sparks hissed and sizzled as flames erupted from the side of the steamboat. The surprising heat of it pushed us back several feet, and Violet drew nearer to me, shivering. I looped my arm about her waist and looked to Marcus.

"We need to clear out of here. Have you any idea where we are?"

Struggling to regain his trademark composure, Marcus nodded. "Stay close and keep quiet."

We crept down the dockside alleys until we arrived at a tavern. A cracked wooden sign declared it to be "The Second Buttonhole," but it certainly didn't rate above the fifth or sixth. The three of us crammed ourselves into a booth in the farthest recesses of the common room, and a dour man with a face like a bowl of risen bread appeared.

"Bit late to be out and about, isn't it?" he remarked. "What will you have?"

"A bottle of whiskey," Marcus said firmly and pressed a coin into his hand.

The payment disappeared into a pocket, and the innkeeper backed away from the table. Half of Marcus's false mustache had peeled away from his upper lip, and he winced as I gently tugged the rest of it off. When he opened his silver cigarette case, a miniature tidal wave streamed out of it. In silence, we set out fans, billfolds, and card holders to dry. The air- and watertight seals on the pocket watches were examined and determined to have done their job. My father's compass and sundial were no worse for wear after their washing, and my winnings added up to a shocking amount.

"Now what?" Waterlogged and worried, I rolled the bottle of Quick-Heal to and fro across my palm.

The innkeeper returned with a large glass bottle, its label yellowed and peeling, and a tray of grimy glasses. He set everything on the table, eyes raking over the miscellaneous items culled from our pockets before pursing his lips and departing.

"I fear we look like a band of thieves meeting up to pool the night's take." Marcus sloshed the liquor into the glasses and lifted one. After a hesitant sip, he grimaced. "Not the best vintage, I grant you, but it'll warm you up."

"A good thing, given the meager fire our host keeps." Though I didn't like to say anything, my Ticker hadn't yet recovered from our impromptu swim. Thumping erratically in my chest, it threatened every few seconds to cease working altogether. Uncorking the Quick-Heal, I downed the contents of the vial. Remembering what Sebastian had said about alcohol aiding in the delivery to the bloodstream, I chased the medication with a shot of whiskey. Instantaneous heat bloomed in my stomach, rushing through every appendage, and I could well imagine what Vinterviken Blasting Oil must taste like.

"What was in that vial, Penny?" Violet looked at me over her glass, her carefully applied eyeliner running down her cheeks like gothic tears. "And should I have asked for some?"

I explained about the Quick-Heal and the revelations made in Private Room Seven. My time in the river had numbed me, but no more than the shock of realizing Sebastian was a turncoat.

"I can hardly believe it," Violet said, biting the corner of her lip.

I couldn't help but remember the mad zeal in his eyes when he tried to convince me to get in the boat. "I certainly never thought he'd get his hands dirty like that."

"How long has he been working for Warwick?" Marcus asked.

"Long enough to help plan his escape from the courthouse," I said. "And to have arranged for my parents' kidnapping. I messaged him when Nic and I were driving across town on the Vitesse. He knew precisely when we would arrive." I wanted to put my head down on the table and cry, but it wouldn't help anyone. "He could have secreted them away and turned right around to meet us at Glasshouse."

Similarly frustrated, Marcus repeatedly bashed at his RiPA to no avail. "Hopefully the secondary unit caught up with him before we ran aground. If not, there's little chance they found him in the chaos afterward."

"True enough," Violet said, finishing her first glass of whiskey and pouring a second.

"I need to get back to the waterfront," Marcus said, gathering his things. "Reporters and more Ferrum Viriae officers should be arriving at the scene."

Violet snatched up her purse. "You stay here with Penny. She needs to rest."

I started to protest, but Marcus was already nodding.

"I suppose I do have a slightly better stature for a bodyguard," he said.

"You have slightly better stature for a brick wall," Violet countered, wresting her dripping dress from the booth. "I'm going after Sebastian. He's going to wish he escaped down a rabbit hole."

Someone else might have cautioned her; Marcus only held up a hand to signal a server. "Call the young lady a hansom cab, please." He turned back to Violet and pressed a stack of coins into her palm. "Go straight to the docks. Find Frederick Carmichael, and take him as your second."

Violet crammed the money in her purse. "How will I find you later?"

"You won't," Marcus said. "We'll contact you tomorrow."

"I hope the two of you behave yourselves," she admonished with mock solemnity.

The muscles along Marcus's jaw jumped before he answered, "I think she's safe from my advances, at least until morning."

"She is sitting right here, and she is perfectly fine, thank you." I strived to make the lie sound convincing. The Quick-Heal's other effects now made themselves known, and it was as though I'd wrapped my Ticker in a flannel blanket and lulled it to sleep.

"You needn't fib to me," Violet said, pressing a quick, fierce kiss to my cheek before hustling out the door.

"I need to get you somewhere more secure," Marcus said, glancing down at me. "Wait here a moment and turn your face toward the wall." He held a whispered conversation with the innkeeper in which yet more coins exchanged hands, and then he returned with a key that appeared well-oiled with kitchen grease. "Come on."

I found my feet but discovered they were much farther away from my head than expected. "I shouldn't have partaken of that second dose." My Ticker lurched, and so did I, but Marcus caught me before I fell. As he carried me up the stairs, I hiccupped and wished I hadn't. "Just leave me here on the carpet."

"Like hell I will," was his grim answer. When we gained the upper landing, he propped me against the wall until he could wrangle the door open.

I stumbled inside to find that the room's appointments were better than we'd any right to expect: one narrow bed that would fit an adult, provided he or she didn't roll over, a wooden chair, several hooks in the crumbling plaster wall, and a blessedly hot radiator that I used to warm my backside.

"It looks as though we are going to have to spend some time in close quarters," Marcus said, shucking his coat. Though it was no longer sopping wet, it left a series of drips on the floor. Hanging it from one of the hooks on the wall, he removed his shoes and socks next and tucked them under the radiator.

"I'm fine with that, given the alternatives." I was surprised to find that I meant it. The anger and resentment I'd harbored toward him for funding Warwick's research had been left behind in the river. "Your clothes will dry out faster if you get them off."

After a moment's hesitation, he started unbuttoning his shirt. "My dear Miss Farthing, what would your mother say?"

"You've worked with her." Already without petticoats, I removed Mama's gown. The silk was ruined, no doubt about it. Standing there in my frilled bloomers, chemise, and corset, I wrapped my arms about me and tried to stop my teeth from chattering. If anyone had told me last week that I would be keeping company with Marcus Kingsley whilst a band of marauding terrorists tried to kidnap me, I wouldn't have believed it. "I'm pretty sure she'd say 'Stop standing on ceremony and get out of those wet things.'"

"That does sound like her." Off came his shirt, and Marcus turned to hang it next to his coat. Scars decorated his arms and chest, ridges and whorls of raised flesh that were the faintest of pinks against his tanned skin.

Stepping closer to get a better look, I murmured, "Careless with a bread knife, are you?"

Caught off guard, he looked down. "Training bayonet got me there," he said, pointing to one of the ridged lines. "The others happened in field practice."

The largest of the scars ran from his navel to his left armpit. "And this one?"

"Combat in Aígyptos." Marcus looked down at me, unashamed of the marks on his body but terribly troubled by something else. "I got off easy in that fight. Lost two soldiers who happened to be close friends."

Sadness bled through the words, and I couldn't help but shudder. I knew that sort of pain. "I'm sorry."

"There's remorse, Tesseraria, and there's the resolve to make certain it never happens again." Reaching past me, he pulled one of the blankets off the bed and draped it over my shoulders. "It's why I struggle to plan out everything the way I do. Viktor was the one with all the combat instincts. He had trained for it since both of us wore knee pants. I was just the one with the head for schematics. Everything would be different if my brother were still alive."

Until this very moment, I hadn't realized how complicated a cipher Marcus was. "You didn't want to be in the Ferrum Viriae? What did you want to do instead?"

"Mechanical engineering, like your parents." Looking down, he studied his hands. "Tinkering, my father called it, until he realized where my true talents lie."

I had an inkling what that might be but wanted to make certain. "And where is that?"

"Weapons," he confirmed. "Small ones in the beginning, like the MAG and the Superconductive Slingshot." Marcus grabbed one of the threadbare towels and rubbed it over his head, the muscles in his back clenching. "I thought I would be able to distance myself from the business later. Viktor and I spoke about it many times, and he knew I didn't want to spend my life developing that sort of technology. But then he was gone, and there was no one to take his place except me."

Thinking of Nic, I put my hand on Marcus's.

His fingers turned over to cling to mine, though he kept his face averted. "My father pulled me out of the College of Engineering and sent me to the Ferrum Viriae Academy. It's been trial by fire, literally, these last six months. So much to catch up on: maneuvers, strategies, history of combat . . ."

"Could you speak with him about it?" Thinking of my own parents, I couldn't imagine them asking me to dedicate my life to someone else's pursuits. "Or your mother?"

Marcus shook his head and gave me a rueful smile. "My mother is a third-generation munitions manufacturer. Her marriage to my father was as much a business arrangement as it was a personal one. I've never brought it up with her, and I never will."

"She might understand."

"A tigress doesn't change her stripes," he said.

I thought of another tigress, one who loved me and my siblings beyond reason, who protected us with tooth and claw. And I thought of what my mother wouldn't give to speak one more time with her eldest child. "What is it that you want to ask Viktor?"

Marcus stiffened but didn't pull away from me. "What do you mean?"

"That's why you're building the Grand Design, isn't it? There's something specific you want to ask him?"

I thought that Marcus might not answer at all. As it was, his next words didn't address my question. "I doubt you've ever seen combat up close, Penny, but it's a terrifying thing. The first time I was on the field, I nearly turned and ran."

"I can imagine."

"Can you?" The words were tight, his throat working as he swallowed. "Can you imagine a thousand guns firing off at once? Searing hot metal screaming past your head only to fell the soldier just behind you? The cries of the wounded? The blood mixed with the dirt? Death all around you?"

"Yes, I can. I do more than imagine it every day." The blanket slid from my shoulder, taking the strap of my chemise with it. Now the top of my own scar was visible, the one from the Augmentation surgery set alongside the Ticker's faceplate. "You're not the only one who's looked death in the face."

Marcus didn't blanch or shrink away from the sight of it, though his was not the detached gaze of a clinician. "Did it hurt?"

"Almost dying hurt a lot more." I pulled the blanket back up and sat upon the bed.

He joined me, the furniture creaking under his weight. "That's what I wanted to ask my brother . . . Isn't there someone else? Someone else better suited to this job?"

Though I'd been cold before, the words were like ice on my skin. "You're doing the best you can."

"That's just the problem," he said softly. "I don't think my best is ever going to be enough."

"Despite *my* best efforts to the contrary, despite Calvin Warwick trying to kidnap me and fléchettes flying in my general direction, Legatus, you've kept me alive. You saw me safely off the ship tonight—"

"And straight into the river!"

"A prime example of how you're learning to think on your feet," I countered. "I might be able to look after myself, but I'm safer when I'm with you."

Marcus reached out, sliding slow fingers through my curls, untangling the knots one at a time until he could run his very capable hand through my hair from the soft spot on the back of my neck down to my waist. In return, I sat very, very still until he wrapped an arm about me and leaned back against the wall.

"Not to frighten you," he said at long last, "but Warwick is just the beginning. There are others who won't be content to watch you Augment factory workers and repair minor injuries when there's potential for so much more. They're going to steal the technology, develop it, exploit it, and destroy everything we hold dear."

I resisted the urge to set my head upon his shoulder, worried what might happen to my already off-balance Ticker if he were to kiss me right now. But Marcus's eyes were closed, purple-black shadows smudging the skin under his thick, dark lashes. If this was a seduction, it was the laziest one on record, so I allowed myself to relax against him. "It must get tiresome, carrying the weight of the world on your shoulders like that."

His answering laugh was a low rumble in his chest. "It does, indeed."

Under the scent of river water and wet wool, there was something about his skin that reminded me of lemon soap and sunshine. "So many burdens weighing you down. Can't you leave off a few?"

"My burdens are the dead who've served under my command and the lives of Industria's citizens," he answered. "So, no, Tesseraria, I'll not set down a single one."

I won't let her fall, Mama.

The broken memento mori on the floor of my parents' study. For a split second, it was as though I held it in my hands again. Then I broke out in gooseflesh. "I know where I've seen the daguerreotype glass before."

Marcus followed the sudden shift in the conversation, opening his eyes and sitting up. "Where was it? When?"

"Just after Cygna died," I said, nearly choking on the memory. "A photographer came to the house."

The woman had posed Dimitria behind the horsehair chaise where Nic and I sat. Mama had placed the baby between us with instructions to hold her gently and stay very still. Cygna, so named because of the swan-soft down upon her tiny head, was dressed in white muslin ruffles and a pink cap. Her little lips were pursed, ready to be kissed, but death had stolen even the smallest of newborn noises from her.

I won't disappoint you, Mama. I won't let Cygna fall.

I'd put my arm about my dead sister and held her for the first time. Nic sat on her other side, stiff and stubborn, the way he always was when trying desperately hard not to cry. Dimitria stood behind us, aloof in her grief.

"It's the only picture ever taken of the four of us together," I said faintly. "I knew there was something about the way Nic had been posed and the quality of the glass that I recognized. Whoever took the daguerreotypes of him specializes in pictures of the dead."

"There isn't enough business to support such an occupation outside the city walls," Marcus said, already deep in thought. "Nic and your parents are still in Bazalgate, then. If the RiPAs resume functioning by the morning, I'll deploy investigative units to all the photography studios."

"And if we can't get a message out, we'll call upon each and every one of them ourselves," I insisted.

"I had a feeling you wouldn't be left out of it."

"You're learning, Legatus." I permitted myself a single jaw-cracking yawn before returning my head to his shoulder. "You're learning."

TEN

In Which There Is a Mouse of Sorts in the Walls

By the time I woke in the morning, Marcus already had slipped out to the Perpetua Marketplace and returned with clothing and the necessary supplies to tint my copper hair the darkest of browns.

"It'll help prevent you from being so easily recognized," he said, sleeves turned up to the elbows and a hairbrush in hand. "No use trying to go black, it would only end badly."

"And you know that because?" I let the question linger in the air, much like the scent of frying ham and burnt toast drifting up through the floorboards.

All I got by way of reply was an enigmatic half-smile. The intimacy of the previous night had gone the way of the shadows. Our RiPAs had yet to resume proper function, though they sputtered occasionally and caused us both to jump. Testing our weapons to be certain the river hadn't similarly ruined them, we kept bumping awkwardly into each other. When the time came to wind my Ticker, I turned my back to buy a modicum of privacy as I unbuttoned the collar of my dress and inserted the key into the chest plate. The clickity-clack of the winding seemed to fill the room; by the time I was done, I was more than ready to escape our cozy confines.

"Come on, then," I said, heading for the door.

"Wait just one moment," Marcus said. "You're not quite ready."

I paused and peered down at my ensemble. The pearl gray frock and lace shawl were neat, clean, and subdued in both color and style. My newly darkened hair caught me off guard each time I glimpsed a loose strand or two out of the corner of my eye, fastened up as it was at the nape of my neck with a dozen hairpins. "Don't I look every inch the respectable miss, visiting from Meridia?"

He held out a gleaming gold circle. "Here to take a honeymoon picture." He already wore a matching band on his left hand.

To gain access to the daguerreotype studios, we needed some sort of cover story. With all our physical differences, it would be difficult to pass as brother and sister. A young married couple made far more sense.

"It is customary, I think, to go down on one knee when you propose, Mister Kingsley." I reached for the ring, but he twitched it away from me.

"Quite right. Wherever are my manners?" The leg of his dark blue trousers hiked up a bit when he bent his knee and took my hand. "My dearest Miss Farthing, will you do me the unutterable honor of wearing this cheap bit of metal that will most likely turn your finger green, pretending to love and honor me as your husband for the purposes of subterfuge and stratagem?"

"My hearts and stars, that will go down in the history books as the most romantic business proposition of the century, I am certain." Still, my Ticker thudded in its new, horrible way as Marcus slid the ring onto my finger. Given the number of diamantés winking back at me, it was far from the inexpensive bauble he'd described. "Fifteen photography studios will make quite a day's work. Let's have breakfast and get going."

"Slowly," he admonished. Tucking my hand under his arm, he led me to the door. "Young couples in love don't rush to the streetcar first thing in the morning. They feed each other bits of toast and discuss the morning news." When I dragged my heels, he turned toward me to add, "A bit of reconnaissance in the dining room is necessary to reassure me we aren't being watched."

So I found myself eyeing the other diners, straining my ears to make out the gossip over the rattle of plates and clink of spoons. Across from me, Marcus sipped cold coffee with the appropriate grimaces, rattled his newspaper, and gazed at me with false adoration every few minutes.

"Shocking," he observed, making no effort to keep his voice down. "This city has gone to the hounds since last we were here. Perhaps we should have taken the steamer to Helvetica instead."

When he nudged me under the table, I hastened to contribute "Of course, my dearest. We ought to have done that" before I returned the favor to his shin. "On the upside, this porridge is delicious." Though it was rough and perhaps contained more sawdust than oats, it went down easily enough with a sprinkle of sugar. I followed that with two hot scones clabbered together with jam and pale butter. When I couldn't find room in my stomach for a third, I wrapped it in a handkerchief.

Marcus peered at me over his newspaper. "What are you doing with that?"

"Putting it in my pocket for later," I said. "No one knows what the day will bring, after all. Are you done with the broadsheets?"

"I am, my love." He pretended to press a kiss to my cheek as he added in an undertone, "And certain no one is overly interested in us. It's safe to go."

The intimacy of the whisper sent a jolt down to my slippers, but I recovered my poise as we made our way outside. Faint as it was, the thin morning sunlight hurt my eyes, but thankfully, my body had otherwise recovered from our midnight swim. The Quick-Heal had dealt with the worst of my bruises and scrapes.

Marcus touched my elbow. "Are you feeling all right?"

"I think so." A half-truth. I could still breathe. The Ticker was still beating, albeit with a highly irregular cadence. That was the most I could hope for at the moment. "Where shall we go first?"

"I thought we might try the Eclipse Studio on the Fourth Etoile Road. Does that meet with your approval?"

"And then perhaps lunch at the Sabaudia Hotel?" I queried for the benefit of the others standing at the streetcar platform.

"Whatever you desire, light of my life, though that might be a bit posh for our modest wallet."

No one tried to interfere with us as we boarded the cherry-red tram. The mechanical horse team pulled us all the way to the West Side; when we arrived, only a handful of people remained on the streetcar, and we were the only ones to descend at our stop.

"So far, so good," I noted. "How far is the first studio?"

"A brisk walk will put us there in less than five minutes," Marcus replied with far too pleasant a smile for the occasion. "Not too brisk, though. We are, after all, on our honeymoon. Hasn't the weather been lovely?"

"I prefer the rain." I caught a flicker of movement out of the corner of my eye: someone dressed in a dark coat over a shiny vest emerged from an alleyway and walked toward us.

Marcus's grip on me tightened almost imperceptibly, then loosened. "The inn is most comfortable."

"I hardly slept a wink." I had to fight to keep my voice even, my pace steady.

"It seems my bride is feeling most contrary this morning."

I could hear footsteps behind us; with our backs to him, we were at a decided disadvantage. With a trilling laugh, I pulled Marcus into the nearest covered doorway. He reached under his coat for his MAG. My hand was in my pocket, thumb already depressing the charging switch on the Pixii.

"If I'm out of sorts, it's because you forgot to kiss me this morning." Standing on tiptoe, I brushed my lips over his.

It was supposed to be a ruse, a stolen moment to ascertain the danger of the situation, but I felt his breath catch in his throat. When the kiss deepened, I forgot about my Ticker, about the very real worry that it might stop working. I burned with white-light, lost in the taste of him. It was almost impossible to concentrate on anything but the feel of his mouth, of his hands circling about my waist and holding me against his chest.

Marcus pulled away first, drawing a ragged breath and pressing his forehead to mine. "Is he gone?"

I still had the stranger in my sights if not my crosshairs, but it was hard to form a coherent sentence. "He's going into the greengrocer's."

We were running out of options. The sky knew it as well; when the rain started, it wasn't a light dousing but a downpour. Waiting out the worst of it under the doorway, we stood pressed against each other, neither of us venturing to speak. The moment there was a break in the weather, we stepped out of our shelter and walked down the street to the first of the photography studios. Sleek and fat as a well-fed feline, the owner rushed to greet us when we opened the door.

"Good morning." He took me by the hand and led us into the main parlor. Everything was upholstered, from the chairs to the walls. The air was heavily perfumed, the scent of lilacs twisting its way into my hair and clothes. “Whom did you want to memorialize today?”

With a rush, I thought of Dimitria. Her last moments with us. How Mama hadn’t taken a final photograph of her, instead seeking solace from the first of many psychics. I forgot all about Marcus and our supposed romantic excursion. “My elder sister. It was very sudden.”

“I understand, I understand,” he said, repeating himself as though hoping to be twice as comforting. “And you want to have a daguerreotype taken before the burial?”

I did my best to speak around the sorrow. “Yes.”

“Of course, of course.” The photographer offered his plush portfolio to me in a most unobtrusive fashion. “I have quite a lot of experience with young people. I think you will find the poses most lifelike.”

Indeed, they were. In sitting positions, in laps of loved ones, in cradles and in coffins, the children in the pictures appeared to be sleeping. Which they were, I realized. The longest of sleeps.

What would have become of Dimitria, had she lived? Would she be fighting alongside me, trying to get Nic and our parents back?

No, because none of this would have happened if she’d lived.

She and Warwick might have been married by now, well on the way to a house filled with laughter and music and fat-cheeked babies. Her death had pushed him to the darkest of places, and he was towing the rest of my family into the darkness with him.

When my hands started to shake, Marcus covered them with his own.

“Perhaps we’ll take your business card for now,” he said. “My wife has had a rather trying day.”

The photographer hastened to retrieve the necessary information. "My rates are most reasonable and studio hours accommodating."

We excused ourselves as hastily as we could. Outside, I leaned against a brick wall and turned my face up to the sky. The rain landed on my skin in intermittent droplets, cold and clean, as I cleared the cloying perfume from my lungs.

"Not the right studio," Marcus said.

"No," I agreed, dragging in another water-heavy breath. "The glass was wrong, never mind that the photographer looked too placid and comfortable to engage in illicit portraiture."

Marcus signaled a hansom cab with a flick of his fingers. "You can never tell what sorts of desperate things people will do."

"I think Sebastian taught me that lesson last night better than anyone else ever could."

The carriage paused before us. Marcus helped me up the metal folding stairs and into the vaguely damp interior. "Are you game for trying the next address?"

"Yes." My Ticker thumped away—two quick contractions, one long, two short again—like it was sending a RiPA message. I closed my eyes and wondered what it was trying to tell me.

Marcus gave our driver the next address, and the mechanical horse took off with a lurch and a bounce. Several minutes passed before he said, "I'm sorry about your sister. I read about it in your file, but it's not the same seeing it typed out as it is to live it."

When I opened my eyes, I found him looking at me, his gray eyes a match to the weather outside. "Dimitria was very sick. None of us knew the extent of it."

"That doesn't make a damn bit of difference to your heart. Grief doesn't take such things into consideration."

I wanted to take his hand in mine but couldn't bring myself to do it. "You're thinking about Viktor now, aren't you?"

"He's always in my thoughts." Marcus shifted in his seat. "There isn't a decision that I make that I don't wonder if he would have done the same. In my head, I see him laughing at me, the way he would when I ate too much cake or tried to climb the tallest tree. I like to remember him laughing. There are days when I think he'd be very disappointed in the way I've turned out, at what I'm doing with his company."

"It's your company now. You're building it into something formidable."

"Not by choice. I think that's the worst part of it. He knew I didn't want this life. Plenty of brothers would have fought over the business when our father retired, but we were happy with the way things were. Too happy, I guess. We must have tipped the Great Brass Balance Scale against us."

"You can't think that his death was supposed to punish you."

"I can, and I do," Marcus said softly.

We endured the rest of the drive in silence, each of us buried in our own painful memories. The cab carried us to a neighborhood where the plaster and bricks were scarred, like soldiers who'd waged a long battle with time and lost. The district was one I'd never visited before, for good reason.

"Stay close to me," Marcus said as we alighted. "We're a bit overdressed."

Indeed, even in our inconspicuous costumes, we were peacocks among peahens. The women passing by were garbed in rough fabrics, carrying baskets, towing children. The men wore threadbare coats and fingerless gloves, and they marked our arrival with suspicion. It was a relief to follow Marcus down a side street to a faded door marked "Lucy Reilly, Portraiture" in flaking gold paint.

Under that, in stronger black letters: "Memorial Photographs." Several faded daguerreotypes were propped up in the window.

I tingled all over. "This is it."

"How can you be certain?" Marcus attempted to peer through the thick layer of grime.

I pointed at the display pictures. "The glass is exactly the same as Nic's pictures. I'd bet on it."

Marcus tried to open the door, but it was locked. Two rounds of knocking yielded no response, and he looked through the window again. "No one appears to be in."

"Guess we'll have to see for ourselves." Before he could stop me, I wrapped my shawl around my elbow and smashed the pane nearest the door.

"That's breaking and entering," he said with a deceptively casual glance over his shoulder. Thankfully, we were far enough off the main street so as not to draw the attention of passersby.

"Technically that was only breaking." I reached inside and unlocked the door. "*Now* it's entering."

The interior was as dark and damp as the carriage, smelling of mildew, stale tea, and acrid chemicals. Miniature coffins stood along one wall. Rubbish had accumulated in the corners of the room and mingled with puddles of developing solution. The hearth hadn't made acquaintance with a fire for quite some time, judging by the amount of ash and the empty coal scuttle.

Marcus sidestepped a stack of glass slides on the floor. "Careful as you go."

His timing was uncanny; the second he spoke, I fell over something heavy and unyielding. Going down with a crash, I flailed at the unseen obstacle.

"Hold on," Marcus ordered, pulling the drapes closed and switching on a gas jet.

The sudden flare of light revealed the body that lay sprawled on the floor, mouth open, eyes staring. I could only assume it was our photographer. "Marcus . . ."

He was by my side before I could draw another breath. Reaching down to her neck, he tried to find a pulse.

I knew just by looking at her that we were too late. "It seems we're in need of some Luminiferous Re-Animator if we want her to tell us anything."

It wasn't altogether a jest. The popular drink earned its name not only for the faint golden glow achieved by means of a top-secret combination of alcohol and alchemy, but also because the concoction was rumored to have brought corpses back from the dead.

"Not necessarily." With his RiPA still nonresponsive, Marcus crossed to an ancient PaperTape machine. Cranking it over twice and bashing it firmly on the side with his fist, he connected with the Flying Fortress. "I'm sending for Philomena and the psychic unit."

Whatever I'd been expecting for a battle plan, it wasn't that. "You're joking."

"Not in the slightest." Marcus returned his attention to the photographer. "What killed her?"

Studying the body, I cataloged more than a dozen Augmentations: her right leg at the knee and ankle, left arm at the elbow and wrist, both ears. The healing was far more advanced than what the timeline would suggest, given that Warwick only escaped custody this week, but my guess was that he administered the Quick-Heal to her as well. No sign of infection or decay. With a frown, I pulled back the woman's unbuttoned collar to reveal the clockwork ventriculator set into her chest. It was more advanced than my own, its polished brass plates nearly seamless against the flesh and its winding mechanism impossibly delicate.

"By all the Bells," Marcus breathed. "The shock of that surgery certainly could have done it."

Only then did I realize I had my hands pressed to my mouth. I forced them back to her body, tracing over the infinitesimal screws used to hold everything in place. "These are from the Gears & Rivets Factory." Checking over the less invasive Augmentations on Lucy's arms and legs, I recognized more parts. "All of them are."

Marcus looked up at me. "How can you be certain?"

I indicated the small identification number stamped along one edge. "These are unique for each piece. We register them to their new owner. The last three numbers tell me it's a batch that just came off the line, earmarked for Currey Hospital. My supervisor notified me they were missing. When Sebastian's men set off the explosion at the factory, they must have stolen inventory out of the stockroom."

Sitting back on his heels, Marcus shook his head. "This is a lot of work to do on one person. She couldn't have needed all of it. Warwick probably brought her in to photograph Nic and then kept her as a subject, to test the Quick-Heal and the heart implant."

"He wouldn't have willingly let her go. She must have escaped." Reaching up, I gently pressed two fingers to the woman's eyelids and closed them for her.

Marcus jerked his chin in the direction of a threadbare carpet-bag, overturned and disgorging its contents upon the floor. "She was packing quickly for a journey."

Thankful for a reason to step away, I crossed the room to examine the luggage. "There's a ticket over here, too. One way to Glacia on a steamship that left this morning."

Falling into an uneasy silence, Marcus and I upended the room, looking for more clues, emptying drawers and cupboards, scouring closets, and pulling up loose floorboards. In various hidey-holes, Marcus located half a dozen burlap pouches containing copper pence and silver denarii.

"Looks like she didn't put much stock in any of Bazalgate's banks," he said.

Up to my elbows in a basket of mending, I nodded. "Or she needed to keep ready cash on hand for something. Perhaps she owed money to someone."

A soft knock drew our attention. Quite unnecessarily, Marcus signaled for me to stay quiet as he went to check the door. Three plainclothes Ferrum Viriae entered, carrying crates of equipment. Philomena de Mesmer strode in at the end of the unusual procession.

She took in her surroundings with a sweeping glance and headed straight for the corpse. "Another of Warwick's victims. At least this one isn't a child." Without sparing either Marcus or me a second look, she set down a leather valise that strongly reminded me of a surgical travel kit. "How long has she been dead?"

"Guessing by the body temperature, a few hours, maybe a bit more," Marcus replied.

The two of them knelt near the corpse, heads close together. Unwilling to waste precious time on parlor tricks, I returned to rummaging. The group made a circle of golden light with lamps. The largest and most scarred of the wooden crates held what appeared to be a portable Cylindrella machine, complete with hand crank and brass trumpet.

Baynard's device for speaking to the dead, I realized. The original Grand Design.

Philomena pulled out a set of wires that ended in circular cotton pads and placed them upon Lucy Reilly's body at various pulse points. The clockwork ventriculator gave them pause.

"Her biological heart was removed," Marcus explained. "Will that impede the reading?"

Sorting through the contents of the photographer's satchel a second time, I noted, "Her lack of pulse should prove more of an impediment."

"Tesseraria . . ." It was all Marcus said, but there was a warning note that I heeded with reluctance.

"Fine. I'll be over here, conducting a proper investigation." I went back to the hastily packed clothes, scrutinizing every piece. Pursued by an unknown madman, Lucy thought them important enough to pack. Faded, worn soft with a thousand washings, some of the shirts and smocks were far too small to fit her.

I turned to tell Marcus, but he wore a Long Ear listening device and a frown of concentration. Philomena had the photographer's limp hand cradled in her own, and it was all I could do to repress a shudder.

One of the aides slowly turned the Cylindrella crank ten precise rotations. I counted off the seconds on my Ticker. After exactly one minute, he turned the crank again. Ten rotations. Another minute of excruciating silence. In the third pause, I thought I heard something. The scrabble of a rodent in the walls, maybe, but it was enough to set my teeth on edge.

"I'm here," Philomena said in a voice not quite her own. My skin rippled with a sudden chill, and I couldn't help but turn to look at the group. It was like staring at a daguerreotype: Marcus and the other technicians holding impossibly still, the light from the lamps glinting as though off glass, Philomena's eyes, open and staring.

Ten more rotations of the hand crank. A minute in near silence. A scrabble from the walls, this one followed by a muffled noise that no rodent would make . . .

A tiny sob.

I stepped toward the sound, running my hands over the plaster, seeking out what was hidden.

"I'm here," Philomena repeated, a bit stronger this time before adding, "Please. You must help."

"Tell us what happened here," Marcus said.

My fingertips located a nodule, and I instinctively pressed it, feeling the panel shudder and start to swing out.

"My heart . . . My own."

"We see what was done to your heart," Marcus murmured, trying to encourage the spirit of Lucy Reilly—if that's who or what it really was—to stay with them.

"My heart, my own." The words were a needle stuck in the groove of a ghostly recording.

"Tell us who did this to you," Marcus said in a hoarse whisper.

A door was hidden behind the panel. Locked, of course, not that such a thing had ever stopped me before. Removing a hairpin, I knelt next to the keyhole and set to work with trembling fingers. It was hard to concentrate, what with the refrain of "my heart, my own" echoing in the background. Then Philomena began to croon a lullaby, so softly at first that I almost missed it.

"Come to me, child of mine, rest your weary head . . ." Filtered by the psychic, the dead woman's voice strengthened, slowly filling the room with the song. "No harm will come to you, child of mine, so long as I watch over you."

The same song that was on Dimitria's Cylindrella player. I wanted to put my fingers in my ears. My hands were shaking so badly that they slipped, jamming the hairpin into the keyhole at an impossible angle.

Impossible, and just what was needed to trip the lock.

"Child of mine, child of mine," the dead woman sang.

In the hissing silence that followed, the trick door opened, and I found myself looking down at a shivering bundle of humanity.

"Mama?"

ELEVEN

In Which Ideas of the Great Hereafter Require Fine-Tuning

I extended my hand, trying to look reassuring. "It's all right. You can come out. I won't hurt you."

"Mama?" she asked again. No more than three or four years old, the little girl was all unkempt hair and enormous eyes.

I tried to keep my face impassive, encouraging, all the while frantically signaling Marcus to cover up the dead woman's body. "Your mother isn't here, little one. Are you hungry?"

No answer, but the glint in the child's eye answered the question. I pulled the scone from my pocket, thankful it hadn't gone completely to crumbs, and handed it to her. She fell upon it with a glad cry, taking great bites of it and babbling to me. Occasionally comprehensible words filtered through the sugared biscuit and blueberries.

"Mama's coming. Steamboat! Big trip." She left off the food long enough for her lower lip to tremble. "Bad man. Very bad man."

I dared move forward, near enough to brush the hair out of her eyes. There was no mistaking the resemblance to our dead photographer. "Do you know the very bad man's name?"

The child nodded yes, shook her head no, then took another bite of scone. By the time I coaxed her out of the closet, Philomena and her team had bundled up the corpse and removed it from the room.

Marcus glanced at the child before murmuring, "The team will see if they can get more using the Grand Design." He got down on the floor so he could meet the little girl's solemn gaze. "Hello there! Are you a fairy queen?"

That silliness bought us the faintest of smiles. "No."

"Are you a mechanical Butterfly in disguise?"

Another shake of her tousled head. "No."

I heaved a sigh. "I suppose you'll have to tell us your name, then."

The child leveled a look at me. "Are you a stranger?"

Taken aback by the force of the inquiry, I could only nod and speak the truth. "Technically, yes. But my name is Penelope Aurelia Farthing, and you can call me Penny. And this," I indicated Marcus, "is Mister Kingsley, Legatus legionus of the Ferrum Viriae."

"I'm Cora." She looked at him, a curious expression on her face. "Are you a clockwork soldier, too?"

Marcus glanced at me before repeating, "A clockwork soldier?"

"Like the boy in Mama's pictures," Cora said. "Did you come to pick them up?"

"We did," Marcus said when he saw I could say nothing. "Does your mum have any more pictures of a man? A clockwork soldier?"

Cora turned and headed back into the hidden closet, beckoning over her shoulder to me and then pointing to a heavy stack of glass slides wrapped in thick twine. I carried them both out of the closet, handed the little girl off to Marcus, and cut the string on the parcel.

Numbered and dated with silver-slick metallic paint, the new daguerreotypes told us that the photographer wasn't the only one to have endured multiple Augmentations in a short period of time. Over the last few days, Nic's elbows, knees, and ankles had been reinforced with plates of dull metal.

I searched through the stack, sweat slicking my palms. "What if they implanted a prototype Ticker in him as well?"

What if he's already dead?

I didn't think I could bear it. Some part of me would die with him, and what remained would simply shrivel up, like a plant denied water and sunlight. I remembered the chasm of grief the family had fallen into when Cygna had died, then again when Dimitria passed; that time, we'd crawled out of the sadness on hands and knees over emotions sharp as glass.

If Nic dies, I don't think I'll be able to find my way out of that dark place again.

But I was spared that sorrow for the moment. The last daguerreotype in the stack showed him sitting up, grimacing into a bright light, his right hand fully Augmented. The metal spark in his eyes was welcome now, because it meant that my twin was still fighting. "He's alive—"

A barrage of MAG gunfire interrupted me. Fléchettes broke through the windows, riddling the walls opposite and tearing open the sleeve of Marcus's coat before he could duck.

He dove to the floor, still holding Cora. "Get down!"

I obeyed without question, clutching the daguerreotypes. Marcus overturned the shabby chaise, put his back against it, and neatly tucked Cora into his lap. Her brown eyes were huge, and she clapped her hands over her ears.

Mama. Her lips moved but no sound came out.

"Send out the girl!" shouted a rough voice from the street. "That's all we want."

I crawled over to Marcus, pushing the pictures in front of me. "They're coming for her?"

"Or you." With his free hand, he flicked off his MAG's safety. "Might I remind you, Tesseraria, that you are also of the feminine persuasion?"

He had a point, curse him. "Give me that."

"The child?"

"The gun."

He shoved it into my hand, and I loaded a round into the chamber just before someone breached the door. Taking a deep breath, I emerged from behind the couch far enough to shoot the intruder high in his dominant shoulder, then low in his left kneecap. He dropped, groaning, and the man behind him fell back with a shout.

"She's armed!"

Behind me came the hissing crackle of Marcus's RiPA firing to life. With a muttered oath, he conveyed to the departing Ferrum Viriae and the ones manning the Communications Center that we were under attack.

"Come out, come out," the attacker outside singsonged before a smoke canister landed on the floor.

Marcus enveloped Cora in his wool coat while I pulled my shawl up over my nose and mouth. Eyes streaming, I used the choking blue fog as cover and crossed to the fallen mercenary. He lay on the floor, still groaning. When I jammed the Pixii under his chin and discharged the full blast, he jerked once and then went slack. Hardly able to see for the smoke, I divested him of his gun and short knife.

"The Araneae will be here in thirty seconds," Marcus relayed to me. "Be prepared to evacuate."

"Two steps ahead of you." And I was. When another mercenary tried to rush the door, I shot him with both MAGs. Fléchettes riddled his chest even as his answering bullets whizzed past me; he succumbed to my better aim. The whine of incoming SkyDarts and the shouts of soldiers in the street told me our backup had arrived. "Let's go!"

With Marcus and Cora right behind me, I edged into the street. Armed Araneae soldiers surrounded us.

The squadron leader shouted through his visor, "Are you all right? Is anyone injured?"

"No one on our side," Marcus said.

The scene beyond the human wall was one of pandemonium, with Ferrum Viriae engaged in hand-to-hand combat and pursuing the attackers who'd fled the scene. Passersby hastened into nearby buildings even as we hustled to the nearest SkyDart. I handed Marcus his weapon without a word, exchanging it for the child. Cora clung to me like a baby possum.

I murmured in the little girl's ear to cover up the shouts of the dead and the dying. "Have you ever been to the Square Park Zoo? They've a Bhaskarian Tiger Exhibit."

After a moment, she answered against my shoulder, "I like the Butterflies."

"Yes! I like visiting the Mechanical Butterfly Enclosure, too." We clambered inside the SkyDart, and Marcus took the controls, launching us like a projectile fired from a Superconductive Slingshot. Fumbling with the lap belt, I somehow strapped it over Cora. "There's the new Glacia Crystal Castle with white maritime bears that walk on the ice. Have you seen that?"

Cora mumbled something into my bodice, and I put my ear down next to her mouth. "What is it, flitter-mouse?"

"He's a bad man," she said, the tremble of her limbs shaking me to the core. "A very bad man."

I patted her, awkwardly at first, then with growing ease. The weight and warmth of her fragile body against mine roused every protective instinct in me, and I could have cheerfully torn apart any threat to her with my bare hands. "He *is* a very bad man, and he's going back to prison."

This flight seemed to take far longer than the last one, perhaps because I counted every shuddering breath of the small creature in my arms. Cora was like a sparrow fallen out of the nest too soon, with bones so light they might as well have been hollow. I had no idea what I would tell her about where we were going, or about the death of her mother. There was little I could say by way of comfort, and the truth was certainly not something I would willingly share with someone so young.

It's no wonder parents lie to their children.

How many times did Mama put on a brave face for my sake? Probably once for every star in the night sky. The urge to bury my face in Cora's dress and hold on with my remaining strength nearly overwhelmed me, but thankfully Marcus circled about one of the white watchtowers and set us down at the Flying Fortress.

Only when we were moving through the corridors at a brisk pace did I realize just how heavy a burden I carried. With Cora's arms about my neck and her legs clasped firmly about my waist, it was akin to jogging with the proverbial millstone tied to me.

"Let me take her," Marcus said as soon as there was a pause in the stream of information from the soldiers who'd met us at the landing platform.

I hitched her up and tried to ignore the ache in my shoulder blades. "I can manage."

"I didn't say you couldn't." His steadying hand found my waist. "I just want to help. You won't be of use to anyone if your Ticker gives out and you drop."

I took a breath, savoring this moment when everything was amicable and easy between us. "True enough." I whispered to Cora, "Do you mind going to the Legatus for a moment?"

For an answer, she held her arms out to him. Physical burden relieved, I stretched out my back and moved with far greater speed. Philomena de Mesmer emerged from a side hallway, flanked by two other members of the psychic unit. I knew whatever information she needed to convey wasn't suitable for little ears.

Hoping Marcus would follow my lead, I tipped my head sideways to address Cora, now hanging from his arms upside down. "Perhaps you'd like a slice of cake and some milk?"

When she began to nod with great enthusiasm, Marcus pulled a thoughtful face. "Ah, no, that's a terrible idea. Whatever can you be thinking, Penny? Children hate cake!"

I clapped my hand to my forehead in the most dramatic fashion possible. "A plate of stewed prunes instead?"

"Creamed spinach," Marcus countered.

"Blancmange," I said, twisting my mouth up at the memory.

"Chicken livers on toast," Marcus said, unable to restrain the puff of laughter that followed.

"I like chicken livers," Cora said with a breathless giggle.

"Is that so?" Marcus pulled her upright and set her on her feet. "I can do one better than that. How about some roast chicken, vegetables or not, bread and butter, and a piece of cake the size of your head to follow?"

"Chocolate cake," Cora bargained.

"Done." They shook solemn hands on it, and Marcus waved over the nearest soldier. "Captain Hunter, take our guest here to the commissary and see to the menu."

"Of course." He passed a small box to Marcus before he offered Cora a gloved hand, which she accepted as gracefully as a debutante at her first dinner dance.

"Hunter won't let anything happen to her," Marcus said under his breath as we watched them go. Opening the box, he retrieved his bracelets and snapped them on in quick succession. When Cora paused halfway down the hall to look back at us, Marcus was ready to deliver a reassuring wave.

My own wrists felt decidedly bare when I raised my hand as well, trying to mirror his cavalier expression. "If you wish to set my mind at rest, Kingsley, you're doing a very bad job of it."

"No one's ever dared attack the Flying Fortress," he said. The instant Cora rounded the corner with Captain Hunter, he added, "Not even during the Great Revolution."

"If the last few days have taught me anything," I said, "it's that there's a first time for everything, and that's usually when you least expect it."

"True words, Tesseraria," Philomena said, her expression wan and lines cutting deep around her mouth. It looked as though years had passed since last we'd seen her, not a scant hour. "I need you in the laboratory immediately, Legatus. Despite everything, I think we've managed to lift the veil." She turned to me. "Your mother's machine is working for now."

Marcus's abrupt "This way" was for my benefit as the two of them took off at a run. Doing my best to keep up, I realized that life couldn't sustain this frantic pace without fracturing. Even now, I felt hairline cracks radiating out from my clockwork heart and down my limbs. Hit me hard, just once, and I was sure to shatter.

With my family gone, who will pick up the pieces?

With impeccable timing, Marcus turned around and held his hand out to me.

"In here, Tesseraria." He used his bracelets to unlock a reinforced metal door set with huge rivets and threatening signs. "This is the generator room," he had to shout over the upsurge of noise. "Careful where you put your feet."

The warning was warranted. Extending hundreds of feet above and below us, gargantuan crankshafts operated with military precision. In place of coal-powered boilers, enormous glowing containers hovered every few feet, radiating blinding white-light with only the merest suggestion of a prism visible through the glare. I expected heat, but instead they exuded a chill so powerful that I shuddered. Frost slicked the surface of the railings that marked off either side of a narrow, grate-floored bridge. Snowflakes drifted past us, dusting our hair and shoulders, clinging to my eyelashes.

"Where did these crystals come from?" I shouted into the din.

Marcus caught hold of my hand before I could reach out to touch the power source. "Viktor and my father discovered them while on an expedition to Glacia ten years back. We've been mining them out of the ice, learning to harness their energy. They keep the Flying Fortress aloft."

Marcus didn't release me until we reached the next doorway and he passed us through. In contrast, the room beyond was blessedly quiet, all noise muffled by the thick marble blocks that composed the walls. The same brilliant light was in evidence, but silver fixtures dispensed more judicious amounts. The air held the faintest scents of ambergris and orrisroot. Homely Bhaskarian-rubber mats were laid out on the floor like mosaic tiles, and insulated cables ran from the body of Lucy Reilly to the generators occupying the nearest wall.

"That's your mother's machine," Marcus said as electricity arced between exposed metal coils.

Even with panels out of place and mechanical guts spilling onto the floor, Mama's version of the Grand Design put every invention I'd ever seen to shame. A thousand parts awaited fine-tuning, as though her hands had merely paused in making the necessary adjustments. "What's the problem with it, exactly?"

"We can't feed enough energy into it without getting a kickback that blows all the circuitry," Marcus said. "That's why we set up the laboratory so close to the source of the white-light. The more time that passes after death, the more power required to make contact."

It made sense now. "My father is the one who handled that sort of thing."

"So your mother said." Marcus was careful not to look at me when he continued, "Apparently he didn't care to work on a project of this scale."

Which meant either Papa thought it a ridiculous waste of time, or he'd chosen the bottle.

Then again, maybe Mama never asked for his help.

Philomena saved me from that line of thought by handing Marcus a typewritten transcript. "I would have gotten more, but we had a power surge that broke the connection."

Marcus pulled me to the side, near a second bank of machines. Needle gauges jumped and danced on various screens while a transcription unit thrummed. "Let's try it again," he said.

Philomena crossed to Lucy's body, which was positioned upon a sturdy table in the center of the room. Someone had taken the time to wash the dead woman's face and hands, to brush her hair and braid it out of her face, but even clean and neat with her hands resting gently at her sides, Lucy was no more at rest than I. There was enough tension in her limbs, at the base of her throat, and just about the eyes to make me wonder if she could be shocked back to life.

Settling into an adjacent chair, Philomena placed a band of metal-studded leather on her own head and matching cuffs around her wrists. Slowly, almost painfully, the assistants turned up the dials on the generators. An answering whine filled the room with crackling feedback.

The vibration threatened to jar my bones through my skin, and my teeth hummed in my jaw. Looking down, I noticed the scorch marks scarring the floor. "Are you certain this is safe?"

"We've got a connection," the lead assistant said before Marcus could respond.

The medium spoke again with Lucy's voice. "Moving. He's moving. Moving. Moving. Pictures. Get the pictures. Moving. Pictures. Catch him, he's moving." Machines spewed out readings that Marcus hastened to read over, even as Philomena continued to mutter. "Going. Going. Catch him."

"Do you think she's talking about Warwick?" I asked, trying to keep my voice low.

He paused, three sets of paperwork in hand. "Let's hope so. I'd rather go prepared into our next battle with him. We'll have to see what kind of useful information she can relay, though."

"Can't you ask her questions?" I glanced back at Philomena. "You interrogated Lucy back at the studio."

Marcus shook his head. "Philomena can't hear anything we say when she's hooked up to the Grand Design. Her body is here, but her mind travels far beyond our reach."

Either the machines were getting louder or Marcus's voice was fading. With ambient electricity crackling over my skin, I struggled not only to pay attention to what he was saying, but to remain conscious. "I wouldn't have believed any of this was possible yesterday."

"Catch him, catch him." The lights in the room flickered, and Philomena's next words were garbled.

"What's happening?" Marcus turned to an assistant.

When the power surged again, I pressed myself against the wall. It seemed more than one machine was malfunctioning; even as the technicians rushed to the Grand Design, struggling to make adjustments before Philomena's connection with the dead broke, my Ticker threatened to send me after her. It was hard to draw a breath. I knew if I closed my eyes, I would most likely faint . . .

I only blinked, but when next I opened my eyes, I sat at the table in Glasshouse's formal dining room. Or rather, a chamber quite like our formal dining room. Here, the flowers on the brocade wallpaper bloomed in three dimensions instead of two, releasing the fragrant scent of roses in summer. The doors on either side of the hearth were gone, removing any chance of exit. The elaborate stained-glass window had been replaced by a vast crystalline sheet; in front of it, a telescope was focused upon the night sky. The midnight canvas was dark blue. Impossibly blue. Wisps of smoke drifted over silk taffeta, the moon a diamanté brooch, the stars beads of iridescent glass. Black velvet shadows swirled around me, but I was far from alone. When I turned to the table, Dimitria sat on her birthday throne. In the corner, a cradle of polished black walnut rocked itself with haunting creaks.

"Tuppence," Dimitria said with the faintest of smiles.

Though the fire in the hearth proved that my afterlife was to be pleasantly warm, my teeth started to chatter. "Demy."

"Thinking of crossing over?" Her voice was as clear and as sweet as violin song.

"I'm not certain that decision is mine any longer." I reached up to touch my finger to the broken Ticker, but under my shirt-waist, the skin was smooth and unbroken. I thought my heart, my real heart, would stop completely from the shock of it. "Haven't I died?"

Dimitria shook her head, tossing a cluster of russet ringlets over her shoulder. "Not yet. This is an in-between place."

Pushing back my chair, I tried to get closer to her, but the room spun around me so that I never left my place at the table. Everything about this room felt disjointed, out of sync, like the music flowing from the broken Cylindrella in the opposite corner.

"Child of mine, child of mine," the recording crooned between gentle creaks of the cradle.

I swallowed hard. "That's Cygna, isn't it?"

Dimitria put a finger to her lips. "Shhh. She's sleeping."

I wanted to touch her, to hug her to me, but I was afraid my hands would pass right through her. "I'm so sorry, Demy."

"Save your sorrows." My sister's face paled until it was as white and lovely as the moon. "I've been trying to reach you for some time, speaking to the dark-haired woman whenever she comes near the veil." Her voice faded a bit, a recording winding down, then surged back when she said, "You have to help him."

"Nic?"

"Warwick. You have to help him. I made him promise me, but he doesn't realize—"

The crystal chandelier popped and showered me with violet sparks. Electricity wrapped me in painful arms, and I fell to the carpet, jaw clenched and muscles spasming. My flesh-and-blood heart gave a single, final thump, and then it was gone, replaced by searing hot metal and clockwork.

Hands grasped me, half lifting me up. "Penny?" The voice that called to me was urgent. I couldn't help opening my eyes. Marcus knelt alongside me, his concerned expression echoing that of Nic. Of my parents.

My Ticker and stomach both sank.

Don't look at me like that. Don't see me as some frail, useless creature.

Fall in love with me, *not the idea of rescuing me.*

I tried to sit up. "It's all right. I just . . . fainted."

Easing me to a sitting position, Marcus ran his hands over my arms and legs, checked the state of my pupils, and took my pulse with grim efficiency. "I'm not altogether certain that's true. Another power surge blew out three of the coils and broke Philomena's connection to Lucy. I picked her up off the floor, and when I turned around, you were slumped against one of the broken generators. I think you might have been electrocuted."

Perhaps that's what restarted my Ticker, the same as it had when Marcus turned the Pixii on me. If clockwork bits couldn't save me, maybe electricity could.

Marcus mistook my silence for shock. "You need rest, and we both need brandy," he said. "I'll take you back to my office. Put your arms around me."

"What about Philomena?" I glanced over my shoulder as he heaved me up into his arms, leaving my legs to dangle.

"She's gone to adjust the main generators."

"I think I owe her an apology." My vision remained blurry about the edges, diffusing the light from the gas globes into soft, golden clouds. Though I tried to blink it away, doing so only produced a curious moving-picture effect. "I spoke with Dimitria. Beyond the veil. Which looked curiously like my dining room."

"You spoke with your sister?" Marcus adjusted his grip upon me.

"Yes. You and Mama were right. It *is* possible." Turning my head toward him, I nuzzled my face against his jacket. "Did you get any other information we can use?"

He cleared his throat before answering. "Nothing of further use, no. It was a success that we even got her to speak, but it's going to take more research and fine-tuning of the equipment to make it function the way we'd like."

"My mother will be able to fix it."

"I know she will."

"You can put me down," I protested, realizing I must be considerably heavier than Cora.

"No need, we're almost there."

"I really do feel better." More than that, actually. With the fog in my brain dissipating, I felt empowered.

He kicked open the door to his office and set me in the chair before the fire. "Can I get you some brandy? Or tea, maybe?"

"Tea, please."

Moving behind his desk, Marcus barked an order into the intercom. That done, he rubbed a hand over the stubble on his chin. "I nearly forgot in all the excitement, but we need to locate Cora's next of kin. I'll have someone at the Bibliothèca messenger up the necessary records."

I stared into the flames, seeing the stuff of a child's nightmares dancing across the embers. "What do you suppose it's going to be like for her, growing up knowing that she would have died if her mother hadn't hidden her?"

Marcus shifted a stack of papers to the side, looking through the intelligence reports that had piled up since his last debriefing. "It's going to be easier if we can tell her that Warwick is back in prison and shackled within an inch of his life."

"I wish you could have known him . . . before. He was a different man then. A good man." Unable to sit still, I strode about the room until I found myself staring up at the maps and plans pinned to the wall.

"We've all had terrible things happen to us," Marcus said without looking up. "Only the weak use it as an excuse to prey upon others."

I didn't argue with him. Instead, I studied a blueprint of the courthouse that was marked where incendiary devices were found and rooms were reduced to rubble. I untacked the diagram and moved back to his desk. "So let's show our strength. We need to organize a ceremony at the courthouse, dedicating the areas that will be rebuilt and celebrating the restoration of justice. Something we can broadcast into all the homes in Industria. Something Warwick won't be able to resist attending."

Marcus's frown doubled when I swept some of his files aside to make room for the map, and not just because I was making a mess of his workspace.

"You can't possibly think a gathering of any size is a good idea," he said. "There's a madman on the loose."

"And this will be an excellent opportunity to lure him in," I said, weighing down the four corners with his letter opener, an ink pot, a single-stroke staple press, and my hand.

"There are other ways of catching him."

"Not ones that have as high a chance of succeeding."

Marcus tamped down his visible frustration before trying again. "I understand your enthusiasm, but I know you a bit better than I did a few days ago, Penelope Farthing, and you'll want to be right in the thick of it, won't you? Fainting spells and assassination attempts on your person be damned?"

“I won’t sit here fussing and fretting while your soldiers do all the dirty work, if that’s what you mean.” The next words gushed out of me like blood from a wound. “Warwick has already gotten to Sebastian, to Nic, to my parents. Who’s next? Violet or Cora? You? We have to stop this now.”

Marcus studied me for a long moment, his gaze tracking over my face. “Can’t you spare a bit of care for yourself?”

“I think you already know the answer to that,” I said.

“Yes, but hope is an ever-blooming flower.” He turned, crossed to the drinks cabinet, and poured out two generous tumblers. Returning to the desk, he offered one to me. “To your good health, Tesseraria. May it endure past noon tomorrow.”

“And to yours, Legatus.” I clinked my glass against his, then emptied it. False warmth snaked through my veins and lent me a desperately needed air of bravado.

“I have to get in touch with the chancellor.” Marcus set his cup down on the blotter, leaving a wet ring on the paper.

I pored over the diagram of the courthouse, noting the entrances and exits, the major streets and small alleys that surrounded it. “If he gives us the go-ahead, we can’t let ordinary citizens anywhere near the site.”

“All the deployments I recalled from Bhaskara and Aígyptos will be here by the morning.” Following me step for imagined step, Marcus pieced together a potential battle plan. “If we go through with this insanity, and that’s a very big if, every person on site will be plainclothes military.” He pointed to the area at the top of the exterior staircase. “We’ll lock down this central area here and put explosive-sniffing dogs at these four locations.”

I continued to study the diagram, wanting to know it as well as he already did. “No matter our preparations, Warwick will be three steps ahead of us.”

In the absence of the tea that he'd ordered, Marcus poured out another measure of brandy. "I'll have my incendiary crew mix up personal powder-flashes. Everyone will carry at least two of them."

"Everyone, Legatus?" I slanted a look at him.

"Yes. They're fairly simple to operate. Light the fuse and throw it at the enemy." After a pause, he added, "*Away* from you."

I would have been insulted, save the fact that his mouth was twitching with inappropriate amusement. "I'm glad you felt compelled to specify that. Light it. Throw it. Then what?"

His smile disappeared. "Then, you run."

"If you think I'm leaving you to the mercy of Warwick's mercenaries, you can just think again—"

"You'll light the powder-flashes, throw them, and run like your shoes are on fire." He put his arms around my waist and drew me against his chest. The soft tribute that followed was no more than the brush of a Butterfly's wing against my mouth.

If my Ticker were going to stop forever, I almost wished it would be now, in this quiet moment, the two of us together. But it beat on, knowing we had yet more work to do.

"I don't like this worse-case-scenario thing," I whispered, my arms slipping up to encircle his neck. "It feels very ominous."

"An ounce of prevention," Marcus said as he bent to kiss me again.

"And large quantities of black powder," I finished the old saying for him just before his lips met mine.

TWELVE

In Which Our Heroine Hits the Ground Running

It took a significant amount of scrubbing and soap, but I got the brown dye out of my hair by the appointed hour the next morning. With help, grander plans for my appearance at the Dedication Ceremony unfolded as rapidly as an opera fan in a socialite's practiced hand.

Once upon a time, I might have preened a bit.

Once upon a time seemed like a very long time ago.

Assuming the most professional manner possible, I rapped twice at the door of Marcus's office. His "Come in" might have sounded distracted, but as I entered, I knew I commanded the whole of his attention.

"Legatus." I paused to enjoy the moment.

"That," he said with careful consideration, "is some heavy artillery."

"Philomena sent out for it." I turned to afford him a better view of the gargantuan bustle and train of coquelicot-colored silk brocade. The crimson skirts were particularly appropriate to my role as a red herring, soon to be crisscrossing the hunting trails to draw the hounds to me. "I must tell you, this ensemble borders on cumbersome."

Marcus let an appraising gaze drift over the gold embroidery on every pouf, puff, and pleat. Heavy Aígyptian-style bangles clinked against my iron bracelets. "You look like a dragon going in for the kill."

I glided forward, accompanied by the gentle sway of the colossal wire hoops supporting the weight of my skirts. They also concealed a pair of highly practical trousers. "Stop teasing and tell me what you really think."

"I think it's a good thing I commissioned a hat worthy of such a dress," he said, producing a box stamped "Exemplar Millinery" in gold lettering. "If you're wearing this, I'll be able to spot you in the crowd."

The item he withdrew from the tissue paper elicited a gasp, which was all I could manage with my tight lacing. "That, sir, is no more a hat than you are a footman."

He held it just out of my reach. "Does that mean you approve?"

"That means your taste is both extravagant and ridiculous, and I commend you for it." Grasping my prize, I went to the nearest mirror, eager to perch it atop my ginger ringlets. The brim dipped low over my forehead, a bloodred rose blooming just at the center. On the left side, a diamanté chrysanthemum anchored a cockade of cream-and-black-striped pheasant plumage. It was, perhaps, the most expensive thing I'd ever worn, and I was only half joking when I said, "This almost makes endangering my life worthwhile."

He handed me a diminutive umbrella. "The finishing touch, Tesseraria."

"I won't be able to raise it over the hat," I protested. "It would hardly help in a downpour, anyway."

"Allow me to demonstrate its practicality." Marcus held out his hand, and I returned the precious bumbershoot with my eyebrows already raised. When he depressed two flanges and pulled the curved ebony handle, a short sword emerged. "Are you suitably impressed now?"

"Perhaps just the slightest bit." I took back the weapon and demonstrated that I could extract it without injuring myself. "I think I can do some damage with this."

"With luck, you won't have to. You're going up in the SkyBox."

Held aloft by eight Montgolfière balloons, the air gondola was luxuriously appointed, fully staffed, and used for occasions of state as well as the annual Eight Bells Steeplechase. It also meant that I was going to be far from the action.

"So I'm dressed within an inch of my life only to be wholly useless?"

"Not necessarily." Marcus completed my arsenal by handing me two powder-flashes. I tucked them into my reticule as he slid two MAGs into their holsters and reached for his uniform cap. "But even you cannot argue with a thousand feet between your boots and the ground, Tesseraria."

The parasol became an immediate weather vane of my mood. Walking out to the landing platform, I lifted it up to jauntily ride my shoulder, hoping to charm Marcus into changing his mind about my priority seating arrangement. When he wouldn't hear a word of my argument, I let the parasol droop. By the time we arrived at the Bazalgate airfield, I employed it as a machete with which to chop at the hedge.

Part of my unease could be traced back to Violet. Still conducting a citywide manhunt for Sebastian, she'd taken a secondary unit of guards to investigate his properties. The search proved fruitless as yet, but she promised to apprise us of her progress and her continued safety. Except now she was three minutes late checking in, and I was ready to send the cavalry after her.

Our surroundings didn't exactly promote tranquility of the mind, either. Despite the fact that crews worked around the clock to clear the main square, heaps of rubble still decorated the perimeter. Half the columns spanning the front of the courthouse had crumpled in the explosion, taking the portico with them. They had carted the worst of the damage away, but the memories of the eleven dead lingered, and it was easy to imagine their blood decorating the stones. Uniformed officers milled about the grounds. Explosives-sniffing hounds searched Combustibles, carts, and conveyances. Dressed in a realistic variety of aristocratic satins and workaday cottons, the soldiers gathered on the stairs could easily be mistaken for Bazalgate civilians.

"This is ludicrous," I told Marcus. "I should stay with you."

"You're too easy a target on the ground, Penny. I won't risk it. Not after what happened to Nic." He signaled to an approaching motorcar, waving it into the restricted area.

Philomena descended from the vehicle, decidedly out of uniform in a butter-yellow frock. At least a dozen amber beaded necklaces dangled about her neck, and a heavily fringed cape striped in honey and black fluttered over her shoulders. Rather than a hat, she'd chosen to wear her countless braids twisted about her head. The enormous knot at the back was fixed with mechanical Bumblebees kept on short gold chains.

"Perfect," Marcus said. "There will be no overlooking either of you."

"That was precisely the idea, wasn't it?" With the brightness of my own dress doubled against the yellow of Philomena's attire, I suddenly felt very conspicuous, which was discomfiting for a girl who didn't give a second thought to ripping about Bazalgate on a motorized cycle. "Thank you for the escort, Legatus. We'll see ourselves in."

Marcus bowed to Philomena, but the kiss he placed against my gloved hand sent an arc of electricity through me. Turning on his heel, he went to join the chancellor.

Philomena leaned close, one of her bee adornments bumbling into my head. "Chin up," she said. "You don't want whoever may be watching to think they have you at a disadvantage."

"They don't have me at a disadvantage." I put up my parasol with a decisive *snap!* "And I have the umbrella to prove it." Walking up the ramp to the SkyBox, I realized there was something I ought to have said much sooner. "Miss de Mesmer, I owe you an apology for my behavior the day we met, and for my cynicism."

"An apology isn't necessary," she said. "Plenty of people are skeptical of my abilities. Might I ask what changed your mind?"

Despite the brilliant sunshine slanting over us, I shivered as we stepped into the octagonal gondola. The painted silk envelopes swayed overhead, restless in the gentle breeze that swept over the dedication site. "Yesterday, when the generators malfunctioned, I found myself in an in-between place. I spoke with my sister. Dimitria mentioned you, said she'd been trying to pass messages whenever you approached the veil."

Sensing I wouldn't want any part of our conversation overheard, Philomena inclined her head toward me. "And what did your in-between place look like, if you don't mind my professional curiosity?"

"The dining room at Glasshouse." Closing my eyes for a moment, it seemed only the thinnest of curtains separated me from that place. "It's where she died."

"That makes sense." After a pause, Philomena added, "Was the little one there as well? I only ever caught the merest suggestion of her."

"Cygna was there. Or rather, there was a cradle rocking on its own." My stomach twisted at the memory; I thought I might be sick, and we'd yet to leave the ground. A servitor passed trays of nibbles and drinks, and I reluctantly accepted a flute of Effervescence. Philomena chose instead a cup of the notorious Luminiferous Re-Animator. When I accidentally inhaled the fumes wafting from the etched-crystal glass, I decided that those revived by the mixture had most likely been killed by it in the first place. "What's *in* that?"

"I haven't the foggiest idea." The end of Philomena's nose turned faintly pink. "Perhaps you should have one as well, to steady your nerves."

"It's hazardous to allow people to imbibe such a drink when we'll soon be aloft," I said. "Take care not to fall out, because I won't jump after you."

"You cut me to the quick, Miss Farthing." When she chuckled, it set the Bumblebees buzzing again.

We both reached for the railing when the ropes were loosened and the ground fell away. With space at a premium, uniformed guards trained to operate the blast valves manned the air gondola. A few brave notables had volunteered to be tucked away in our little jewel cask, including members of Parliament, scientists of note, and a patent holder worth millions. The chancellor remained on the ground with Marcus, wearing a nervous smile and wielding a pair of gold scissors. From our growing vantage point, the red ribbon that spanned the square looked like a blood trail.

A trumpeted fanfare interrupted my observations and signaled the start of the Dedication Ceremony. Everyone leaned over the sides of the gondola to peer through binoculars. Tinny speakers broadcast the chancellor's speech into the SkyBox.

"And so . . ." he said between dramatic pauses filled with hiss-and-crackle feedback, "we will heal our great city . . . by dedicating this site to the repairs of . . . the courthouse . . . which will serve as a reminder . . . of Industria's justice, strength, and bravery."

Watching through my binoculars, I had to give the chancellor credit for his own strength and bravery. Despite the beads of sweat standing out on his brow, the man wasn't turning tail to run. He stood front and center on that staircase, trusting that the Ferrum Viriae would keep him safe. Shifting the glasses, I took in Marcus just to his left, the row of soldiers behind him, the plainclothes extras gathered beyond the stage . . .

And my brother, wending a slow and careful path through the crowd.

The surprise was a blow to my midsection, and I sucked in a breath. The very next moment, the speakers cut out with a screeching whine. The other occupants of the SkyBox murmured to one another, frowns spreading like smallpox as I adjusted my binoculars to home in on my twin. Though Nic wore the gray livery of a soldier and a hat drawn far down over his forehead, there was no mistaking him. I whirled about, nearly felling Philomena.

"My brother is down there!" Hitching up my bustle skirt, I tapped out a message to Marcus on the new RiPA he'd assigned me that morning:

NIC IS BEHIND YOU - STOP - HE ESCAPED - STOP -
HE WILL KNOW WHERE WARWICK IS - STOP

But I didn't get a response.

"Here, I'll try." Philomena tapped out a message, but the silence endured.

Glancing from the speakers overhead to our communications devices, I was the one having a premonition. "Something is jamming the signals. I have to get Marcus's attention another way."

"Follow protocol," one of the officers announced. They immediately opened the blast valves to take the gondola higher.

"Protocol?" I grasped the nearest of the soldiers by his uniform-clad arm. "I need you to put us down this second."

"Apologies, Tesseraria," he said, not sounding at all contrite, "but I don't take orders from you. The Legatus said that in case of emergency, we're to remain aloft until the area is secured."

Distant screams drew our attention. I raised my binoculars in time to see black iridescent water pouring down the sides of the buildings adjacent to the courthouse.

"By all the Bells, what *is* that?" Bringing the picture into focus, I realized that the metallic waves were actually hundreds of mechanical Spiders skittering down bricks, over cobblestones. The tiny creatures clambered up the legs of the soldiers and into their ears; within seconds, most of the victims stood as though paralyzed, rendered catatonic.

At the top of the stairs, Marcus and the chancellor retreated, only seconds ahead of the arachnids. Blasts from Marcus's Superconductive Slingshot bought him precious moments, but Nic still headed for them at a dead run. Marcus pulled out the first of his powder-flashes and lit it. The brilliant explosion that followed knocked my twin back several feet.

"We have to get down there," I said, this time to Philomena.

"How far up are we, would you guess?" she asked with great practicality, wrestling open the nearest wicker bench. Stowed within were a dozen parachutes, just as Marcus had promised when we rode in his SkyDart.

"You can't mean to jump."

"Not me. You."

I stared at her for a long moment. "If I die, I'll haunt you this lifetime *and* the next." Off went my skirts with a desperate rip and yank. The glorious hat landed atop the silken heap. I wished I had my goggles, but was thankful beyond measure for my trousers.

"Looks like you expected some mayhem," Philomena said with approval as she helped me sort out the straps and buckles. The Ferrum Viriae aboard were busy trying to keep the basket level. With all the passengers heaving about, they'd yet to take any notice of our actions; otherwise, they surely would have tackled me.

"Just read me the instructions."

"According to the pamphlet, you clear the side of the gondola, count to two, and pull this ring. These toggles control the steering lines and will let you guide the parachute down, though you're going to get a crash course in directional wind."

"As long as it's not a crash course in equipment failure." I climbed up on the ledge, clinging to the ropes tethering the balloons to the basket. One of the guards caught sight of me and shouted a warning, but I fixed my gaze upon the staircase below, held my breath, and jumped.

The rush of wind in my face was different than the Vitesse, different even than the SkyDart, and decidedly the most thrilling and exhilarating thing I'd ever experienced. A week ago, the free fall would also have been the most terrifying, but it was nothing compared to the number of times I'd nearly died in the last few days. When I pulled the brass ring, the silk parachute deployed. Wind filled it with a series of ruffles and a final *snap!* as the fabric went taut. Though I struggled with the toggles, I finally wrapped my brain around the subtleties of gliding down, down, down. The winds were in my favor, carrying me all the way to the top of the staircase. My own sudden weight startled me; legs buckled and knees protested, but I didn't stumble, and I couldn't stop to reflect on my good fortune. Unclipping the harness, I freed myself of the silk lines and parachute.

Not a hundred yards away, my twin raised his arm and pointed a MAG directly at the fleeing figures of Marcus and the chancellor.

"Nic, no!" I screamed.

A second wave of Ferrum Viriae rushed at Nic, weapons drawn. I followed, thinking that somehow I could prevent a bloodbath, but my brother shot the first soldier to come at him and disarmed the next four, breaking bones as though distributing petits fours at afternoon tea. Even years of sparring at Mettlefield's Gymnasium couldn't explain the lightning speed at which he moved or the gold glint in his eyes when a semicircle of groaning soldiers lay on the ground before him. Reaching into his pockets, he disgorged a dozen more Spiders that skitter-scattered over their bodies and straight into their ears.

"Nic!" I choked out, still running toward him.

"With me!" he yelled, and the Spider-afflicted soldiers fell in behind him. Nic turned and fled through the crowd, the turncoats clearing a path for him. Leaping aboard a new-model Vitesse, Nic gunned the engine and roared off down an alley. As though triggered by his passing, an explosion detonated inside the courthouse.

Ducking to the ground, I could do nothing but hold my breath as debris and dust engulfed me. A glancing blow to my arm suggested I'd been hit by a stone or a bit of mortar. Before the worst of the cloud had cleared, the Ferrum Viriae who'd followed my brother were gone. I located a mounted officer who was still responsive.

"Get down! I'm commandeering your mount!"

"Tesseraria?" the soldier said, evidently recognizing me from the Flying Fortress. Bewildered, he obeyed the command.

"Help me up."

He made a cradle of his palms, sputtering protests. "You're not trained for this!"

"I beg to differ," I retorted. "I was born to it."

At the far side of the square, Marcus shoved the chancellor into an idling Combustible. A third wave of Ferrum Viriae approached at a run.

"The streets are locked down to everything except the Emergency Rescue Squadrons!" one of them shouted at me.

"That's a good thing," I said, backing out of the knot of new arrivals. "It means I'm less likely to hit something."

I dug in my heels. With a metallic whinny, the horse leapt clear of the crowd, metal shoes sparking when she landed. I clutched at the reins as we clattered down the narrow avenue leading to the main road. The steady hoofbeats, the rhythmic twin streams of scorching hot steam issuing from my steed's copper muzzle, and the distant wail of sirens drowned out everything but the frantic beating of my Ticker.

I caught sight of Nic at the far end of the boulevard; it was easy enough to spot him with the rest of the traffic at a standstill. Vehicles were haphazardly pulled over to the sides of the road, and panicked pedestrians squeezed close to the buildings. Some of the onlookers shouted, gesturing to me with their hats and purses. Jostled by the crowd, a bystander fell into the street, directly in my path. I sucked in my breath, squeezed with my knees, and held on for dear life. A frisson of energy passed over the mechanical horse as it bent its knees and sprang forward, soaring with ease over the woman's head . . .

We landed, and I kept my seat and my life. I stood up in the stirrups as I'd seen jockeys do at the steeplechases, encouraging my mount to go yet faster. Around corners, past the Heart of the Star, down the First Etoile Road.

"Come on," I urged. "We have to catch up with Nic!"

The Ticker began to wind down in my chest, and everything slowed to match: the pedestrians, the wind whipping at my bare head, the clatter of hooves. Just ahead of me, Nic wove in and out of traffic with a deftness that belied all the time he had spent snubbing the Vitesse.

The brother I knew didn't move like a soldier. He didn't raise arms against a crowd. He hadn't known they were Ferrum Viriae in disguise; they appeared to be normal citizens of Bazalgate. And there was the traitorous behavior of the afflicted soldiers to consider as well.

The Spiders. The Spiders can be used for mind control.

What has Warwick done to you, Nic? And where are you taking me?

He led me back to the West Side, past Lucy Reilly's photography studio. The buildings climbed toward the sky until they blotted out the sun. Broken windows were boarded over like coins on the eyes of the dead. Rooftops sagged against one another, too tired to stay where they should. Brickwork crumbled to dust before my eyes. Under the sad air of neglect was something rancid. Something choking.

Nic rounded a final corner. By the time I did the same, he'd abandoned the cycle and disappeared. I dismounted, my head buzzing and my legs so wobbly they might as well have been made of Dreadnaught's blancmange.

"Nic?" It was like a deadly game of hide-and-seek. He always triumphed over me, fitting into cupboards, leaping down from wardrobes, grabbing my booted ankle from under the four-poster beds. "Come out, come out, wherever you are."

No answer, save the patter of retreating footsteps down the alley to my right. I gave chase as best I could with the Ticker's terrible irregularity. I pressed a hand to my chest, tearing at the buttons of my bodice, fumbling for the key. Before I could wind my traitorous heart, Nic appeared in front of me like a conjurer. The game was over, and I'd lost. He wore a stranger's face, cheekbones jutting out in defiance of the pale skin stretched over them. The faint glint of his ocular Augmentation was the only light in his eyes. What was left of the blood in my extremities drained away. I'd abandoned my parasol sword in the SkyBox, but I wouldn't have had time to draw it anyway.

"I told you to stay put until I messaged you," my twin said before his fist connected with my jaw.

I collided with the crumbling brick wall, pain spreading eager fingers through my head as I slid to the ground. The street seemed to tilt under my hands. Disoriented, I tried to focus my eyes as Nic heaved me up, tossed me over his shoulder, and carried me a short distance to a waiting carriage.

"Reckless and selfish," he said. "The family would have healed after Dimitria's death if it weren't for you. It was your own fault you fell off Andromeda. You might never have needed the ventriculator if you only listened. Precious, delicate clockwork doll. Wind her up, watch her dance. Watch Mama hover. Watch Papa climb inside a liquor bottle . . ."

With a small grunt, he tossed me inside. I landed on the floor in a tangle of limbs, the ache in my head still blurring my vision. I could just make out when he leapt in after me and took my reticule containing Pixii, RiPA, and the two powder-flashes. When he rapped on the roof, the mechanical horses jerked forward and the conveyance moved down the street. Blinking hard, I looked up at my twin and then over at my host.

Calvin Warwick had aged terribly during the year he'd been absent. Resembling the island prison where he'd been incarcerated, his forehead was now a sheer cliff. Silver strands crept through his brown hair like tendrils of fog. His dark eyes haunted his poet's face, and though I scrambled back as far as I could, I couldn't escape his disconcerting gaze.

Reaching down, the surgeon helped me achieve the seat opposite him. I couldn't count the number of times those cool, slim hands had checked my pulse. If he pressed his fingers to the hollow of my throat now, he would know that my Ticker raced faster than any hummingbird's heart. I flinched away from his touch as though it burned. In an instant, Warwick's hopeful expression crumbled into lines of disappointment. He squeezed my hands until my bones ground together.

"I'm afraid we're going to have a difficult time of it at first," he said. "Once you understand what I've been doing for you, you'll relent."

I turned back to Nic. His strange new eyes were fixed upon something only he could see. Every muscle under his dark suit was clenched, primed for a fight. The pain in my jaw served as a reminder that he had his orders but no idea what he was actually doing. "Nic, look at me."

No reaction at all, not even a flicker of his eyelashes.

"Copernicus," Warwick said gently, "look at your sister, please."

Nic's head obediently swiveled in my direction.

"You used the Spiders on him, didn't you?" I could almost imagine the horrible things skittering behind his golden eyes.

"Yes." Warwick shifted forward, encouraged by my question if not my tone. "I was an intern at Currey Hospital when several

Bibliothèca patients were brought in. Quite by chance, I discovered the Beetles themselves caused the initial paralysis, the ensuing silence prompted by suggestions made by the Unseen. During my incarceration, I revisited my theories, building the first prototypes out of spare parts borrowed from other machines. Then there was the simple matter of one Spider for the guard, several more delivered to Mister Stirling via message cylinder . . ."

Sebastian.

"That's why he helped you arrange everything." I tried to lick my lips, but I might as well have rubbed them with sandpaper.

Warwick pulled his watch from his vest pocket, rubbing his thumb over the gold lid. Such a gesture must have been habit, because he'd burnished off all its decorative engraving; whatever message my sister placed there for him existed only in his mind now. "The Spiders allow me to exert a bit of influence. Mister Stirling's business acumen, for example, was easily exploited. Once the Spiders were in place, I merely suggested to him via RiPA that a sizable amount of money could be made through Augmentation. The rest was his own doing. Your friend possesses a ruthless streak that spilled over into strategy. I never would have thought to plant explosives at the factory, nor would I have inflicted so much damage at Glasshouse."

I wasn't about to let him blame everything on Sebastian. "What about my parents? Was it his idea to kidnap them?"

"Not entirely," Warwick admitted, toying with the watch. In the flickering light from the carriage window, I realized the fob had become mourning jewelry, with an intricate braid of Dimitria's hair forming the strap. "Your parents refused to speak with me. I sent letter after letter, but they never responded. Nic and I conversed for a while, and he understood what I wanted . . . *needed* . . . to do for you."

"Yes, and look at what you did to him!" Anger overtook every one of my senses, bleeding red around the edges of my consciousness and polluting everything with hot iron. "You turned him into a monster."

"The monster was inside him all along, Penny." Winding Dimitria's hair about his fingers, Warwick tucked the watch back into his pocket. "I didn't expect his resentment of you to be so strong."

"Don't be ridiculous," I snapped. "Nic doesn't resent me."

"Of course he does." The surgeon's tone grew cold, the analysis suddenly clinical and detached. "He was angry, Penny. Tired of shouldering the family's responsibilities. He was relieved to be brought here, anxious to set down his burdens. The Spiders were hardly in place before he spoke of that day at Carteblanche, how you climbed atop that horse despite his efforts to make you see reason. How you selfishly took the family's chance to heal and threw it away."

The words struck harder than Nic's fist. "He can't hate me that much," I whispered.

"If he didn't, there isn't anything I could have said to make him behave in such a fashion, I promise you." Warwick spoke as though delivering grim news to a patient's family. "You're a burden he's longed to set down for some time now."

It was the truth, every word. If I doubted it, I need only remember the furrows in Mama's brow, the gray hair at Papa's temples. Nic had finally had enough of me.

Worse than any slap or shout, Warwick saw the realization in my eyes and returned it with sympathy. "But you won't be a burden," he promised. "Not after today."

I dragged each breath into my lungs as though it might be my last. "Why didn't you send *me* a Spider? I could have come to you for my surgery willingly and saved us all a lot of trouble."

"I couldn't risk it for the same reason I didn't use them on your parents," Warwick said, perturbed by the very idea. "The Spiders most likely would have exploited your familial tendency to rush headlong into danger. You might have killed yourself before that damned faulty Ticker gave out. But I'm going to fix it. I will do the same for you as I've done for your brother: correct the imperfections of the flesh and improve upon nature. Shouldn't that be Man's greatest aspiration?"

The carriage jerked to a stop.

"Help her out, Copernicus," Warwick instructed.

"No, thank you," I said, but like a serpent striking, Nic's hand flashed out to clamp down on my arm, Augmented strength pouring out of him.

"As much as I have always admired your spirit," Warwick said, "you don't have the luxury of refusing my invitation. Resign yourself, Penny, this is going to happen."

Nic wrestled me to the sidewalk. Before us, columns rose four stories high, supporting a colonnade carved with muses in various attitudes. Nic towed me up the grand staircase of gold-flecked granite, the metallic glints mirrored in the decorative railings. Shuttered windows lent a secretive air, as did the chain and padlock on the front door.

Only then did I remember the words Philomena had uttered, entranced by the corpse of Lucy Reilly. *Moving. He's moving. Moving. Moving. Pictures. Get the pictures. Moving. Pictures. Catch him, he's moving.* The photographer had been trying to tell us where to find Warwick: Sebastian's moving-picture house. He'd acquired the lot as part of an undeveloped land parcel. I remembered looking at plans for half a dozen restaurants and an open-air shopping boulevard, but all construction was at a standstill. The metal archway leading to the deserted promenade resembled the gates to the underworld, and cranes loomed overhead, colossal birds of prey. There was no telltale hammering, no shouts of the work crew, no one to see Nic carrying me, no one to hear me scream if I'd been able to draw half the necessary breath.

Lined up along the wall stood another set of Ferrum Viriae soldiers, among them Frederick Carmichael. My step faltered at the sight of his blank gaze, because this was the secondary unit that should have been guarding Violet. From the end of the row, Sebastian emerged from the long shadows.

"Penny," he said easily enough, though he leaned upon his walking stick rather than swinging it.

"How's your knee?" I flashed at him.

Warwick answered on his behalf. "Augmented, thanks to your sharpshooting."

I kept my gaze trained on Sebastian. "Where's Violet?" Even staring into his eyes, I could see no trace of the mechanical Spiders controlling him. "Have you any idea your strings are being pulled?"

"Let us go inside, Mister Stirling," Warwick suggested.

With Sebastian in front, our curious parade bypassed the main door and circled around to a side entrance. Once we were inside, he padlocked the door behind us.

"This way," Warwick said, assuming the lead. "Mister Stirling, would you please fetch our other guest?"

"What about my parents?" I asked as Sebastian disappeared down a corridor. "When can I see them? And what have you done with Violet?"

"In due time, my dear," Warwick said. "Have patience."

That was a commodity in short supply at the moment. Lit by frosted gas globes that didn't do enough to chase away the shadows, the carpeted passageway seemed to extend forever. Nic barely permitted my feet to touch the floor as we rushed along. Harder to bear than my precarious circumstance was the way he looked at me. Looked *through* me.

Now I had proof that a girl with a clockwork ventriculator could have a broken heart.

"Just remember your name, Nic. It's yours. From our father and our grandfather before him. Copernicus. Emery. Farthing." I punctuated each word with a kick of my boot to his calves as he towed me along. "Nic, you've got to remember."

His only response was the ungentle prying of my fingers from his coat.

"Why would he want to remember that version of himself?" Warwick asked. "He's stronger now. Faster. Relieved of his weaknesses, the many little faults that break down this flesh, killing us from the inside out, tearing us from the arms of our loved ones." Zeal built up in his voice until the very walls echoed with his mad passion. "Don't you see, Penny, how much better off we'll all be when mere muscle and bone are left by the wayside?"

"Nic." I wrapped my fingers about my twin's wrist and squeezed, willing all the shared memories of our youth to transfer from my skin to his: playing in the nursery, capering at the grounds of Carteblanche, carriage rides through Square Park, ice-skating on the pond, countless pranks and midnight feasts. I summoned the bad memories as well, for those were just as powerful: Cygna sitting between us on the chaise, Dimitria's party, Mama's tears, Papa's drinking. Just like I had at the Bibliothèca, I tapped out a message, hoping it would reach my twin wherever his mind wandered.

THIS IS NOT YOU - REMEMBER WHO YOU ARE

I wanted to shake him until the message sank in, but nothing seemed to have an effect on him. Warwick reached another door, and beyond that was utter darkness. My other senses struggled to compensate as I inhaled a whiff of dusty velvet. My outstretched hand caught the hemp graze of rope. Lights flickered on, blinding me for a moment. Pristine muslin draped everything, but I knew we stood on the stage. Overhead, I could just make out the white silk of the projection screen, billowing like a ghost ship sailing into a forgotten sea. More frightening to contemplate were the metal tables, containers, and instruments set out in gleaming rows.

It was unmistakably an operatory.

"I think you'll marvel at everything we've managed under circumstances that are . . . well, perhaps less than ideal. The equipment. The supplies." Warwick pulled back a sheet of white cotton to reveal an assortment of Augmentation parts that included metal plates, tiny screws, and infinitesimal gears. "I've taken great pains in my preparations."

"I see that." Struggling to remain calm, I looked over the amassed collection. "Those are from the Gears & Rivets Factory?"

"That's right," he said, pleased I pieced that together. "Everything's ready."

Sebastian arrived, pushing a bound and gagged Violet ahead of him. Her eyes widened, but the length of cotton wadded up in her mouth muffled whatever she wanted to say.

I leapt forward. Unable to do anything for her bound wrists, red and raw under the ropes, I tugged the rag from her mouth. "Are you all right?"

"Penny! By all the Bells, get out of here!"

"That's hardly polite, Miss Nesselrode," Warwick said.

"Get stuffed!" Violet shot back at him, impotent fury pouring out of her.

"Why are you doing this to her?" I demanded.

"Your friend stumbled upon us this morning, and we had to forcibly detain her. It would have been easier if we could have used the Spiders on her, but she's apparently immune to suggestion. I'll have to address such resistance in the next upgrade." Warwick reached out, taking me by the arm as though about to stroll through a midnight rose garden. "Come, my dear, it's time."

Violet reared back and connected one of her black boots with Sebastian's unAugmented knee. With an unholy howl, he fell to the floor.

I plowed my elbow into Warwick's ribs. "Get the key, Violet. It's in Sebastian's pocket!"

"Copernicus!" the surgeon called out.

Nic pounced on me like a cat on a mouse. The two of us landed hard on the floorboards, rolling one over the other as we had in our nursery days. But in all the times we'd wrestled imaginary lions and tamed vicious beasts, Nic had never once wrapped his hands about my throat and tried to choke the life from me. And he was strong. So much stronger than I remembered. Dots of color appeared before my eyes.

"This isn't you," I tried to tell him.

With her hands still bound, Violet threw herself at Nic. It wasn't much of an attack, but enough to lessen his grip on me. Sebastian staggered to his feet behind her. Warwick sought out the nearest of the tables, hand closing down on a hypodermic syringe.

"Violet, go!" I cried out.

Hesitating one crucial second, she turned and ran. Nic's gaze tracked her attempted exit, so I reacted without thinking, jamming both my thumbs into his ocular implants. He fell to his knees, clawing at his face as bits of metal sparked and hissed. I gained my feet and turned to run, but an arm looped about my waist. Something delivered a sharp, stabbing pain in the side of my neck.

No.

Numbness spread down my shoulders and into my arms. Sebastian caught Violet just as she reached the door. She kicked and screamed until he clamped a hand over her mouth. She must have bitten him, because he flinched but didn't let her go a second time. As my legs failed me, Warwick picked me up and carried me to the largest of the metal tables. Muttering all the while, he strapped down my arms. When I turned my head, I could just make out Nic crouched upon the floor, whimpering like a kicked pup, hands pressed to his face.

"I'll see to your brother in a moment," Warwick promised before turning to contemplate the surgical implements, the bits of cotton wadding, the dark glass bottles standing in soldiers' rows before he finally found what he was looking for: my new clockwork heart. It was a lovely brass gleaming thing, small, compact, far more refined than the device dying by inches in my chest. "First things first."

My old Ticker was done. I could feel it winding down as it had so many times before, but each beat lingered a bit longer than it should, a vibration of finality in every contraction. The entire mechanism thrummed gently, as though trying to rock me to sleep.

"I'll fight you with my last breath," I told him.

"Good." Warwick's voice faded, and the improvised operatory stretched out before me like a train tunnel through a mountain pass.

My Ticker gave one last thud.

It seemed only seconds later that pain was a hot coal shovel lodged deep in my chest. I struggled against it, against the flesh that held me captive, against the straps pinning me against cold metal. My eyes flickered open, and I caught sight of Warwick, bloody up to his elbows, bright red splashes fading up his chest to the dull color of rust.

"I brought you out of sedation." His desperate words belied the grace with which his hands moved as he dripped Quick-Heal into my mouth. "You need to fight. *You must.* Your survival depends as much upon your own will to live as it does this device. Fight to live. Fight as she couldn't, damn you!"

I felt pressure on my chest, then heard a wet sucking noise. With a shudder, the new ventriculator began to work, moving pain through my body in spurts of summer lightning. Had I not been strapped down, I would have curled in on myself and whimpered.

"Why?" I could hardly give voice to the word, so faint was the breath leaving my lungs. "Why are you doing this?"

"Don't you understand? We've both had our hearts broken." Warwick bent down to whisper in my ear. "Death took from me the thing I loved most in this world. Now I am going to cheat it at every turn."

"Dimitria wouldn't want you to do any of this," I said.

"Oh, but she would." Warwick clamped a white rag over my nose and mouth; instead of chloroform, I smelled only roses. "Her last words to me were 'Save Penny.'"

THIRTEEN

In Which All the Turns in the Waltz Are Reverses

It was some time before I woke again; I could tell by the crust on the edge of the bandages crackling nastily against my skin, by the sharp reek of disinfectant cutting through the copper tang of blood. My throat was raw, probably from screaming. Four blue glass bottles of Quick-Heal sat on the nearest table, three of them empty. Closing a hand down upon the fourth, I uncapped and drained it in one swift movement.

Returning the bottle to the table, I jangled the wires and rubber tubing attached to my arms and chest. Holding my breath, I tested each one, then pulled them out, singly and in pairs. I wore only my shift, and the room was Glacia cold, as though Warwick had decided we were best served chilled, just like one of Dreadnaught's fancy melon ices. My breath turned to mist with every exhalation, and I couldn't feel the end of my nose.

Circulatory complications, my inner clinician noted with detachment.

The lamps burned spots into my retinas, and I experienced one brief, panicked moment thinking Warwick had Augmented my eyes as well. I forced myself to breathe, to give myself time to adjust to the circumstances. The surgeon was conspicuous in his absence, though the space around me still reverberated with his grief-fueled convictions. Sebastian was also missing, but Violet lay on another table some distance away. I wasn't certain if she was alive. Hands at her sides, skin pallid, she took a sip of air only after several long seconds. Still wearing his gray costume livery, Nic slept next to her.

I levered myself to a mostly upright position, sweat gathering at my temples. The skin on the backs of my hands was a horrible shade of gray. My circulation was definitely compromised. I couldn't tell if the fault lay with the new Ticker or my own body; either way, I needed a stimulant.

My Pixii sat on a nearby workbench, but there was the small matter of getting to it. I counted off the steps it would take, calculated the amount of energy I would need. Shoring up my reserves, I slid from the metal operating table. My feet rasped against the wooden floorboards. My thin cotton gown wasn't enough to protect me from the chill of the room, and my teeth began to chatter. The sound of ivory on ivory filled my head until I could hardly think over the noise of it. I had to rest against the counter for forty-nine beats of the Ticker before I could close my fingers around the Pixii's handle. By the time I located the depression switch, my knees wobbled. Charging the device took another twenty-seven seconds. Gritting my teeth, I set the metal foreprongs against the skin just below my chin.

The second I depressed the switch, I staggered back. Though I tried to brace myself, a blinding rush of energy roared straight to my head. Within seconds, my entire body radiated warmth. My veins thrummed, and my hands turned pink.

Tingling all over, I almost missed the soft cadence of boots against the stage floor. Ducking behind the nearest table, I could feel my pulse, a god's hammer on an anvil. The acute cold faded into the distant background as I recharged the Pixii. The curtain nearest me parted, and Sebastian entered. His handheld torch cut a swath of light across the operatory, over Nic, over Violet. When he reached my empty makeshift bed, I leapt forward and jammed the Pixii's foreprongs under his chin. The discharge suffused the white draperies with blinding blue light. Before it had completely faded, Sebastian crumpled to the ground.

Seconds later, at least a dozen mechanical Spiders staggered out of his ears. Dull brass instead of the black ones I'd seen at the courthouse, they twitched and jerked in disoriented circles before their legs gave out completely.

It's like using an electrified net on the Butterflies.

Sweeping aside the Spiders with my arm, I knelt on the floor and checked Sebastian's heart rate and his pupils before hastening to Nic. Delicate metal plates covered my brother's entire left hand. A set of brass screws marked the line of his jaw—perceived weaknesses of flesh and bone, I could only assume, given Warwick's fervid speech on the subject.

Forcing myself to move quickly, I set the Pixii under Nic's chin, held my breath, and discharged it with a zing. He convulsed, his body stiffening with the transferred energy, then he fell back, limp and pale.

No response from him, and no Spiders.

Trying not to panic, I recharged the device, nearly cracking the dial in half as I twisted it up to the maximum setting. A second burst of light, a second round of waiting.

Still nothing.

Blinking back the burn of tears, I smashed the Pixii against the side of the table and peered at its shiny innards. With a few bits of wiring removed, I could dial up its power to twice what I'd used on Nic before. There was the chance that I'd kill him . . .

Or that he'd rouse from this sleep and kill me first.

Holding my breath, I braced the disembodied prongs under his chin and gave him everything the little machine had. A muffled pop was the only noise for a long moment, then a sudden wave of bugs poured out of my brother like a plague. Silver this time and at least twice as many as had been in Sebastian, they rushed forward as though drawn by invisible wires to the Pixii. Scrambling back, I struggled to piece the device together as they gave chase. Their legs tappity-tapped against the floor in a hellish sort of waltz; I hadn't thought it possible for creatures with eight legs to move in perfect three-quarter time, but they did. My skin crawled as though they were already upon me.

Balancing the broken bits of the Pixii in my shaking hands, I somehow generated enough crackling energy to make my hair stand on end. Attracted by the warm hum of power, the Spiders leapt at me; the moment they alighted upon my skin, I pressed the discharge button. The blast knocked me off my feet, and I fell hard on my backside. Everything smelled of singed cotton and fizzled copper wiring. A straggling strand of my hair smoked, ready and willing to burst into merry flames. I licked my fingers and put out the threat of fire with a small, final hiss. Spiders surrounded me, their clockwork corpses twitching in a danse macabre.

"Penny?" Nic groaned.

"I'm here." Three steps closed the distance between us, and then I had my arms about him. His body, under the tattered shirt, was stiff and unyielding.

"By all the Bells, don't squeeze me," was the somewhat muffled protest as my brother sat up. "There's precious little on my person that doesn't ache. Even my hair hurts."

I responded by hugging him all the harder. "There has to be another bottle of Quick-Heal in here somewhere."

Pale and disheveled as he was, Nic's eyes gleamed with the faintest golden light. "I hope to Cogs my memory is faulty," he said with a groan, "but did I actually punch you in the face?"

In spite of myself, I took a step back. "You did. And I jammed my fingers into your ocular Augmentations, though it seems Warwick repaired them."

He turned his head aside as though too ashamed to meet my gaze. "I never meant to hurt you."

"I know," I said. Warwick and his Spiders had done more than prey upon Nic's resentment toward me; they'd sown wild seeds of doubt between us. "We'll talk about that later."

Looking very much like he might vomit, Nic stumbled against the nearest table. "Where's Warwick?"

"In absentia."

"The Spiders?"

I pointed to the smashed bits on the floor. "Obliterated."

"Well played," Nic whispered. "What about Sebastian?"

"Resting, for the moment," I said. "Where are Mama and Papa?"

"Tidied away in a storage closet like a pair of brooms last I saw them." Nic's every word emanated furious purpose. "We'll see this ended, Penny."

"Yes, we will," I agreed.

As one, we moved to Violet's side, but it was Nic who leaned over, brushed a strand of dark hair from her cheek, and adjusted the crooked collar of her walking-out dress. I held my breath, wondering if he'd kiss the sleeping princess awake, but he was too much a gentleman for that sort of behavior.

"Violet," he said, soft and urgent all at once. "We have to get out of here."

Though her eyelashes fluttered, she didn't rouse.

"There's a faster way to get her up," I said, nudging her roughly. "You've slept over your alarm, Nesselrode. Customers are waiting at the counter, and the sticky buns have risen out of their pans."

When she sat bolt upright, she nearly took my nose off. "What's happened?!"

I clamped an arm about her before she bailed off the table. "Calm yourself, it's all right."

"What about the buns?" Violet pivoted her head about. "This isn't my room. This isn't *your* room. Where are we?"

"In dire circumstances," Nic said, helping me lower her to the floor. "You ran afoul of Warwick."

Violet's face paled, but her grip on us intensified. "I remember now. And Sebastian . . ." She ran her gaze over us, the same keen glance that took inventory of the bakery stockroom in less than ten seconds. "Sebastian ambushed me!"

"He wasn't altogether himself," was all I had time to say before Violet turned and flung herself at Nic.

"Never mind that now," she said, blinking back tears. "You might have died, and all I've been able to think about was that stupid fight."

Nic slipped his arms about her and murmured something in her ear as I crept away from the string of apologies that followed. Still, I caught snippets of "No, it was all my fault" and "I was afraid I'd never see you again" from both of them, followed by enough kissing to set my face ablaze.

As they made their amends, I located the smelling salts and turned my attention to Sebastian's prone form. "Mister Stirling, it's time to wake up." Waving the bottle under his nose earned me a frown. A stiff and well-deserved slap to his cheek roused him the rest of the way.

"Penny, my darling," he mumbled, "I hoped that someday I would wake to find you by my side. I just didn't think it would be because you tried to kill me."

"If I wanted to kill you, you'd be dead." I looked down at him. "Whatever you say next, don't bother to be charming. I'm not in the mood."

Sebastian's eyes suddenly widened, and he jerked up as though I'd taken the Pixii to him again. "We have to warn Marcus."

I caught hold of him by the shoulders. "About what?"

"A hundred SugarWerks Carry-Away Boxes distributed around the city. At the train terminals. The Meridian port. The airfield." Sebastian heaved himself up, wincing as he jarred his Augmented knee. "I personally delivered the damn things to diplomats and government officials, every prominent aristocrat, shipping baron, manufacturer, and registered member of the Edoceon movement."

Violet whirled about, looking as if she might strangle him. "You stole boxes from SugarWerks?"

Less concerned with the containers than the contents, I stared at Sebastian. "What's in the boxes?"

"Mechanical Spiders. More than enough to bring the city to a standstill. Marcus needs to know before the timers go off." Noticing that I wore only my shift, Sebastian shrugged off his jacket and draped it over my shoulders.

"We also need to get Mama and Papa," I said. "What do we have in the way of weapons, other than my Pixii?"

As it turned out, there were plenty: razor-sharp scalpels, syringes of sedatives, and the metal legs off the operating tables, which would serve as clubs. Nic hastily patched the Pixii back together with some spare plates and wires, but the poor thing was prone to buzzing and sparking without warning now. Still, I felt safer with it at the ready.

"Let's go," Nic said once we were armed.

We tiptoed across the stage, eased open a door, and entered a long corridor. Unnatural quiet surrounded us, broken only by the sound of our muffled footsteps upon the rug. After the brilliant illumination of the operatory, my eyes struggled to adjust. Nic's ocular Augmentations must have compensated for the lack of light, but he still moved with caution that matched my own.

Doors on either side of us bore small luminous nameplates identifying the contents of each alcove: film canisters, construction supplies, cleaning equipment. Warning signs marked the rooms containing nitrocellulose, and we gave those a wide berth. At the end of the hallway, Sebastian pulled a key from his pocket and unlocked the door.

The room beyond smelled of stale tea and sweat. A lantern with a red glass globe burned atop a table littered with overturned cups and crumbs. Blindfolded and bound, our parents huddled together on the floor. Their clothes were grimy and rumpled, like those of naughty children caught playing in a coal hole. Far from being chastened, though, our father reared up his head like a bull about to charge.

"Coward!" he roared. Despite the dried blood crackling in his beard and the rusty flecks decorating his linen, he vibrated with indignation and strength.

This wasn't the empty shell sloshing with alcohol we'd known this last year. This was my *father*.

Nic closed the door as I flew across the room and pressed my fingers to Papa's mouth.

"Quiet," I ordered him. "It's not Warwick."

"Penny?" When I jerked his blindfold off, he flinched away from the light.

"By all the Bells!" Mama whispered, trying to twist closer to me.

I reached out and pulled the cloth from her eyes. For a fleeting moment, I looked at a blurred picture of Dimitria, her copper hair falling over her shoulders, eyes filled with tears; then everything came into focus and I held my mother in my arms, breathing in the trace of rose water under the acrid scents of fear and fury. "Are you all right?" I asked.

"Get out, the lot of you, before he comes back—" A bout of coughing curtailed my father's order. Apparently he hadn't been taken without a fight, and Warwick must not have spared any Quick-Heal for him.

Nic landed alongside me, his Augmented fingers attacking the knots. "Save your strength. We're going to need it to get out of this place."

The moment Papa's hands were free, he reached into his breast pocket for his spectacles. He wrapped the wires about his ears as Nic turned to Mama.

"Let me see what he did to you," she demanded. When her ropes dropped to the floor, she grasped Nic's Augmented hand and turned it over.

"I'm fine, I promise." He averted his gaze before she could look into his eyes. "We've no time for an examination."

"Where's the nearest exit?" Mama asked, finding her feet and looking over the group like a hen counting her chicks.

"The stage door, but it's rigged with sensors and explosives." Sebastian led us out of the storeroom and down the hall. "The front entrance is farther, but at least we'll leave with our limbs intact."

I charged the Pixii to its full capacity as we hurried. "We need to get everyone out and signal Marcus for help. We still have the Carry-Away Boxes to worry about."

"I expected the almighty Kingsley to be here by now, astride a white horse, colors flying," Sebastian observed as we made our way up a twisting staircase.

The unexpected blast of a black-powder shot interrupted our progress. Papa hunched over with a groan, blood oozing from a bullet wound in his shoulder. With a wordless cry, Mama grabbed him by one lolling wrist and tried to pull him to the upper floor.

I shoved at Sebastian. "Go! Get them out."

He obeyed, vaulting up the last few stairs to help my mother. Two more bullets tore through the spot where Sebastian had just been. I ducked down behind the iron railing with Nic and Violet just behind me. Peering through the bars, I saw Calvin Warwick aiming a revolver at us.

"You can't leave," he said flatly, firing once more. "It isn't safe for you out there until I take care of the Edoceon and the city council. Once the Spiders are in place, the officials and the protestors will be more amenable to my methods. Nothing will impede my good work, helping others like you. Like Dimitria."

Afraid he might take another shot at us, I reached out and jammed the Pixii into the nearest light switch. The energy transferred with a hiss and zing, mercifully into the outlet and not up my arm. A series of fireworks cascaded from the light fixtures before every incandescent bulb in the hall exploded.

"This has to end!" I shouted at the shadows pooling in the hallway.

“I agree.” Warwick’s voice twined about us like a specter. Hollow footsteps signaled his approach. “Don’t be unreasonable, Penny.”

“Unreasonable?! You shot my father!”

One plus two plus one . . .

I counted four bullets fired; he had only two left.

“I’ve killed before to save you, and I’ll do it again,” was his chilling response. “Dimitria wanted it that way.”

Nic shifted behind me. “My sister never would have wanted any of this.”

“Don’t tell me what I do and do not know. I was the one who heard her breath stop. I was the one holding her when the light left her eyes.” Something cracked open, and all of Warwick’s grief poured out of him. “Dimitria’s last words weren’t for me—they were for Penny! And then she was *gone*!”

“My mother’s building a machine at the Flying Fortress,” I said, hoping such news could shine a bit of light to his heart. “The Grand Design. It lifts the veil between this world and the next. You can speak with Dimitria. She’ll tell you . . .”

His slow footsteps resumed. “Don’t try to trick me. I’m a man of science. A man of logic.”

“Then listen to yourself!” I shouted, more angry now than frightened. “You’re the one about to unleash mind-controlling devices on thousands of innocent people. You’re the one terrorizing the city and plotting to overthrow the government. It would be a mistake to call you mad. A mistake and a kindness both.”

“Stop,” he warned me, but I couldn’t.

“You might be able to correct the weaknesses of the flesh, but you can never mend a heart that’s broken the way yours is!”

To silence me, he fired off another shot. The bullet embedded itself in the plaster just over my head.

One bullet left.

Violet squeaked, shoving me up the last three stairs and into the lobby. There was nowhere to hide in the cavernous space. Sebastian had unlocked the revolving door and helped my parents out to the terrace. I could see Papa leaning against a marble column with my mother bent over him. Nic grasped Violet's hand and made a run for it. The parquet floor spread out before us, dark wood against light like a chessboard. No time for subtleness, strategy, Knight's Maneuvers, or trying to spare the Queen.

We reached the exit, and I ducked into the compartment behind Nic and Violet, momentum carrying us forward until Warwick grasped the back of my borrowed jacket. The fabric caught between the revolving panels and the wall; the door ceased to turn. I was trapped, with only a pane of glass between us.

"Hold on!" Nic tugged at the metal frame, forcing it to yield by inches.

"Stay with me, Penny," Warwick pleaded, jerking the jacket and the door back toward him. "You're not like them. You understand . . ."

Full up with loathing, I rounded on him. "I understand this: It's *over*, Warwick. We know how to deactivate the Spiders. If we want to fight the Edoceon, we'll do it in a courtroom. You kept your promise to Dimitria, and now you have to stop! What would she say, if she could see you now?"

Warwick looked past me to my father bleeding on the terrace, Sebastian in the street waving at the rapidly approaching Ferrum Viriae, then down at the gun in his hand.

One shot left. I dragged in a panicked breath, waiting for him to raise the revolver.

"You lived," he said.

"I did."

He let go of me and reached for his pocket watch. His thumb traced the gold case, then he wound the intricate braid of Dimitria's hair about his fingers. "I saved you."

"Yes," I choked out. "You did just as she asked."

Warwick's terrifying anger slipped away, and something akin to peace spread across his face. Whatever else he might have said was drowned out by the wheeze of brakes and the screech of tires. Marcus bailed out of the vehicle like it was on fire, taking the stairs three at a time. When I looked back to Warwick, he gave me a sad smile before opening his pocket watch and disgorging a dozen gold Spiders. He kept his eyes on mine as the mechanical bugs crawled up his sleeve, over his collar, across his face, and into his ears.

Dimitria.

His mouth formed the name as his smile faded, exactly the way the light does only moments after the sun sets. I watched the last vestiges of the man I'd known disappear into the darkness, leaving an empty shell behind.

"Get her out of there," said Marcus from just outside. When the door yielded with a final desperate jerk, he caught me in his arms.

"It's about damn time, Kingsley," Nic said. "What took you so long?"

"I got here as fast as I could. There's a tracking device in Penny's bracelets, but we couldn't activate it until after we discovered and dismantled the device blocking all the communications systems at the courthouse." Marcus peered over my shoulder at the catatonic form of Calvin Warwick. "It seems I missed the exciting bit?"

As tired as I was, there were explanations to be made about the SugarWerks Boxes and how the Spiders could be neutralized with different levels of electrical current. Sebastian ran through all the information, with Marcus relaying everything he said to the

Communications Center. An ambulance arrived, and two soldiers placed Papa inside. Mama climbed in after him and closed the doors herself.

Watching them go, I finally exhaled. Not even the most brazen of the tabloids would fully believe this story. Oh, they would tell the tale and sell the papers, but they wouldn't believe it.

Marcus trailed a gentle hand down my back. "I seem to be forever catching you in your undergarments, Tesseraria. What is this? Three times in as many days?"

"We do seem to be making a habit of it." Leaning against him, my ear to his chest, I could hear his heart beating, a rhythm now more familiar than any piece of music. My new Ticker paused for just a moment, and I panicked, wondering if it, too, were faulty. Then it thudded once, twice, in perfect time with the heart of the man standing before me.

Just as steady. Just as strong.

"Silver denarii for your thoughts, Tesseraria."

"Surely you know me better than that by now, Legatus?" I smiled up at Marcus, welcoming the sunshine on my upturned face and neck. "My thoughts are worth a golden aureii, every one."

FOURTEEN

In Which There Are More Stories Than Those Reported in the Papers

---

All of us crammed into Marcus's motorcar for the ride to Currey Hospital. Papa was in surgery by the time we arrived, and Mama paced the hallway.

"I want to stay," Marcus said, watching her wear a groove into the floor. "But seeing as half my forces are under the influence of the Spiders and there are infested Carry-Away Boxes scattered about the city . . ."

"Go," I said, only half meaning it. "Take Sebastian with you."

"I suppose I have to leave you at the mercy of the doctors. Or perhaps I got that backward." One last squeeze and he tucked a finger under my chin. "Permission to call this evening?"

"Don't you need to submit your requests in triplicate?" It wasn't flirting. Not after everything we'd been through.

For an answer, Marcus lifted my bare hand to his mouth and kissed it thrice. "Will that do?"

"Quite," I said, slapping at him. "Now go, before my face bursts into actual flames."

After Marcus departed, Violet sat with my mother while Nic and I were hustled into an examination room. The Augmentation specialists took pages of notes, focusing primarily on my new clockwork ventriculator and my brother's ocular corrections. No doubt a study would be published in the medical journals just as soon as ink could hit paper. We were admonished to get plenty of rest and food, and then excused. Before I rejoined the others, I donned the dress Mama had ordered from a nearby shop. Grateful for my good health and that of my loved ones, I didn't offer a single complaint that it was the most trying shade of amaranth pink imaginable.

Nic was just outside the examination room when I exited, and we regarded each other with eyes that were no longer twinned mirrors. The memory of his fist connecting with my face and the accusations he'd made in the alley still burned, but I tamped down that fire.

"*Tempus est clavis*," I whispered, reaching out a hand.

Time will heal all wounds, outside as well as in.

The moment I touched his arm, Nic relaxed his shoulders. "How are you feeling?"

"Impossibly energized." I paused to consider the matter further. "And starving. I don't know when I last ate. You?"

"Fit as the proverbial fiddle. We really should speak with Marcus about an Augmentation contract. If a soldier can come out of battle feeling this way, he'd be nearly unstoppable."

"Warwick promised him something similar," I said without thinking.

Nic looked down at me. "It sounds as though there's more to that story."

"I'll explain later." I gazed up at him, uncertain what else to say. "I didn't want to venture anything in front of the doctors, but we could remove the upgrades . . . all except the ones in your eyes, I think. You could be as you were before."

"I don't think any of us are going to be as we were before." Nic took my hand in his newly Augmented one, metal fingers sliding alongside mine, the whir of gears and balance wheels like a pulse, new yet familiar. "Don't fret. I'll get used to them in time."

"They're a forever sort of souvenir." I thought about the machine beating away in my chest, of Warwick, of the look upon his face when he whispered Dimitria's name one last time. "And how long will it be before we sleep without nightmares and walk down the street without looking over our shoulders?"

"Or see a Spider without jumping out of our skins?" Nic reached up to rub a finger about his ear.

"That's not funny," Violet said, joining us with Mama just behind her. "Your next project is to redesign the Carry-Away Boxes. Otherwise, I won't be able to load them with cake without wondering first if they're full of mind-controlling arachnids."

"Done." He drew her into his arms. "But I won't be able to manage it on an empty stomach. Will anyone join me for a meal?"

"Your father ought to be out of surgery soon," Mama said. "They removed the bullet, and thankfully it missed everything vital. I'll stay here to wait for him to wake up. He'll be as cranky as anything."

"I'll wait with Mama," I said. "Bring me something from the canteen?"

"A piece of pie?" Violet asked as Nic led her toward the stairs.

"An entire pie," I said, sitting down alongside Mama. "And a bucket of tea with a dozen lumps of sugar."

My mother permitted herself a small laugh as she noted, "I'll help you drink it. It's been too long since I had a proper cup."

We'd both been through such a lot, and yet there was one more thing to tell her. "I owe you an apology, Mama."

"Whatever for, dear heart?" She wrapped an arm about me, her rose water perfume instantly transporting me back to the dining room, into the company of my elder sister, listening to the cradle rock in the corner.

I should have believed my mother. She knew it was possible all along.

"I thought you were crazy, consulting all those psychics and mediums, trying to reach Dimitria and Cygna." I nestled against her. "Why didn't you tell me about the Grand Design?"

"I signed papers. Gave Mister Kingsley my word. And I didn't like to say anything before it was working properly. False hope, and all that."

"But it *does* work." I explained about reanimating Lucy Reilly's corpse, about my own near-death moment spent in the in-between place that resembled our dining room.

"You saw her, then," Mama said. "You spoke with Dimitria?"

"Yes. She looked just as she did . . . on her birthday." I couldn't bring myself to word it any other way.

"And Cygna?"

"I didn't see her. Just the cradle rocking."

"I wish I could have been there with you." Mama's eyes filled with tears, but she hugged me hard.

"We'll try again," I surprised myself by saying. "I'll go with you to see Philomena."

"I'd like that," my mother said. "Very much."

My RiPA delivered a message from Marcus.

HALF THE AFFLICTED SOLDIERS HAVE GONE ABSENT WITHOUT LEAVE - STOP - BRACELETS DEACTIVATED - STOP - WARWICK PROGRAMMING PROVING DIFFICULT TO DECODE - STOP

More news followed, none of it particularly good. The soldiers who'd recovered from the Spider removal—Frederick Carmichael among them—were still in the process of tracking down the Carry-Away Boxes and neutralizing the remaining threat. The broad-sheets had picked up the story, and bulletins had been issued to every RiPA and PaperTape machine in the city, warning Bazalgate's citizens to be wary of unexpected gifts of cake.

"The Legatus will see things set to rights, never fear," Mama said when the stream of messages ceased, her mouth quirking a bit. "He's a very remarkable young man."

I didn't ask what she meant by such a leading comment because a doctor interrupted us.

"Mister Farthing is out of surgery and recovering nicely. If one of you would like to go in, that ought to be fine."

Mama and I exchanged a look, and I gave her a little push. "Go. We'll meet you back at Glasshouse."

But I wasn't going to head straight home. Life ought to be celebrated at every possible opportunity, and we had a lot of catching up to do.

After sending Nic ahead to prepare Dreadnaught, Violet and I made our way to Perpetua Marketplace. We had the meat dishes, vegetables, creams, and ices sent back to Glasshouse, but I carried the turtle myself.

It was an accident; I'd never intended on buying such a thing and had even less intention of eating it, but with the costermonger and the Meridian fishmonger extolling the virtues of their wares in each of my ears, I'd somehow come away from the transaction with several lobsters for pastry vol-au-vents, twenty pounds of fresh peas, sparrow-grass and cowcumbers, and one largish and very much alive Bhaskarian turtle.

"Every bit of it can be used," the fishmonger had said as he took my money and ignored my protests. "Boil the belly, roast the back meat, and put the innards in a *beyootiful* soup. Tell your cook that the shell can be used as a tureen!"

He had wrapped the poor creature in damp burlap and handed it over as Violet snickered into her gloved hands. The turtle's significant weight left no doubt in my mind that it would indeed serve eight to ten, as the fishmonger repeatedly assured me.

"But—"

He'd already turned to help another customer. "Of course the oysters are fresh, sir! I am appalled you would even ask such a thing!"

Ducking the spray as he enthusiastically shucked shellfish, we hastened to exit the marketplace.

"All we wanted was a bit of light supper," I muttered as we wended our way through the stalls. "Dreadnaught is going to have a fit when she sees this."

"The creature is the very opposite of 'light' dining," Violet said, helping me carry it.

There was a trick to heaving the turtle into a hansom cab, another to convince the driver that it wouldn't eat the upholstery. Once we were on our way, I poured my remaining coins into my lap, looking from the copper pence to the impulsively purchased chelonian.

"Who would have thought you could cost so much?"

The creature's head emerged from its shell, and it regarded me with something akin to reproach.

"I would have helped pay for it!" Violet informed me.

"You did enough, what with the marzipan and the cream and the pineapples. Whatever possessed you to buy such ugly things?"

"Wait until you taste what I bake with them—almond soufflés and pineapple tartlets." Violet clapped her hands together. "And you're one to speak about buying ugly ingredients."

When the turtle snapped at our toes, we squeaked and pulled up our skirts.

"I don't much care for the idea of eating something whose face I've seen, I can tell you that much," I said as we pulled up at Glasshouse. The turtle turned its head and nibbled at its burlap wrappings. "You certainly are a useless and nonsensical thing. I'll call you Brimborion." I leapt over him and out the door in one mighty bound. "Help me bring him around to the kitchen garden, Violet, and mind your fingers."

The second we exited the carriage, the press descended. Violet and I retreated to the sanctity of the kitchen, where Nic and Dreadnaught met us.

"They won't leave us in peace until they get their story," I said, suddenly weary down to my toes. "Take Violet into the back parlor and show the reporters in."

Nic donned a new pair of smoked-glass spectacles to hide his eyes before Dreadnaught permitted the representatives from the *Bazalgate Pictorial: An Illustrated Weekly, The Gazette,* and *The Evening Express* access to the front parlor. She did not offer them tea or refreshments, not that they cared. They stampeded in, shouting questions.

"Our readers want to hear about your encounter with Calvin Warwick! What happened?"

"Is it true he proposed to you, Miss Farthing?"

"That he threatened to blow up the entire city?"

"What about the Spiders?"

There was the brilliant light of a camera flash, and I flinched at the *whoosh!* of burning potassium permanganate and aluminum. "It all happened terribly fast. The Ferrum Viriae arrived and bundled us away."

The reporters weren't satisfied with such a bland answer and pressed closer, pencils poised above their notebooks, RiPAs at the ready.

"What about the doctor?"

"Is he in custody?"

I didn't want to say as much, but Marcus had dealt with Warwick himself. Under the influence of the golden Spiders, he'd been docile, silent. Guilty, doubly so, and destined for the gallows, he'd been escorted back to Gannet Penitentiary.

But will the surgeons be able to remove the Spiders? Or will Warwick be trapped within his own mind as well as the prison?

Those were thoughts for another day, and nothing I was going to share with the newspapers. "I think we've answered enough questions for now."

The most insistent of the reporters wagged his pencil under my nose. "What do you have to say about the city of Bazalgate lauding you and your friends as heroes?"

"No comment," I said firmly.

"But surely you have an opinion!"

"There are no heroes in a situation like this," Nic said. "There are only the dead and the survivors."

Closing my eyes, I wished all these horrible people would go away and leave us alone. Like a genie granting my request, Dreadnaught appeared in the doorway. "You have other callers, Miss Farthing."

The reporters paled when Marcus and Sebastian entered the parlor. Both of them had found clean clothes in the interim, but it was Marcus's demeanor as much as his uniform that brought everyone to attention.

"Am I interrupting something?" the Legatus calmly inquired.

Our unwelcome guests bowed their heads and filed past him with much stumbling over furniture and hastily packed photography equipment.

"A most welcome interruption." I rose from the chaise but made no move toward them.

Sebastian took the first step. "I need to apologize for my behavior and make amends. Instead of flowers or chocolates, I've rung my barristers. The factory and courthouse will be rebuilt, and a hundred thousand aureii will go into a trust, to be divided between the families of the victims. My insurance doesn't cover acts of terrorism and valiant stupidity, so this will be coming out of my own pocket."

It was one thing for Sebastian to admit to wrongdoing and quite another for him to part with such a sizable chunk of his wealth. And yet . . . "It wasn't your fault. Not really."

"That's not altogether true, is it?" Like a child, he smiled and scuffed a toe against the carpet. "Warwick explained it to me, my dear Penny. I remember, though it's all a bit hazy now. He couldn't have suggested I do things that weren't in my nature. If I wasn't a greedy bastard, he wouldn't have been able to manipulate me."

Hitching up his shoulders, he stuffed both hands deep in his pockets. Those bluer-than-blue eyes were darker than I ever remembered seeing them before.

I pressed my hands to his face, forcing him to meet my gaze. "You will make amends, Sebastian. And you have the love and support and *forgiveness* of your friends to see you through it. You were a victim, too, and I'll not hear a single word spoken against you. None of us will."

He flushed then, and I could see the struggle to retrieve the pieces of his lackadaisical dignity. "Well then, if you're not going to cast me out on my ear . . ."

"I'm not."

"Maybe I could sit down? It's been a long dashed week."

I shifted to one side to permit his entry into the study. A second later, Cora peeped out from behind Marcus's jacket, her shy smile widening with each passing second.

"Hallo!" She scampered across the room and enfolded me in a mighty hug.

I crouched to better look at her. "That is a very pretty dress."

Hopping back, she twirled to show off the flare of her charcoal skirts. "Not a dress. A uniform!" She held up her wrists to display matching silver bangle bracelets.

"So you've joined the army, have you?" I hazarded a glance at Marcus. "Young for a recruit, don't you think? You could have waited until she was done with primary school."

He was careful to wink at me when Cora looked away. "She apparently insisted sometime between the roast chicken and the cake. According to Captain Hunter, she also explored every inch of the Fortress and redecorated one of the guest barracks to suit her."

"I like it there," Cora chimed in. "And Mama said it was all right for me to stay near Philomena and the great big talking machine."

I stiffened, as did Marcus, and both of us said, "Talking machine?" as one voice.

Cora admired herself in the hall mirror, turning this way and that to take in the sight of her iron-gray skirts. "The one past the ice room. I can hear her plain as day in there."

Marcus hunkered down next to her. "You can hear your mother when you're near the Grand Design?"

Cora leaned forward until the tip of her nose was touching his. "Yes, Legatus."

I could tell there was more he wanted to ask, but I shook my head and beckoned to Nic. "Cora, this is my brother, Copernicus Emery Farthing."

She peered up at him, tilting her head as though listening to something only she could hear. "The clockwork soldier."

I broke out in gooseflesh, but Nic only nodded and took care not to scare her with his newly Augmented hand. "It might look that way, but really I'm an inventor. I make things."

"Windup toys?" Evidently deciding to trust him, Cora drew him over to the cart and pointed to the cream slices just out of her reach. "Can we have tea and cakes?"

Seizing the opportunity to speak to Marcus alone, I joined him in the doorway. "Do you think she's actually clairvoyant?"

"It could simply be her active imagination, but I'll speak with Philomena about it." In case Cora should glance over at us, he kept his expression placid. "Either way, what's the harm if it gives her solace?"

"What about her family?"

"None we can locate yet." Marcus glanced at the child coercing the largest cream slice out of my brother. "We tried to pull her cards from the Bibliothèca, but she hasn't a birth certificate we can find."

"Sloppy record keeping isn't one of the Eidolachometer trademarks." It was all I could do to remain smiling, though the charade gave me something of a headache. "You'll keep trying, though?"

"Certainly," Marcus said. "In the meantime, she'll live at the Flying Fortress as my ward. It will be quite the feat not to spoil her. She already has every member of the Ferrum Viriae wrapped about her finger."

"Including the great Mister Kingsley, I should imagine."

"She does, though it undermines my authority to admit it. And you'll visit regularly, of course." Marcus glanced across the study at Nic and back to me. "We have matters to discuss, Tesseraria."

"Don't mistake him for a soldier," I warned. "He won't ever walk that path."

"Not just that," Marcus admitted. "We've tried several levels and varieties of energy on Warwick. Nothing has proved effective yet on the Spiders he used on himself."

"His were gold," I said, remembering the look of them upon the surgeon's hand, before they disappeared into his ears. "Sebastian's were brass and easily deactivated. Nic's were silver and took a third pulse. But the ones at the courthouse and in the Carry-Away Boxes were black, and Warwick's were gold. Perhaps he designed his own so they can't ever be removed."

Sebastian called to us, "I'm for a drink. Does anyone want anything?"

I felt the dust settling around us and wondered if I could trust the floor not to open up again underfoot. I'd had quite enough excitement to last me two lifetimes.

Realizing the press had gone, Violet hustled in from the back parlor. "Legatus," she murmured in passing.

"Miss Nesselrode." Marcus inclined his head.

Dreadnaught entered, studying a small but startlingly vivid bouquet. "These just arrived for you."

"Whoever are they from?" I said, accepting the floral tribute of roses in every possible shade: Dark pink for gratitude, light pink for joy of life, yellow for friendship, and red. Quite a lot of red. No mistaking the meaning in that. "There's no card."

"No need for one," Marcus said with a cough. "They're from me, though I meant them to be delivered later this evening."

"Don't we merit tributes as well?" the irrepressible Mister Stirling asked as he poured himself a measure of Gentian Amaros.

"Indeed you do." Marcus distributed paper-wrapped parcels to Sebastian, Nic, and Violet. Opened, they contained matching sets of iron bracelets. "Honorary, of course, but they'll provide access to the Flying Fortress whenever you might require it."

As the others put on their new jewelry, Marcus returned to my side, looking down at me with that steady gray gaze I'd come to know so well. "I hope I conveyed the right message. With the flowers, I mean."

"You did indeed, sir . . ." At that moment, a lumbering gray-green mass appeared at the edge of the settee. Nic caught sight of Brimborion and started with surprise. Thinking that Marcus would hardly approve of taking tea with a turtle, I raised my voice to draw his attention. "You have my thanks."

"Only your thanks?" he asked. Before I could answer, he touched two fingers to his hat. "If you don't mind watching Cora for the rest of the afternoon, I fear I must take my leave for now."

I abandoned the bouquet and followed him into the hall. "Must you go already?"

"There's still a lot to be done about the city, even if the primary threat has been removed." He paused at the door and turned back to me. When he held out a hand, I took it. "Get some rest, and tell

Dreadnaught there's a turtle behind the chaise lounge. It probably could use a bit of carrot peeling or some nice lettuce."

I flushed up to the roots of my hair. A look over my shoulder confirmed that Cora was attempting to ride Brimborion about the study. "I haven't the slightest notion what you are talking about, Mister Kingsley."

"I think you do." Marcus drew me closer than necessary to add, "You are the keeper of vital information, are you not?"

I experienced an elevated pulse that couldn't be blamed upon my new Ticker. We might never acknowledge it aloud, but we had Warwick to thank for both my new heart and my ability to offer it to someone. "I am."

"Then allow me to share with you the intelligence, Tesseraria, that I wish to be your escort to the theater next weekend." He claimed my other hand, which still wore his diamanté ring. "You haven't taken this off."

"No. Would you like it back?" My breath caught just a little at the idea of returning it to him.

Marcus thought it over for a moment before saying solemnly, "Perhaps you should keep it, Penny. See if you think it suits you."

"It suits me just fine." Standing on tiptoe, I added, "*You* suit me just fine."

"Thank the Bells," he said, inhaling softly, breathing me in.

Then there was only him. Only us. Two heartbeats synced, his flesh-and-blood heart keeping time with my clockwork one. I closed my eyes, etched this moment in my memory, made space for it between all that had happened and all that was yet to come.

When I finally pulled back, I glanced at the others. They were crowded about Brimborion, studiously avoiding the interlude in the hallway.

All save Cora, who clapped her hands and crowed, "Kiss him again!"

The world spun around me as Marcus caught me about the waist and dipped me low. "Shall we oblige her—"

Before he could finish asking, I silenced his mouth with my own, because no one knows better how to seize a moment than a girl with a clockwork heart.

ACKNOWLEDGMENTS

As always, I would like to convey my love and appreciation, this time distributed in SugarWerks Carry-Away Boxes and accompanied by gifts of cake.

To the fans of the theater books who kept asking when I would have another novel out. Thank you for asking for an encore performance and for the roses you've thrown onto the stage.

To my husband and children, who understand that my corporeal body might be present but my mind occupies several alternate dimensions simultaneously. And to my mother and sister, who know why I don't always pick up the phone and yet they continue to call, to make offers of childcare, and to deliver hugs and dessert.

To my literary agent, Laura Rennert, for her enthusiasm and fellow feeling. Thank you for loving Penny's story and finding it a home.

To the Skyscape team: Miriam Juskowicz, for giving Penny a place to park her Vitesse; my editor, Robin Benjamin, for her meticulous notes and eyes so keen, I suspect they might have been Augmented; and my copyeditor, Rebecca Friedman, who put the final coat of polish on this massive brass contraption.

To the steampunk community, including artisans like Richard "Doc" Nagy (sadly lost to us) and musicians like Professor Elemental, Steam Powered Giraffe, Vagabond Opera, and Abney

Park. You are an endless source of joy and inspiration, there from the very beginning of Penny's journey, planting seeds in a garden that is just now blooming.

To my first readers, second readers, third, fourth, and fifth readers, who saw so many different drafts of Penny's story that they will have to read the final published version to see what made it to the page: Lori Hunt, Jennifer Ford, Sunil Sebastian, Glenn Dallas, Noël Furniss, Stephanie Burgis, Tiffany Trent, Shannon Messenger, Melissa Bleir, Rafe Brox, Kari Armstrong, Heather Clawson, Lianne Marie Mease, Amanda Mitchell, and Derek Silver.

Last but certainly not least, credit for the word "crimstone" goes to Nancy Jeanne Hedge, with my gratitude.

ABOUT THE AUTHOR

© Angel Mantchev

Lisa Mantchev is the author of the acclaimed Théâtre Illuminata series, which includes *Eyes Like Stars*, a nominee for the Mythopoeic and Andre Norton awards. She has also published numerous short stories in venues such as *Strange Horizons*, *Clarkesworld*, *Weird Tales*, and *Fantasy*. She lives on the Olympic Peninsula of Washington with her husband, children, and horde of hairy animals. Visit her online at: www.lisamantchev.com.